I0617684

I went to Palm Springs

and all I got was

Three Dead Blondes

Anne Stinnett

Copyright © 2012 Blue Eye Books
All rights reserved.
ISBN: 0578106019
ISBN-13: 978-0578106014

LCCN:2012908018

To my sister Sabrina - For her tireless encouragement, her countless perusals, and her ability to be ever unfazed by my crazy. Sorry for all the times I couldn't talk about anything else.

Acknowledgments

Profuse thanks to Kathy Stinnett and B.J. Burns, mother and aunt extraordinaire, for their support, input and encouragement. Thanks also to Kimberly Liphardt who would be the perfect friend if she weren't so far away and to Tyler Kent for his amazingly thoughtful and detailed notes. Thank you to everyone who offered encouraging words along the way; Ben, this includes you (obviously) and, because sometimes you really can rely on the kindness of strangers, thanks to Sharon Endsley and Julissa Loza for lending their time and insight.

One

"It sounds like he's right," Zuzu said. "You don't support him."

I felt my eyebrows snap together and my eyes narrow in response to the laughter erupting from my phone.

Zuzu Jones had been my best friend since we split my candy cigarettes on the last day of first grade. In return, she had infected me with chicken pox. Our mothers had spent weeks alternating the care and feeding of their spotted, cranky offspring; allowing themselves time off and affording our mutual misery company. In the twenty plus years I had known her, she had transformed from my personal Typhoid Mary to a Florence Nightingale, spreading succor instead of disease.

Right now I could do without her.

"Zuzu, he wants to do porn. I would have supported him if he had wanted to do something besides boff other women. On film."

Zuzu snickered. I did not. The breakup had gone from ludicrous to ugly. Jason had called me an uptight bitch and I had retaliated by wishing him leprosy and flinging a book at his head. In my defense, the book was titled *69 Ways to Make It or Fake It: A Beginner's Guide to Getting and Giving Onscreen O's,* and he had presented it to me a tick-tock prior to the flinging, with the air of someone who expects to be lionized.

I had never thought of Jason as my one true love, but I had grown accustomed to his...presence. I'd believed in his affection. His loathsome revelation had left me battered and pulpy and somehow ashamed. The call to Zuzu had been intended to elicit sympathy; I had forgotten my audience. I shook my head at Gulliver and he licked my elbow in a canine show of solidarity.

Zuzu continued to shriek with mirth. I tried to dredge up an accompanying laugh. I managed a joyless and deceitful chuckle, and silently wished Zuzu would wet her pants.

"Sorry Evin," she finally managed. "I'm just a little shocked you managed to downgrade from the guy who peed in the shower."

"Thanks." That had been disgusting. The final straw had been when he peed while we were in the shower together. Nothing had ever doused an afterglow faster than that stream of urine hitting my new pedicure.

"At least now you'll..."

"What?"

"I don't know," she said. "I started talking, but I lost the follow up."

"Please. I'm suffocating in all the silver lining."

"Where are you?"

"Close." I was speeding down the I-10 just west of Indio. We had been ripping along since 5:00 A.M.

having abandoned our shoes-in-the-shower motel under cover of darkness.

"Are you sure you don't want to stay with me?"

"I'm sure," I said. "Leonie's still up north, so it's safe to go home."

"How is she anyway? Still not speaking to Jack?"

Jack was my stepfather. At least for now. My mother had expelled him from the house months ago and departed on an extended vacation to meditate on the appeal of divorce.

"Still not," I confirmed.

"See? It's good you're back. It will cheer Jack up. I don't need cheering, but I can't wait to see you."

"Me too."

I also couldn't wait to sprawl by the pool. The air was toasty with sun and felt gorgeous on my face. The convertible top was down, and Gulliver was wearing his harness, so he could ride safely buckled in. It was only February, but it was well after noon, and heat was the norm here.

I could see the windmills now, white tidy ranks flanking the freeway ahead, which meant my exit was coming up. I told Zuzu I would call her later and grabbed my off ramp. The trip had taken about forty-eight hours; Minneapolis to Palm Springs, freezing rain to balmy sunshine, miserable independence to the comforts of home.

Soft wind whipped my hair into a frenzy and set Gulliver's ears flapping. We took Indian Canyon into town. The windmills dwindled in the rearview mirror. Before long, we were cruising Palm Canyon.

Downtown was picturesque as ever. People thronged the streets. Though the cars all flowed the same direction, the bodies milled every which way. Winter is the high season in the desert, mild and generally sunny. In late April and early May, the city would be abandoned drove by drove, leaving only the diehards to bake in a summer sun that harassed the mercury into triple digits for months at a time.

For now, snowbirds flocked everywhere. People from all over descended on our sunny town to escape inclement weather and bask in the sun. For the weekend, the month or the entire winter they came. While the unfortunate East Coast bundles up to shovel snow, Palm Springs golfs, shops, and swims. The strip was packed. Residents full and part-time mixed with tourists from Canada, Vermont and San Francisco. Restaurant patios were at capacity and sun-tanned, or reddened, humans abounded. Two hours to the west, L.A. dwellers might be all about the spray tan, but Palm Springs was an oasis for the true sun-worshippers.

Gulliver had his head out the window and his mouth ajar, the better to show off his massive teeth. A paranoid mother gaped at him and yanked a small child away. I thought about chasing her down to deliver a lecture on the unfairness of stereotyping, or failing that, let Gulliver give her a good scare. I like to fight prejudice, or at least punish the transgressors. But I was in a hurry.

We went as far as Ramon, seeing everything there was to see, then made a double left and were back on Indian. The sedate sister, Indian was more business than vacation. There were some sights to see, but the real party was always a block to the west.

It took five minutes and fewer turns to get home. I pulled up to the gate and hung out the window far enough to key in the date of my birth. Inside, I let the Thunderbird shudder off in front of the garage. I try to love my car. I tell myself that it's a classic, which it is, and that soon it will be restored to its proper glory. Manifestation had failed miserably, so I'm not clear on how this will be accomplished.

The house sat on a double lot at the end of the street. It was one story, the roof long and nearly flat. Mature hedges and fruit trees worked the perimeter like sentries, holding the world at arm's length. The yard had been the setting of many a backyard campout. In winter, marshmallows were roasted over the little portable grill; summer found giggling pre-teens sweltering in tents, often creeping in the night from yard to house in search of the cool streams of air expelled by the gently humming AC.

Gulliver bounded off to explore. I hefted a duffel bag out of the trunk and headed inside.

My key still worked which was a relief. Not that Leonie had any reason to change the locks on me but, as I had belatedly realized at some point between Flagstaff and Phoenix, she might have changed them on Jack.

The house was cooler than I'd expected. It was eighty outside. My shoes whispered across the tile as I moved from the entryway to the kitchen.

I plunked my duffel on the floor and for no reason other than habit opened the fridge. It was nicely cold and fully stocked. *No.* She had promised not to be here.

It finally sunk in that the refrigerator was not just full, but full of beer and enough red meat for a block party barbeque.

So, not Leonie.

This was going from bad to...well to slightly less bad, but still. I had driven for two days to enjoy a little sunshine and quiet. I was tired and ready to smack anyone who might upset my temporary oasis. I muttered some moderate profanity, let the door swing shut on the illicit groceries, and searched the house.

I found him sleeping or maybe just passed out. They were interchangeable when he was troubled, and he'd been troubled since Leonie's departure. He was sprawled face down in the guest room. That was something. I would have hated to have had to drag him out of my mother's bed.

Long limbs and a tousled head jutted out from rumpled sheets. If it hadn't taken so long to get here, I'd have turned around and left the shit and the fan alone to do what they would. As it was, I sighed and did something.

"Hey." I was still in the doorway, prepared to duck out if I suspected nudity.

He didn't stir. I tried again. Still nothing. I went for help, planning to unleash Gulliver on him. Instead, I got sidetracked by the arsenal in my room and returned with a loaded super soaker.

"Hi Jack," I said to my abruptly conscious and dripping stepfather. "You know, I talked to Leonie a couple of days ago and she didn't say anything about you moving back in."

He cleared his throat. It sounded phlegmy. Ugh. "Hey, Ev," he said.

"Get up would you?" I said. "I'm going to go drink your beer."

"Wait, I'm coming."

"Not until you shower," I said. The room reeked of sweaty male and stale beer. "And take your time; I'll be killing you when you're done."

I sat out by the pool with Gulliver and a cold bottle of Bass. Now that I'd had a look around, I realized Jack had been here for awhile. The motorized pool cover, which stayed on when no one was in residence, had been retracted. Pushbutton efficiency meant it had only taken a minute to lose the cover, but the pool chairs had been set up, the skimmer was out, and there was a rainbow of foam noodles strewn about the yard. The noodles may have been Gulliver's doing.

My mother had lived in this house with two husbands. The first, my father, had died when I was three; leaving Leonie a wad of life insurance she was too devastated to spend. I knew no more about him than you could see in a picture.

He had been handsome, strong jawed with light blue eyes and dark brown hair. I had inherited the hair, but not the eyes. Not entirely. When I was a kid I had liked to think I'd inherited my blue eye from him and my brown one from my mother. It was really just a pigment problem good for provoking uncomfortable conversation.

Pictures also suggested that my parents had adored each other. In the old photo albums, they were forever entwined and laughing. Phillip and Leonie had been young and in love. At least as far as I could tell. It was something we didn't discuss. To mention my father in Leonie's presence was to invite a barrage of tears followed by a long stretch of sharp, pouty silence. I hadn't mentioned Phillip Hart in front of my mother since sometime during elementary school. I wasn't sure if it was the pain of his loss or her anger that he could have prevented it. That he had been stupid enough to get in the car after numerous double bourbons. That he had ended up just another drunk spread on a tree. A bang and a whimper all rolled into one.

Four years after the death of her first husband, Leonie had thought nothing of whiling away an afternoon crying into her pillow, while I at seven years old, was on my own for dinner, homework, and a bath.

She was an oblivious proponent of the, "It takes a village," theory of childrearing, no matter that for years, I had been the only other resident of our village.

Then came Jack. There had been occasional others, never serious. Leonie was beautiful and fond of men in self-affirming doses. Jack had come into our lives when I was in second grade. For whatever reason, he had stuck long enough for attachments to form and marriage to ensue. My step was the only father I knew.

Jack emerged from the house, now attired in shorts and a golf shirt, what I thought of as the Palm Springs uniform. He had two beers in one hand and a cold glass in the other. I didn't reach for one of the beers because neither was for me. Jack drinks black and tans, Guiness floating comfortably on a foundation of Bass ale, among other things. I don't see the point of going to the trouble of layering beer; it only slows the inebriation process.

He was halfway through assembly when there was a sharp bark of joy and 150 pounds of Gulliver came bounding around the pool. The tan hit the deck followed closely by Jack, whose attempt to scramble out of the way culminated with his becoming one with a piece of patio furniture. It was a dreadful tangle of limbs and chair; then dog jumped in. Out of loyalty to Jack, I will not go into detail about the screams, but they were plentiful. I gave them a highly entertaining thirty seconds to get acquainted then stepped in to subdue Gulliver. Man and dog were drenched in beer. The man swore, the dog drooled and I laughed, but mostly on the inside, because Jack was livid.

I went inside and fixed Jack a fresh beer as a peace offering. It was enough to motivate him out of his prone position. He took the beer, flipped the chair upright, and made proper use of both. Gulliver flopped at Jack's feet and graced him with a friendly swipe of the tongue.

"Is he serious?" Jack said.

"He was just saying hi. He gets excited when he meets someone new."

"That's the puppy? What is he, Golden Retriever mixed with bear?"

"He's a Leonberger."

"Did you say he killed his last owner?" Jack swiped away his foam lip with the back of his hand.

"No, I did not." Gulliver's first person and my former landlady, Aida Leftwich, was residing in a senior community after having burned to the ground our shared abode. Jack knew all this, as I reminded him.

"And they don't allow dogs?"

"There's a twenty pound limit."

"Good policy."

Jack saw me getting ready to defend Gulliver and went on the offensive.

"What are you doing here? Did you break up with another boyfriend?"

"Yeah."

Jack ignored the warning in my tone. "Because he cried all the time, right?" Jack said.

I sighed. "No."

"Really? You didn't mind that?"

I had minded desperately. "That was a different guy."

"So what was the problem with this one?"

"Don't worry about it." No way was I explaining to Jack about the porn. "What's going on with you? Won't Leonie kill you if she finds out you're here?"

"Understatement."

"Jack." Besides what he would suffer at Leonie's hands if she found out, it was almost unbearably pathetic.

"Yeah, I know, but I just needed to crash for a few days. Maggie can't find me here and I needed some peace."

Ugh. *I* needed some peace.

"How is Leonie?"

"She's great," I said. "I talked to her the night before we left Minneapolis. Maggie?"

"Just a friend. I'd talk to her if she'd let me." He meant Leonie.

"I know. It's just a thing of hers. One of many. You should quit worrying about that and worry about what she'll do if she catches you here. Besides, she's still doing the Absolute Truth thing." I didn't know why Jack couldn't be happy about dodging that bullet. "Why can't you stay at your place? It's nice. I love your place."

"I hate my place. It's impersonal."

It was impersonal because Jack had bought it when Leonie evicted him and he'd been too busy pining to make it his own. Or too stubborn. I said none of this.

"I know I shouldn't be here. You won't tell her, right?"

"You know I won't."

"Yeah."

"So, Maggie is the hairdresser? That you met like two months ago?"

"Ev? Could you be a little more subtle with your judgment."

"Sorry. Continue." I swallowed the last of my beer.

"That's it. I hate my condo, and Maggie's been putting the chain on the door. She got mad about something. I'm just here for a few days. I changed the filter in the air conditioner."

Jack was sweet, even if not respectful of personal property. "Why is she mad?"

Jack looked at his beer and said, "I drive her crazy."

I choked on a laugh. That had been Leonie's reason for fleeing the desert. Jack had been ousted for betrayal, not the traditional coital variety, but for apologizing to one of the victims of Leonie's merciless tongue on her behalf.

After evicting her turncoat husband, she had made it a point to revisit her prey to explain that she was not, and never had been, sorry. Then with a clear conscience, Leonie had flown up north for an extended visit with a friend. Pity the friend.

Deprived of the object of his moping, Jack had found a distraction and somehow pissed her off as well.

"You think it's funny?" Jack said.

"A little."

"I don't know what I'm supposed to do about it."

"Stop?" I suggested.

Jack rolled his eyes. I took that to mean he didn't know how to stop.

"If Maggie's avoiding you, why do you have to hide?"

"She kept wanting to talk."

"About what?"

"Leonie. She thinks I still..."

"Oh." Maggie thought Jack still loved Leonie. I knew he did. Gulliver was trying to stick his nose in my glass. I nudged him away.

"I don't want to talk about it. It's not her business."

"If you're dating her, it kind of is."

"I'm not anymore. But I do need my stuff back."

"What stuff?"

"My ring."

"Your wedding ring?"

Jack nodded. I enquired frostily what had possessed him to leave his ring at Maggie's.

"I panicked. She used to complain if I was wearing it, so I would leave it at home, but one day I forgot, so I stuck it in a drawer before she noticed."

That sounded right. Totally normal and healthy.

Jack hit me with a sigh and eyes that rivaled Gulliver's when he works me for extra treats.

"You said it wasn't serious."

"It's not. We had fun. She took my mind off everything." Jack hit the kitchen again and returned with a straight Guiness. "Since you're here…"

"Since I'm here, what?"

"You could drop by Maggie's and-"

"And what? Have your horribly uncomfortable conversation for you?" I said. "No way. Besides, if you just have fun she can't be that irreplaceable."

"I need my ring Evin. When Leonie comes back I have to be wearing it."

I didn't have the heart to suggest she might not be back.

"That's such a high school thing to do." My voice was high and fast. "I hated high school. No. You go talk to her. You have to be an adult. You can do it Jack, everything will be fine, I swear. Besides, I don't even know this woman. It would be excruciating. For both of us. You know I don't like new people. I'll help you figure out what to say to her though. Ok?"

When I was five, I told my mother I would only eat Twinkies when I grew up. When I was seven, I swore I would never kiss a boy. There were other unlikely claims over the years, documented by Leonie in a prim little linen-clad book. My clandestine searches failed continually to unearth the ledger, but it never failed to appear in my mother's perfectly manicured hands when she was in the mood to rehash some bit of foolishness. When I was sixteen, this practice led to a battle so tempestuous that I stormed out swearing, dramatically and inaccurately (as documented) never to return. By the time I arrived at Zuzu's house where I'd planned to take refuge, Jack was waiting for me. He had apologized for the necessity and taken me home. It had taken me two months to forgive him.

Three months after that, on my seventeenth birthday, Jack had pulled me aside and presented me with the ledger. Whether he charmed it out of Leonie or swiped it, I never found out, but for this and more, I considered myself obligated to help him if I could.

I made him work for it though. For the next twenty minutes he persuaded and I protested. We both knew I would do it; we have an insufferable habit of not letting each other down, for which, of course, I blame Jack. But damned if I'd be first to blink. If it had been in me to refuse, things probably would have worked out better, at least, for us.

Lacking any clairvoyant tendencies, I nudged aside my reluctance and I went.

Anne Stinnett

Two

Maggie's house was small, with a rustic charm reminiscent of an upscale summer camp. There was natural desert landscaping in the front, including a palm tree and some plump aloe vera plants. Desert willows gave a bit of shade and pink and yellow lantanas lined the walk. I pulled into the horseshoe shaped driveway and cut the engine. Before I could knock, a bright blue, sparkling clean VW Bug rocketed up the other side of the driveway and slid to a halt nose to nose with my little Ford. Good brakes. The driver emerged, beeped the VW locked and sauntered down to the mailbox on superbly shaped and tan legs.

"Maggie?" I said when she approached me.

She agreed that she was and we shook hands. I explained who I was and that I was hoping to have a word. Her eyes lit up when I mentioned Jack so the whole question of my admittance wasn't too suspenseful. She had been at a Pilates class and asked me to wait while she made sure the house was presentable. I said I was sure it was fine, but ended up waiting on the stoop anyway. I shifted uncomfortably and hoped the woman who lived here was not expecting tidings of love.

Inside there were hardwood floors, ceiling fans

and a view of the backyard, which was on the small side, but not so small that Maggie had to do without a pool.

There were also gorgeous built-in bookshelves filled with some great books. They needed organizing though; I paused to examine her library and found a copy of *The Stand* wedged smack in the middle of what looked like a comprehensive Hemingway collection. The shelves also offered science, poetry and history. Maggie freely admitted she had scant interest in reading.

"My uncle Benjamin left all of those to me and I adored him, but I'm not much into books myself. Before he died, I kept my car keys there."

"Really?"

"No, honey. Not really." Maggie laughed.

I tried not to look openly acquisitive, but since the fire, I had been hurting for reading material, and knowing this collection was sitting here unloved was killing me. I spent a few minutes browsing her shelves, until Maggie told me I was welcome to borrow anytime.

I sighed to myself. The offer would probably be rescinded by the time I left. I thanked her anyway.

"Any friend of Jack's," she said. "Or step-daughter. You know, I think it would be nice for us to sit outside. It's such a beautiful day."

We adjourned to the patio to lounge and drink iced tea. Maggie was chattering about her morning; I was trying to identify the origin of her accent.

"Now tell me about that man. I can't believe it," Maggie said. "I can't believe he sent you over here."

"Yeah, me either. But I owe him."

"Owe him for what?"

I added more sugar to my tea before answering,

"Lots of stuff. My teenage years. He just wants to make peace."

"Peace? What does that mean?"

I assumed she wasn't asking for an actual definition. "He thinks you're mad at him. He has this weird thing, where he hates it if people are mad at him. Especially his friends." I kept my eyes away from hers as I delivered that last bit.

Maggie regarded me, and after awhile said, "Yeah, I suppose that's what we are. If anything. Well, I'll tell you, but it's need to know only, and Jack doesn't." She patted her superbly highlighted hair and leaned forward, blue eyes on mine. "I was just trying to teach him a lesson. He kept insisting he was over that woman, sorry, I guess she's your mother, but he isn't over her at all. Being a man, he just refused to talk about any of it. Started avoiding me completely, made me figure out the whole thing on my own. So yes, I was mad, but I got over it. Or I will. You can tell him no hard feelings, but I don't want a man that's constantly thinking of another woman. So, here's his ring to prove it." She handed me Jack's familiar platinum band. "Which I'm guessing is what he really wants, right?" She let out a wispy sigh. "Do you want to swim? I see you're wearing your suit."

"I swam earlier."

"What the hell, honey. Swim again. While we're at it, let's switch to wine. Red or white?"

I considered. "White, please."

"How about you just go on and uncover the pool, and I'll be right there."

"Yeah, sure." I secured Jack's ring before heading over to the switch Maggie had indicated and giving it a flip. I pulled my sundress over my head and tossed it on a lounge chair. Soon the sun would start going down, another hour or so, but it wasn't too cool for a quick dip, as long as the pool was heated. I wandered over to the edge and stuck a toe in. Goldilocks would have been pleased, and so was I.

My pleasure was short lived. The next second I was screaming. Not because of the water. Because of what was in the water, which was a person, or had been, once. A very small, blonde person with improbable boobs and an even more improbable knife stuck between them. I screamed again. Or still. My eyes were locked on the knife jutting grossly from her flesh. Then Maggie hit me and my mouth snapped shut.

She left once I was quiet, but I didn't realize it until she reappeared with a little white pill, which she instructed me to place under my tongue. I let it dissolve there, gagging on the bitterness.

"There's a knife in her," I told Maggie.

"I know." She helped pull my dress back on and deposited me on a patio chair.

I sat for awhile breathing from the belly, sitting on my hands, waiting for their tremors to lessen. Sirens wailed in the distance. Help was rushing our way though none would suffice. The sun still shone, and the woman still floated, but the pill was doing its happy work.

When the police arrived, Maggie was gone.

***

The uniforms came first. I roused myself and met them at the door. The tidy little living room was now in disarray. Drawers had been pulled, cushions were askew, and the floor was littered with the remnants of a vase and its former contents. I never heard it fall. I escorted two officers named Hoffman and De la Cruz into Maggie's, and indicated the pool. I told them what I knew about the body, which wasn't much.

Officer Hoffman was tall, with sandy brown hair that had started to edge away from his forehead. He had the physique of a keen chess player and had been regarding me with what I felt were unnecessarily hostile eyes. Thankfully, he now turned them in the direction of the patio and headed out to the pool.

I remained with Officer De la Cruz. He had muscles everywhere and he'd set his expression to stern. But he had kind eyes and looked nineteen. We established some relevant facts, first, that this was not my house, and second, that Maggie, like Elvis, had left the building.

"I don't know why she took off," I said to De la Cruz. "She was here when I found the body. She called you guys, right?"

"No. We received multiple disturbance calls from neighbors. Your name?"

"Evin," I said. "Maggie was just here."

De la Cruz gave me an expectant look. "Your full name, Ma'am."

Ma'am? "Evin Jaymes Hart. I was supposed to be a boy," I said. "I mean, not in a bad way, like they wanted a boy and were so disappointed they forced me do stuff like go hunting and fix the car. Just that they thought I was a boy, before I was born. I was going to be Evan James." I spelled the difference for him.

"We only need your actual name," he said carefully.

"Right."

I heard the squawk of a radio at the patio door, and then Hoffman stepped in and nodded to his partner. "I called it in," he said.

De la Cruz asked me to take him through everything that had transpired since my arrival. I did my best to be coherent and thorough. While I talked, he made notes and when I finished, he escorted me out the front door and down the street, to a black and white cruiser. He placed me in the backseat where I sat like a foiled criminal; at least he spared me the handcuffs. He gave me a nod and said the detective would be along to speak to me, then departed back to the house in his quiet way.

In the driveway, my battered little Thunderbird still sat. Maggie's Volkswagen had vanished as thoroughly as its mistress.

I waited.

More officers arrived. The street was now clogged with black and white cars. I watched a dark haired female officer with a serious face help De la Cruz string yellow tape around Maggie's cute little house. I waited.

By the time the detective arrived, I felt better. Enough so, that I was faintly embarrassed by my earlier damsel in distress act. On the other hand, I was growing increasingly disturbed by Maggie's disappearance.

After huddling with De la Cruz, Hoffman and other members of the crime-solving brigade, Detective Gerald Quick made his way over to release me from the cruiser and introduce himself. He had dark grey brows over light grey eyes and a sharp, bold nose. Behind the eyes was an intensity that undoubtedly caused the wicked to tremble in their ill-gotten shoes. He assessed me down to what may have been my soul, while his long, thin hand engulfed my own. I felt guilty and judged. I hadn't killed the woman in the pool, but I had done ninety on the freeway coming into town.

Quick led me to a nondescript gold sedan and leaned against it. Like De la Cruz, he produced a notebook to record what I uttered. I blurted my concerns about Maggie first thing.

"You didn't see her leave?"

"No. Sorry. It was kind of a shock, and I had something to calm down."

"What?"

"Xanax?" I hazarded, keeping my gaze firmly on Quick's chin. It felt like Xanax.

"Was it your Xanax?"

"Before or after I took it?"

"I'm glad to see you're enjoying this."

"I'm not. I was upset. Maggie was trying to help." Since Maggie had left me here to deal with a body, she could take the fall for my illicit drug use.

"It's never a good idea to take other people's medication." He stared at me until I was compelled to raise my eyes to meet his. "It's also illegal."

"Even in an emergency?" The grey eyes let me know he was not impressed with my emergency.

He made a notation in his little notebook and changed the subject. "What time did you arrive?"

"About quarter to four, I think." He wrote on his pad while keeping his eyes trained on me.

"And the reason for your visit?"

I explained about the Jack and Maggie saga. "Jack kind of hates confrontation, so he asked if I could come over and make sure everything was cool. Anyway, that's why I came, because why should two adults have to actually discuss what's going on between them, right? Next time, I'll just tell him to pass her a note in algebra." Quick had a Queen Victoria sort of look on his face, so I shut up.

The detective made another notation. "Continue."

I took a breath and tried to organize my brain. "Ok, so I came to talk to Maggie about Jack."

"Where did you talk?"

"Outside, in the backyard."

"At any point did you enter the house?"

"Yes, when I got here, and then after...to let you guys in."

"What condition was the house in when you arrived?"

"It was good. Nice. Neat." I shivered. A chill was easing through the night air. "I didn't see all the mess until I went back inside. It seems like Maggie did a pretty thorough rummage for something before she took off."

"What do you think she was looking for?"

"I don't know. How could I possibly know? I've never been here. I was just sitting there drinking iced tea." To my mortification, my voice had started thickening during this little speech, an occurrence inevitably followed by hot tears spilling down my face.

Detective Quick for the first time, mercifully slanted his eyes to his notebook.

I pulled myself together, fast, and apologized. "I'm never this overwrought," I said which was untrue, but not demonstrably so.

"It happens." He returned to his inquiry. "Did you see Ms. Connor searching the house?"

"I didn't, no. Now that I think about it, why would she need to?" My stomach tightened. "Do you think someone else was here?"

"Did you see anyone else?"

"I would have said so."

"Did you search the premises?"

"No. Of course not," I said. "Do you think whoever killed her searched the house?"

"What happened next?" Quick said, quid pro squat.

"Then Maggie said we should swim and when I opened the pool cover..."

"She asked you to open the pool cover?"

"While she went to get us some wine."

"Drinking while you swim?" I could see him wonder why I didn't use what little sense I had. I wondered too. If I had used my sense, I would be at Leonie's right now, watching TV with Gulliver and ignoring Jack's sad eyes. Instead of addressing these issues, I nodded.

"How long did it take Ms. Conner to answer the door when you arrived?"

I told him about our meeting in the driveway. "She was
just getting home from Pilates. Her car is gone. It's a little VW Bug."

"Where did she take pilates?" I had no idea, but suggested Body Kinetics since it was close and employed marvelously ruthless trainers.

"So that's your Thunderbird? It's nice. V8?"

I thought nice was a stretch. Maybe he was mocking me, but I chose to believe not. I responded with dignity in the affirmative.

"Did Ms. Conner invite you in immediately? Or did she step inside alone prior to inviting you in?"

"She went in alone for a minute or two, to make sure the place wasn't a mess." I said.

"How good a look did you get at the body?"

I blinked. I had been trying hard to expel the visual from my mind. "I saw the knife in her chest. Other than that, not very."

"Ok. Come with me," he said.

Anne Stinnett

Three

"The M.E., that's the Medical Examiner," I said to Jack, who nodded impatiently, "thinks she was killed sometime between twelve and one this afternoon. Lucky for me, I was stopping for gas a hundred miles away about that time. But it was really bad." I rubbed Gulliver's big head for comfort and looked at Jack. "I can't get the knife out of my head. Or her face. I saw this picture once of an orangutan right before a jaguar got it. Its face was so fierce and desperate; you could tell how much it didn't want to die. Her face was like that."

"So after you looked at the body they let you go?"

Thanks for listening. "After that and more questions. There was also fingerprinting, which in case you were wondering, was not at all humiliating. By the way, he told me not to talk about anything I saw tonight, so don't you say anything either, Jack."

"Maggie's not answering her phone." Jack was circling the kitchen.

"The detective seems to think-"

Jack whirled on me. "Do you? Think?"

"I don't. No." I fidgeted with Gulliver's ear. "I don't know. I think she needs to talk to them. She'll be a fugitive."

"You said she had an alibi. Why would she leave?"

"I don't know, Jack. She said she was having a mental health day. Massage, breakfast, pilates, we were just chatting. She wasn't trying to account for her time. But it doesn't make sense that she'd hide a body in the pool just to have me find it a few hours later. And the ransacking is throwing me off too."

"What about it?"

"I'm not sure. But if Maggie did it, what the hell was she looking for and who put it there?"

"Someone else could have torn the house up," Jack said. "Like whoever stabbed the blonde."

"I wasn't too out of it to notice someone-"

"What are you talking about? You didn't hear anyone going through the house, whether or not it was Maggie."

"So it's my fault we don't know what happened?"

"Yeah, that's exactly what I just said. Don't make me tell you you're just like your mother."

"Don't even think it. And stop yelling." I paused to tidy my thoughts. "There wasn't a lot of time for someone else to come, search, and sneak out before the cops showed up. I think we have to assume Maggie made the search."

"So?"

"So, how did she know there was something to look for? And why did someone stash something in Maggie's house without telling her?"

"Maybe they just didn't tell her where."

It was possible. I nodded.

"That reminds me. Did you get my ring?"

"Jack." Talk about sensitive. I handed it over and glared at him.

"Sorry. It was probably the dead girl. Who hid something."

"Dead woman. If she hid something at Maggie's and Maggie knew to look for it, but not where..." I sighed. "Sorry. I lost my train of thought. Maybe she was staying there. Visiting. Before she was a body, I mean."

"Evin, I know Maggie wouldn't hurt anyone."

"How? I know you don't want anything to happen to her," I said. "But she had a body in her pool. I'm thinking she's at least peripherally involved. I'm not convinced that she killed anyone, but you said your relationship was casual. You don't know-"

Jack slammed the granite countertop with both hands making me jump and sending Gulliver into a crescendo of throaty barking.

Eventually I convinced Gulliver he could stop protecting me from Jack. Jack had helped by having a seat and composing himself, at least outwardly.

"Sorry Ev. Look, I haven't known her long, but I know she wouldn't kill someone and go out to yoga and breakfast or whatever the hell she did, like it was nothing. Hell, she takes spiders outside instead of stepping on them like a normal person."

I sighed pointedly. The next spider I rescued was making a pit stop in Jack's bed.

"Sorry, I forgot."

"You better not be squishing spiders." I said.

"You have my word," Jack flashed a grin then sobered. "We have to do something."

"Why is that?"

"You're right. We don't. I do."

Crap. "So where would she go? Do you know any of her friends?"

"She's been talking about Hazel a lot lately. And the people from her salon. I don't really know them though."

"What's the matter with you? You know the name of every guy in the valley that has better than a ten handicap but you can't name more than one friend of your girlfriend's?"

"She's not my girlfriend. I just want to make sure she's ok."

"Because you feel guilty about leading her on? You have your ring back. Isn't that all you really wanted?"

"Don't be an asshole." That was Jack; always asking the impossible.

"Fine. What's her last name? Hazel's? Do you know?" I was starving. I couldn't recall the last thing I'd eaten. I fired up my laptop and tried to remember. It may have been a Mars bar.

"New something, I think. Newland."

"Ok. Good." There was nothing edible in the whole damn house. For the life of me, I could not understand how Jack could go to the grocery store, spend a hundred bucks on beer and steaks, and absolutely shun everything else. My stomach growled audibly. I tried 411.com for Hazel Newland. Nothing.

"Is she married?" I asked Jack, wishing he would be a little more proactive. He was pacing again, hair standing on end, under close observation by Gulliver.

"Yeah. Yeah, she is."

I waited.

"To that cheating bastard Bobby." Jack looked pleased with himself. I raised an eyebrow. Jack shrugged, "That's what Maggie calls him. See, I know about Maggie's friends."

"Impressive." For a man.

I fiddled around with "Bobby" and "Robert" then tried some variations of the last name. I'd only descended as far as mild frustration by the time I plugged in Robert Neuland. That cheating bastard was a doctor and he lived in a pricey pocket of town. "Ok, there's no phone number, but the address is here," I said. "Let's go." I sounded eager, but that was only because I was planning to stop for food on the way home.

I drove. Jack took shotgun and Gulliver rode on his lap, except for his head, which rode on my shoulder. Almost five hundred pounds of people and dog crammed in a two-seater isn't a great idea. I didn't feel like going back, so we suffered.

Hazel Neuland and her cheating bastard lived about two miles from Leonie's. We took Palm Canyon and made a right on Tahquitz. There were only a few houses up here and they were monsters.

"I don't see Maggie's car," I said. I cruised by and coasted to a stop in a little turnaround at the top of the street in an attempt to avoid alerting anyone with the roar of my badly tuned engine.

"We should go in and talk to Hazel," Jack said.

"Fine. Let's go."

"I think it might be weird if I go."

"Weird for whom?"

"For everyone," Jack said unblushingly.

"Right. So by 'we' you mean me?" I fixed my gaze on Jack and thought rude thoughts.

"Don't give me that look," Jack said. "It's less suspicious for you to go. She's married."

"You said it was a crappy marriage. Besides, why does it matter how it looks?"

Jack said nothing, so I didn't either. We sat there in stubborn silence for so long it began to feel ridiculous. When my stomach let out an audible growl I gave in.

"Fine," I said, and climbed out of the car. "Get in the driver's seat in case we have to run away or something. And try to calm Gulliver down, he's starting to freak out."

"Wait," Jack nearly shrieked. "How do I calm him down?"

I smirked and walked away. Gulliver would never freak out in the car. He was forever happy in the car. I was still basking in my minor revenge as I approached Hazel Neuland's front door.

The door was actually double doors about eight feet tall. Up close, the house loomed over me. Impressive yes, but it lacked the coziness that I appreciate in a dwelling.

My watch told me it was almost 7:30. My social barometer told me it was a little late to drop in on a stranger, especially since it had been dark for almost two hours. I reminded myself that Hazel was Maggie's best friend. She would want to help. I took a breath and gave the bell a quick push.

After a modest interval, the door opened to reveal a not so modest girl. She had enough height to look tall, but without fear of looming over any eligible suitors, and I'm sure there were plenty. She was wearing sky-high heels and a scrap of a dress, over a body that pulled it all off.

"Hi," I said. "Are you Hazel?" Even as the words came out, I doubted it. She looked a little young to be Maggie's bosom bud.

"Definitely not," she said, scorn for me, Hazel, and probably anyone who wasn't her, clear in her voice.

Ok. I cleared my nervous throat and asked if Hazel was home.

"Nope. So sorry."

Right. I was going to throttle Jack for putting me through this. I pushed on and inquired whether the adulterous doctor was in, but not in those words because I'd long since exhausted my daily supply of pluck.

I was sure she was going to answer in the negative, but she surprised me by offering a grudging, "I'll get him. I guess."

Before I could express my dubious thanks, the door shut in my face. I waited until a tall, dense looking man wearing two pieces of a three-piece suit and a surly expression reopened the door. Since he was presumably finished working for the day, I thought his attire hinted at uptight. I shifted from foot to foot like a kid standing in front of the principal. Even with three feet between us, I felt slightly overwhelmed by him, due as much to his grim demeanor as his size. In addition to the frown, he had dark hair no grey, a strong chest, and arms to go with it. Definitely a religious gym goer. He might be attractive if he stopped working so hard at being intimidating. His eyes were brown and focused on my chest.

"Hi," I said, suddenly wishing I had a coat to wrap around me even though it was probably sixty degrees, which felt tropical after Minneapolis. "I'm here to see Hazel. You must be Bobby."

"I'm Dr. Neuland. Who are you?"

I didn't want to tell him who I was. I did want to wrap this up before I had another encounter with the rabid girlfriend.

"I'm so sorry," I said, and flashed my dimple. "Did I get the wrong Neuland?"

"Hazel doesn't live here anymore, so yes, you did." The door started to swing shut.

"Wait. I'm sorry," I said again, and got a glower in return.

"I hate to bother you." I really did. "I just thought I'd look her up. Since I'm here. In town, I mean." I was still smiling furiously. Jack and I were beyond even for the teenage years.

"Hazel is gone. She's been gone for two weeks. If you're her friend, why don't you know that?"

"I'm an old friend."

"Fine. What's your name. I'll tell her you stopped by." Said the spider.

"Mary. When do you think you'll be talking to her?" I was backing away from the door. Behind Dr. Bobby, I saw the girl strut past. She glanced over and our eyes met briefly, then with a sneer and a clatter of heels, she was gone. Clearly, he wasn't missing his wife.

"Never, if all goes well. That's the upside of your spouse leaving you."

"Ok. Thanks anyway." I turned to trot down the stairs.

He called after me, "I'll give Hazel your message, if I speak to her." I turned to flash a thank you smile. "If you see her first, you give her my message: This won't be a repeat of the mess with Verona. If she thinks she can gouge anything of significance out of me, she is mistaken. Goodbye, Miss...?"

"Hart." I said. "Um, who is Verona?"

Bobby Neuland was looking at me sharply, "Your name is Mary Hart?"

Crap. I was an idiot. I nodded once and said, "Ok, thanks, bye."

I turned and forced a casual stroll. When I heard the door slam behind me, I gave in to my inner sprinter. I hit the car hard, yanked the door open and tried to fling myself inside. Failed. Gulliver was filling the passenger seat so I had to shift my own weight and more in dog before I could slink in and cower under the dashboard.

"Shit, Jack. I told him my real last name."

"Ok. Real first name?"

"No. Mary."

Jack burst out laughing.

"Shut up," I said. "He's scary. I panicked." I peeked over the dash and saw that Dr. Bobby had withdrawn into his lair.

"I'm guessing she wasn't there," Jack said when he stopped laughing. I was getting tired of being a source of such amusement for my nearest and dearest.

"He said she doesn't live there anymore. Maggie didn't say anything about Hazel leaving him? Maybe something to do with the whole cheating bastard situation?"

"I don't think so." He sounded unsure.

"Jack. Jeez. Don't you listen to her when she talks?"

"I tried."

Unbelievable. I felt a vibration in my pocket and pulled out my phone.

"Be quiet, it's Leonie." I pushed talk and said, "Hey, Mom."

I made it a point never to address her by her given name, although I tended to think of her as Leonie. She would have preferred I lose the maternal moniker, but I liked to remind her that in this one relationship she was expected to be the adult.

"Did you make it then?" she said. "Because I was expecting to hear from you and I don't appreciate having to take attention from what I am doing to worry about whether you arrived safely."

"Sorry. It was kind of a busy day. I'm just out getting some dinner," I said. I was planning to after this, so it was somewhat true, unlike what I said next. "But I'm driving right now, so how about I call you in the morning."

"You shouldn't drive while on the phone, darling, but I am pleased you're getting up in the mornings now. So much less depressing for you." Unlike this conversation.

"Mother, I was working nights." Ugh.

"Community theatre is not working."

"It was a professional theatre company." There had definitely been money involved. Just not a lot.

"Darling, it was a waste. You don't even enjoy acting." That was true. In exchange for six weeks of rehearsal all you get is a bunch of strangers staring while you sweat under hot lights. What I had loved was the backstage hubbub, though that had felt more like a pleasantly distracting hobby than a career path.

"Forget it. How are things up there?"

Leonie was taking an extended vacation in San Francisco at my aunt Blu's. Aunt Blu wasn't actually my aunt, just a college friend of Leonie's that I could only dimly recall from a couple of visits when I was a kid.

"I'm fine, darling, except, Blu is excessively trying right now. She's upset about some bad liposuction. Very bad. I told her that if she had spent the money on a trainer instead of giving up and resorting to surgery, her thighs and stomach might be a little plump, but at least she wouldn't be lumpy and scarred." I heard Blu objecting in the background, but Leonie was unfazed. "She was angry, but of course I'm quite used to people who refuse to appreciate the Truth."

She should be.

"Even if it is the truth, it doesn't do her any good for you to inflict it on her now."

"Yes, darling, but the Truth can't be suppressed

just to prevent a few hurt feelings, so I said it."

"Ok, well I better get off the phone and drive." Before any truths were aimed at me.

"Well, then. We'll talk soon."

"Ok." Great.

"By the way, have you seen your stepfather?"

"Uh...no. Not yet. Why?" I glanced at Jack and rolled my eyes.

"Because darling, I'm planning to let him come home soon."

"Really? Does he know that?" I looked at Jack, who was focused on me with the intensity Gulliver shows taunting squirrels.

"Of course he does. It would hardly be Truthful to keep it from him."

Ok. "Why the wait?"

"Darling, I'm not ready for him to stop being miserable. When I feel he deserves to be happy again I'll be home."

I thought the opposite might be true, but I bit my tongue. It would do no good to comment on Leonie's petty sadism.

"And in case you're worried," she went on, "I'm aware of that waitress he was seeing. As far as I'm concerned, that's worked out nicely. He'll always feel a bit guilty which will keep him in line in the future."

"I think she's a stylist," I said. Jack was gesturing for me to shut up.

"Same thing, darling."

Turned out the truth wasn't in the details.

"Ok," I told her. "I really have to go."

"Fine darling. Goodbye."

"Bye." I ended the call and told Jack, "Leonie asked about you. Congrats on the pending reconciliation. Is that why you dumped Maggie?"

"It wasn't dumping."

Right. Maybe Jack did deserve to suffer further.

"I wasn't kidding about dinner," I said, "I need to eat now."

"What do you want?"

"Native Foods."

"I want a burger," Jack said.

"They have burgers." They had veggie burgers, veggie nachos and a variety of other meatless delights. "Don't bitch; I just had to stand up there for five minutes while that beefy creep stared at my boobs. And you wouldn't believe the twelve year old girlfriend he's got in there."

"Twelve?"

"Early twenties. Same thing."

"Ok."

"Food please." I looked at Jack as he turned the engine over and saw that he wasn't going to complain further.

"It's in Smoketree Commons," I said.

We were rolling down the street, Jack trying not to kill the engine as he shifted from first to second, and me trying to shift Gulliver on my lap so he wasn't smashing anything important, when a nondescript gold sedan rounded the corner and headed toward us.

In the glare of the car's headlights, I saw nothing, but as we rolled past, I looked left and glimpsed a patrician profile. "Jack, wait," I said.

"What's wrong?"

"No. Don't stop."

"You said to wait," Jack said, more patiently than I probably would have.

"I meant hurry." Jack had some trouble getting the car going again. It took a long string of seconds to make it around the corner. When we were out of sight,

Jack braked sharply, forgetting about the clutch, causing my poor little car to lurch, and then shudder to a halt.

"What's the problem?" Jack said, clearly not expecting a reasonable explanation.

"That was the detective. I didn't want him to see me," I said. "And when was the last time you drove a stick?"

"Five years at least. There's a reason they hardly make them anymore. You're the one who said he suspects Maggie. Of course he's looking for her."

"I didn't say suspects. I said he wants to talk to her. But who told him to look for her here? I didn't."

"They might have talked to someone from her salon." Jack shrugged. "That's where she first met Hazel, and what does it matter if he saw you? We're not doing anything wrong."

"Maybe you're not. I just told Bobby Neuland, who's kind of a scary jerk, that I'm Mary Hart. There's no way he won't mention me to the cops. This is exactly why I didn't want to go to Maggie's."

"Exactly?"

"Well, I didn't know about the body, but I had a bad feeling."

"The only bad feeling you had was laziness."

"Shut up," I said. "And drive."

***

We sat on the patio while we waited for our order. After some persuasion, Jack had deigned to order the Reuben. I'd gotten the Native nachos and the Portobello and sausage burger. My eyes were always bigger than my stomach but I thought I could come damn close.

We surreptitiously passed Jack's flask back and forth in an effort to take the day's edge off. It was stainless steel and engraved with a J and D, which were Jack's initials, but could also have referred to its current contents. Gulliver slurped water from the bowl our server had provided then rested his drippy jowls on the edge. Intermittent calls to Maggie's cell phone had gone unanswered. If Jack hadn't heard from her by morning, we were planning to hit the salon and see what her fellow stylists knew. For now we sat, drinking and thinking.

"Maybe I should talk to Harry," Jack said.

"Who?"

"Harry Chalmers. You know him. He's Stella's nephew."

"Stella your P.I. friend?" Jack nodded. "I remember her. I thought she was completely awesome."

"You were afraid of her."

"Yeah, that too. Didn't she die?"

"Yeah," Jack said. "She died. He's still alive."

Stella Chalmers' nephew was still alive in spite of her untimely demise. Check.

"I still don't know him."

"Yes you do. He came over with Stella sometimes. You were a teenager."

"You mean that pain in the ass? The skinny little kid with greasy black hair and a skateboard?"

"Yeah." Jack shook his head at me.

I remembered. And no way were we calling Harry Chalmers. I'd kissed him once. Well, mostly, he'd kissed me once. But there was no need to dredge up the past. I'd driven thousands of miles to escape the past. I had forgotten the past was here too.

"It's bad enough we've involved ourselves in this

mess," I said. "We shouldn't drag in other people."

"He's a P.I. He took over Stella's agency."

"I don't care. We don't need anybody else." I thought it was high time for a subject change. "Do you know what she looks like?"

"Who? Hazel?"

"Yeah. Hazel."

"Blonde. Blonder than Maggie. Like...platinum."

"Big boobs?" My stomach started slowly to turn. "Like way too big for her body? I know you'd notice that."

Jack laughed. "Yeah. How'd you know?"

"I think she was in the pool."

Anne Stinnett

Four

We were having a ferocious debate about whether to return to the Neuland house. I was sensibly against. Jack was under the impression that it would not be grossly uncomfortable and potentially dangerous to return and ask the unpleasant and large Dr. Bobby if the police had stopped by with news of Hazel's untimely demise.

"Jack. No. I'm not doing it. We can find out in the morning. In the paper. Or, on the news. We're going home."

Jack continued to hound me, but I'd had the foresight to hop in the driver's seat so I ignored him and hightailed us back to Leonie's.

By the time we got there, Jack had calmed enough to wolf down his Reuben and love it, so I talked him into trying a bite of my burger.

"It's all right," he said. "Doesn't taste like real sausage though."

I thought it was much better and said so. Jack wanted to try the nachos too, so I parted with a bite, and then selfishly ate the rest myself. At ten o'clock, the news came on.

The body in Maggie's pool was the lead story. The woman had been identified as Hazel Neuland, Palm

Springs resident. "I don't know what to do with this," I told Jack. "Do you think it was Bobby? If it's not the butler, it's the husband, right?"

"How do you know there isn't a butler?"

Good point. There could be an extensive live-in staff stashed away in the Neuland house. I was still rooting for Dr. Bobby.

"I'm worried like hell about Maggie. I need to find her."

"Jack." I peeked at him from the corner of my eye. "Maybe we should back off. This is serious."

"If she's in trouble, it's partly my fault. If things had gone better with us I would have been there, or she would have been able to come to me for help."

"If you hadn't been using her as a Leonie patch we wouldn't even know about this," I retorted.

"Exactly. It's my fault."

"That's not what I meant." Obviously, neither Maggie's disappearance nor Hazel's death were Jack's fault; however, our involvement was.

"You should forget about it, Evin. It's not your problem."

I let my head fall back on the couch while I contemplated my shitty personality. "No, it's fine," I said. "I want to help." I couldn't think of anything I wanted to do less. I should be quietly licking my Jason inflicted wounds and contemplating life in the convent. The most irksome element of the porn fiasco was that from the moment I caught him staring at my ass in the Best Buy checkout line, I had never taken him seriously. He was young and unfocused, hardly a prime candidate for two point five and a picket fence.

But he had been fun and spontaneous and endlessly entertaining.

Apparently I had not.

But, since I didn't have the privacy necessary for a really good wallow in my own woes, maybe Jack's would provide some distraction.

"We'll drop by the salon tomorrow and see her partners," I said. "Maybe they've talked to her. Or maybe she was so shaken up after seeing Hazel like that she took off to think; to be alone for awhile."

"You don't believe that."

Not for a second. I changed the subject. "What could she have been looking for? It couldn't be anything too big. She looked in cabinets and drawers."

"We still don't know it was her." Jack said. "What if whoever killed Hazel was still there? Or came back at some point while you were having your break with reality by the pool?"

"I don't know." When I seriously considered that possibility, I got a little chill. I shoved the thought away, hard. "You never met her, did you? Hazel, I mean."

"No. I'm only concerned with making sure Maggie is safe. There's nothing anyone can do for Hazel." Jack finished the flask and left without another word. I flipped channels looking for something distracting and mindless. I settled for a reality show about three sisters, two of whom were nothing but skin and vanity. When Jack hadn't returned by the time it ended, I knew he'd gone to bed.

I found Gulliver's leash and took him for a quick walk, then we did the same.

***

My cell rang just after six the next morning. I didn't bother checking the caller I.D. before silencing it. Only one person would call me at such a time.

My dog was the next to wake me. Instead of a phone call, he plunked a giant paw down on my face. I struggled out of bed and to the bathroom, where I spit out whatever Gulliver had stepped in the day before. Then I released him to the yard and got my caffeine fix brewing. It was eight-thirty.

I hauled the rest of my bags in from the car, grabbed a shower, downed two cups of coffee then set to work waking Jack. I had no doubt he was worried, and invested in finding Maggie, but left to his own devices he wouldn't crawl out of bed for another two hours.

I started by knocking. Just the basics, Ma'am. Nothing. I called his name. I opened the door and yelled. Still nothing. It was time for the big gun. I lured Gulliver to the guest room with a handful of peanut butter treats, which I tossed on Jack's snoring form. Gulliver was a half second behind. I shut the door on my stepfather's howls and returned to the kitchen.

They emerged shortly, one a sight more cheerful than the other, no visible injuries. I waved Jack toward the coffee. I knew he needed a few minutes to wake up so I took the opportunity to call Leonie back. No answer. Perfect. I would get credit for a phone call, without the excruciating conversation.

While I waited for Jack, I stretched out on my bed and had a completely undeserved rest. I thought about the Neulands and wondered where Maggie fit in. It seemed she'd been lending more than a sympathetic ear to Hazel. I hoped she wasn't now in the same condition. My brief impression of Bobby Neuland, was that he was a chauvinist and a bully. How close did that combination bring a man to murder? And did I really want to know? For now, I lay peacefully with my eyes closed, feeling the blaze of the winter sun on my SPF 30'd face.

Just as I was settling into a blissful doze, I heard Jack and Gulliver trouncing down the hall. Gulliver arrived first and launched himself onto the bed before Jack showed himself in the doorway.

"You about ready?" Jack said.

"Yeah. Let's go."

In response, Gulliver leaped off the bed and toppled the bookcase, strewing young adult literature everywhere. Presumably, he had missed his mark, though I couldn't say for sure.

"Damn," I said.

Jack echoed the sentiment, but with more salt.

"No one was talking to you," Jack told Gulliver who was happily unaware of anything amiss.

"He likes to go places." I started gathering strewn books while Jack righted the bookcase.

"These should be bolted to the wall." Jack said. "What if we have an earthquake?" I was re-shelving my collection of horse books. I had been mad for anything to do with animals as a child. Walter Farley, Marguerite Henry, and Anna Sewell were all represented, among others. Some of them I had read twenty times. I was glad that I hadn't taken them with me when I left for school, they'd be nothing but ash now. Since all my grown-up reading material *was* now ash, I set "King of the Wind" on the nightstand to read later.

"If there's an earthquake, I guess we'll die under an avalanche of literature. At least this one isn't that tall. It's the ones in the living room that will kill us when the big one hits. Why do I have two copies of Watership Down?" I set my familiar and worn paperback copy on the nightstand and brandished the much larger hardback edition at Jack.

Jack looked up and grinned. "One of them is mine," he said.

"I thought you didn't read books. Especially long books. About bunnies."

"Look inside. In the middle."

"Jack!" Watership Down concealed a clever little compartment that held another sleek flask and a tin of curiously strong mints.

"It's left over from when Leonie decided we were drinking too much."

I twisted the cap off and sniffed. "Patron?"

"I don't remember, but I trust your nose."

Hmmm. I put the copy with the flask in it on the nightstand as well. It would be plan B for getting to sleep tonight. Jack put his last handful of books back on the shelf and I followed suit. I'd organize them later.

"Come on," he said. "We can take my car."

***

Root to Tip was on Palm Canyon between Antique Collective and A La Mod. We arrived just before ten, hoping to find the place staffed but not busy. We peeked in to see a petite, attractive redhead finishing up with the welcoming touches: straightening magazines, turning on the sound system, tidying a flower arrangement. She caught sight of us, and quickstepped over on Betsy Johnson heels so high I would rather have stabbed myself with them than put them on my feet.

"Hi there," she said when she turned the key and cracked the door open. "We're not open just yet, but I suppose it would be okay for you to wait inside. Do you have an appointment?"

We explained who we were.

She introduced herself as Violet Beeme.

"So you're the famous Jack Dekker," she said. "Maggie showed us your picture in the paper with that singer." Jack is a golf pro. He instructs famous visitors and well-heeled locals in the fine art of the backswing and other arcane procedures. It was true that he was mildly notable. In the desert.

"Maggie's not here yet as you can see, but I just took a peek at the appointment book and she should be along shortly. Can I get you something while you wait? Coffee, tea, Fiji water?"

"No thanks," I said.

"Your eyes are amazing," she said, her own too intent on my face. "One brown and one blue. That's so unique. My cat has one blue eye and one yellow and he's deaf. You can hear, right?"

I unclenched my teeth and told her that I could.

"What's it called again?" she said. "Something iridis right?"

"Iridium. Heterochromia Iridium," I said. "Iridis is two colors within the same eye."

"Listen, Violet," Jack said. "Maggie's been...out of touch since last night."

The flow of Violet's incessant movement paused. "Out of touch? I'm sorry, what does that mean?" Her small pale hands with their bright red nails fidgeted with the tie on her wrap dress.

Jack shot me a look; I didn't see any pressing reason not to tell her. I gave her the lowlights.

"Oh, no. I mean, oh my gosh. I just can't believe it." Violet's tone was hushed. "I knew Hazel. I met her here. She came in all the time. She and Maggie were so close. I feel terrible for her poor husband and kids. I met her daughter once. Well, stepdaughter, she was really. That's just the same sometimes though, right?"

I didn't think so. I doubted Jack and I would be such fast friends if he had spent my adolescence trying to discipline me. I glanced at him and got a shrug back.

"What's the stepdaughter's name?" I asked Violet.

"Reina. She has a brother named Rex. They're twins. I heard Hazel and Maggie talking about them. I met the daughter once. Sorry, I already said that. I think Mrs. Neuland brought her along trying to bond, you know how it is. Just between us, I don't think they were exactly braiding each other's hair. They were close enough in age to be sisters even though they didn't look alike. Not that there was any reason why they would. Hazel was a platinum blonde; Reina's brunette. That was the problem I'm sure, the closeness in age. Not the hair color, of course." She laughed at her little joke.

I supposed someone had to.

"Daughters don't usually appreciate their daddies marrying someone who could be their playmate. But there's always some issue with family. Don't you think?"

I silently agreed with that.

Violet stopped for breath, cheeks pinker than when she had begun, and looked at me like Gulliver had the time he'd brought me that poor bird. Aloud, I agreed that inappropriately young stepmothers were often an annoyance to their new daughters.

"What we really want to know," I said, wresting back control of the conversation, "Is whether you have any idea where Maggie could be."

"No. I haven't talked to her since we closed up together the night before last. We don't spend much time together outside of the salon. Eddie should be along shortly. He and Maggie were friendly; they often go out for a drink after work. Just be sure to call him Edward if any clients are within earshot. He's straight, you know, but he tends to act slightly... well, some clients expect that. I mean, it is Palm Springs and he's a stylist, right?"

While we absorbed that, Violet flitted over to inspect the appointment book. "I'm sorry, and of course you're welcome to stay and wait for Eddie, but I need to set up Maggie's station. If she isn't going to make it in, Eddie and I need to cover her appointments. Not that I'm not worried about Maggie, of course, but we can't afford to alienate any clients."

A discrete chime followed by a small rush of warm air had me pivoting toward the door in anticipation of Edward-the-straight. For my trouble, I ended up face to face with Detective Gerald Quick. I sucked in a hasty breath and used it to say hello.

"Ms. Mary Hart," he said. "How was your talk with Dr. Neuland?"

"A little creepy," I said, without hesitation. I hope that no one ever confides a state secret to me. I would give it up at the first hint of torture. "That's why I didn't tell him my real name."

"You told him your real last name."

"I panicked. We weren't trying to interfere. We didn't even know it was Hazel in the pool until later." I shrugged.

"My fault then," Quick said with grave humor. "I should have kept you in the loop. Of course, I'm surprised you didn't stop to compare notes when you saw me at the Neuland's."

"I was worried I wasn't supposed to be there."

"Sometimes it's good to trust your intuition," he said, the shape of his lips closely resembling a smile.

"Got it."

"Let's talk outside."

Five

I wasn't nearly naïve enough to think that Quick cracking a joke meant he'd sworn off arresting me and orphaning Gulliver. With no expectation of pleasure, I followed the lanky detective in his grey pin-stripe slacks and white shirt into the midmorning sun.

"What do you do, Ms. Hart? Your occupation." He clarified, leading me toward, then past, A La Mod.

"Nothing. I'm figuring out what I want to do." With my degree, I was less employable than a high school dropout.

"You were passing out samples at King's Groceries before a fire at a previous residence, correct? Now you're living on the payout from your insurance company. It's nice when what seems like a tragedy works out so well."

My criminal career has consisted of numerous moving violations, crossing outside the crosswalk and against the light (simultaneously) and when I was at my most rebellious, I had stolen lipstick on a regular basis. Therefore, although in my just barely more than thirty-one years, I have perpetrated many a petty crime, the implication that I had conspired at arson provoked a hot flash of temper. I took a moment and forced a civil tone. "If you know that, you know the fire was determined to be an accident. You can't actually believe that Mrs. Leftwich torched her home of sixty years, for a little insurance money. Or is it that you think I'm some demented firebug? Because I didn't even have renter's insurance. The only reason I got anything was because my car was in the garage and burned, with everything else, to the ground."

"At least you got a great car out of the deal."

He didn't have to drive the damn thing. I had preferred my Acura. Everything had worked.

"It wasn't a deal," I said evenly. No one would make a deal that involved losing everything they had. Clothes, books, Wuby, the wind-up, musical bear that hadn't wound up since I was four, all gone; photo albums documenting my cherubic childhood, gone. I'd told Leonie I had saved them. No amount of money would make up for the hell I was going to get when she found out I hadn't.

"Aida felt bad, so she gave me the Thunderbird. It was supposed to make up for her telling me I was covered by her homeowners insurance when I wasn't." It hadn't. "I'm not talking about this anymore." I went on talking. "But if you think we conspired at arson, you're crazy."

"I don't. Really." He said, and smiled down at me. I was growing to hate him. Really.

We stopped, obedient to a flashing Don't Walk signal. Sweat trickled between my breasts and I felt a blister developing on my left heel. I sat on the curb, feet in the gutter. Under the offending shoe, I found a sweaty, liquid-filled welt.

"I told you before we're not trying to interfere." I said, rummaging through my purse in search of a band-aid. "We just want to know Maggie is safe. Jack is worried; so am I." I slapped on my found bandage, and worked my shoe back on. I rose, brushed the curb off my ass and turned to face the detective. He was gone. I wondered with annoyance how long I had been talking to myself. I peeked in surrounding shop windows until I spotted the too familiar profile in a little coffee shop that hadn't been here the last time I was. I considered a get-away, but Quick knew where to find me. I followed him inside.

"Is this your way of telling me we're done with our talk?" I said and gave him my best smile, dimple and all. He turned and handed me a cup containing iced coffee with room at the top.

"You look like you're not used to the desert."

"Thanks," I said. "So now you're nice?"

"I'm always nice; sometimes I'm doing my job."

I added soymilk and more sugar than was good for my thighs. Quick was drinking his steaming and black. We made our exit and retraced our steps. I told him what Bobby Neuland had said about Hazel, Verona and his money. As expected, he made no comment.

"We know you couldn't have done it," he said after a pause. "In addition to the charge receipt we have the surveillance video from the gas station."

"So, I have nothing to worry about?" I said.

"If you were worried, maybe we should take a second look at you."

I thought he was joking. I hoped.

"Cops worry everyone," I said. "When I'm driving and I see one behind me, I practically can't breathe. Even if I'm not speeding."

"That happens to everyone. We have fun with it."

I bit back a laugh, and drank my coffee.

***

When we got back to the salon there were two more bodies; both alive, neither of them Maggie. An older woman was sitting under a dryer leafing through a glossy Palm Springs Life with Zooey Deschanel on the cover. Quick raised his cup at me in salute then stepped over to Jack. There was a murmured exchange and they walked outside. Jack shot me a look over his shoulder as the door closed behind him. I tried to take this philosophically, but my stomach was already tying knots. Violet was yammering in my ear, which didn't help.

"I'm sorry, what?" I said, forcing a smile for Violet and expanding it to include the new addition who she introduced to me as Eddie Daigle, Edward to his clients. He had three inches on me, at most, which made him about 5'7", with exceedingly well-groomed facial hair. His features were perfect; his clothing was not. He was wearing Ed Hardy, which I find exhausting, but there are worse sins. Based on appearance, I suspected vanity was one of his. He showed me a mouthful of beautiful white teeth and shook my hand.

"So Maggie's off to parts unknown, huh?"

"That means you haven't heard from her either," I said.

"I told them you two went for drinks sometimes," Violet said, her pale little hands now fidgeting with an empty paper cup. I wished she would either be still or go away.

"We did."

There was a change in the composition of the background noise and Violet excused herself to wrest her charge from beneath the dryer.

Eddie moved over to the coffee pot and poured himself a cup. "But no, I haven't heard from her," he said. "She must be devastated about Hazel. I wonder if she just took off to get her head together."

Spare me from other people whose heads weren't together. I had enough trouble with my own.

"She must have known the police would want to talk to her." I said. "I mean how flakey is she?" Sure, "flakey" wasn't the most sensitive word, but I was running out of patience with the Maggie quest.

I was keeping an eye on Jack and Quick through the door, remaining vigilant lest Jack be hauled away to rot in jail without my knowledge.

I focused back in on Eddie. "Sorry, I've been scattered since all this happened. What did you say?"

"Just that Maggie is usually completely reliable. I also said it sucks about Hazel. I only knew her from when she came in to the salon, but I went to school with the twins."

"Palm Springs High?"

He nodded.

"Same class?"

"They were a couple years ahead of me, so I didn't know them that well."

I nodded acknowledgement of high school heirachy. "Different circles."

"Yeah. They were much more popular. People are always fascinated by twins, you ever notice?"

I wasn't sure about that. I'd gone to middle school with a grossly unpopular twin set, though it was true that they had been fascinating in an Addams family kind of way.

I switched to small talk. "What year did you graduate?"

"I hate to date myself," he said, and let me drag it out of him.

Turns out, he had graduated nine years after me.

I'd been torn screaming from my twenties, was newly single, again, and all my man-catching parts were poised to commence sagging. Now I had to listen to a twenty-two year old grouse about his age. I managed to keep my lip from curling and moved on.

"Are you still in touch with either of the twins? I'd like to find out if Hazel ever talked to them about Maggie, maybe something to give us an idea of where she might be. I'd also like to know if Maggie contacts them about what happened to Hazel. Although Violet said Hazel and Reina didn't like each other much. Do you know anything about that?"

"Nah. Not really. I know they would come to the salon together once in awhile. I think Hazel was always trying to make friends. I don't know a lot about their relationship. I hadn't seen Reina for years until recently."

"Here?"

"Yeah."

"And?" I said, because he looked like something was about to burst.

"Well, it's work." Eddie lowered his voice, "I don't fawn over the beautiful girls. I fawn over the rich ones. But, Reina suggested we have lunch yesterday." I watched him preen at himself in the mirror behind me, and thought Reina must be my polar opposite. I find guys that I have to fight for mirror time revolting.

"How was that?"

He looked startled at my asking. "It was really cool, I was glad she asked me, but...I mean we didn't...we didn't talk about Hazel."

Too busy making the most of his chance with his high school dream twin. It didn't matter. At lunchtime yesterday, Hazel hadn't even been found.

"What about Rex?"

"I don't talk to Rex much. I ran into him a few months back, he's a bartender at the Yacht Club."

"Ok. If I give you my number, will you call if you hear from Maggie?"

"I guess. But, I mean, what if there's some reason she's not calling your friend?"

"There's no reason she wouldn't want Jack to know she's ok. If she is."

Eddie pulled out his cell phone and plugged in my number then gave me his card in return. "So you're just looking for Maggie? You're not looking at what happened with Hazel?"

"No. That's what the cops are for," I said. "We just want to know if Maggie's ok." Well, one of us did.

"Me too," Eddie said. "Let me know if there's anything else you need help with. Seriously."

I thought I might as well look through the appointment book. Since I was there it seemed stupid not to, but nothing stood out. I didn't see the names of any Neulands in this month's calendar. I waved goodbye to Violet and thanked Eddie for his help.

"Anytime." He tore his eyes from his reflection and flashed those gorgeous teeth in farewell. I went to retrieve Jack.

***

Jack was still conversing with the detective when I emerged from the salon. I made a beeline. The crease between Jack's eyebrows was in full effect, and he was stiff with tension. Quick said something I couldn't hear and passed Jack a card like the one I had gotten the night before. He treated each of us to a nod and made his elegant departure.

"What's up?" I said to Jack.

"Nothing. It was great. He asked if I had ever met Hazel, but he didn't believe me when I said I hadn't. He thinks I might have killed her."

"What? Why would you kill Hazel?"

"I don't know Ev. He's thinking I was overcome with rage when Hazel convinced Maggie to break things off."

"That's not what happened at all. Didn't you tell him about Leonie?"

Jack looked horrified. "You want me to drag your mother into this?"

More like she'd have to be dragged out of it once she found out. Leonie never turned her back on drama. "She'd love it," I said.

"He suggested I might have killed Maggie too."

I looked around; Quick had disappeared.

"He's just throwing around ideas, trying to get a reaction," I said. "And I think he likes to screw with people. How did he come up with that idea?"

"I think it was suggested last night at Neuland's."

I knew I didn't like Dr. Bobby. "When did you stop seeing Maggie?"

"A few weeks ago."

"So, before Hazel left Bobby."

Jack nodded.

"So that's how Bobby knows about you. He's trying to shift the blame elsewhere; you're just handy. It was probably him. He would have lost a lot of money when Hazel divorced him. The police went to question him first thing. He's guilty and panicking."

"I hope so."

"I told Quick what Bobby said about Hazel not getting his money like Verona did. The cops will figure out what really happened."

"Maybe." Jack sighed. "So Verona is the ex-wife?"

"I think so, but Quick didn't tell me anything. Please Jack. Don't worry. He has to check everything out." I tossed the watery remnants of my coffee into a nearby trashcan. "His sense of humor is a little sadistic, but I don't think he's corrupt or anything."

"I hope you're right."

"I'm right."

"You hungry?" Jack said.

"A little."

We walked to the old Las Casuelas on Palm Canyon. I had a strawberry Margarita and Jack had a Dos Equis. We picked at an order of cheese quesadillas.

"I loved those commercials. Remember them?" I asked Jack when he ordered a second beer.

"The most interesting man in the world?"

I nodded.

"I remember."

We sat and sipped.

"Maggie's always been such a pain in the ass," Jack said. "Almost as bad as your mother."

"Really?" Not that I disagreed with either assessment.

"No. No one comes close to Leonie." It sounded like a compliment.

"Maggie will be ok," I said, wishing I believed this to be true. I watched Jack dial her cell again. Then again. We left the restaurant and cruised by her house to see if anything had changed. Maggie's house was still wrapped up tight in yellow tape, like a wound on the cheerful street. Fitting; Maggie was like a wound in our lives. I hoped for everything to heal up soon.

Anne Stinnett

Six

I woke up in the dark. Consciousness had been too depressing, so I had pulled the curtains and checked out. Now the sun was gone for the day, but our troubles remained.

Gulliver was asleep with his huge head on my stomach and that point of contact was the only bit of warmth remaining. I had ratcheted on the air conditioner when we got home; it had performed admirably. I roused Gulliver and prevailed upon him to rise, which allowed me to do the same. I took my second shower of the day, shaving all the parts that needed it.

I was going out.

I toweled my hair to damp and combed it out, cursing every painful tug. Except for my sophomore year of college, when I had chopped it to my chin in a fit of frustration leading to a week spent in tears, this had been a daily ritual since I turned eleven, when Leonie had abdicated the care and feeding of my rowdy mane.

That chore done, I surveyed the clothes strewn around my room. Everything was draped over furniture or hanging out of suitcases. A few items that were expensive, delicate or both hung in the closet out of harm's way.

I was building an outfit around my almost new brown boots. They were nearly broken in, with stacked heels that made me tall without crippling me. I decided on my darkest jeans and a lightweight sweater that generously displayed my cleavage. To help the sweater give its all, I donned my favorite push up bra.

I gave my hair a quick few minutes with the blow dryer to speed it along without creating frizz, and then allowed it to finish on its own. Next, I assessed my face, tweezing a few stray hairs from my brows before shading my eyes to smoky. I was ready except for lips. I went straight for my current kissable favorite, Hibiskiss in Breeze. Not that I planned to do any kissing tonight. Not that I planned to do any ever. I eyed myself in the bathroom mirror. Everything seemed to hang together. I looked more free love than family values, but not so slutty either Jack or I would cringe when I saw him on my way out.

I filled my pockets with gloss, ID, and some cash. I plucked my keys off the dresser and made a face at my reflection, which responded in kind. I looked at Gulliver and said, "I need someone to go with me."

I love going to the movies alone. I'm comfortable eating at a restaurant by myself, and shopping with a cohort is not my first choice. However, the thought of walking alone into a packed club on a Saturday night had me feeling slightly ill. Jack couldn't go with me; at some point in the past, there had been an incident involving Jack, a nine iron, and Fred Fennell, the owner of the Yacht Club. The story ended with Jack spending the night in jail.

I called my go-to number for these and other pressing matters.

***

As a kid, Zuzu had been coltish. The summer after our freshman year, she grew even further, up and into her long limbs. Her hair was jet and always short. She had worn it in a slew of avant garde styles over the years, but I'd never seen it long enough to touch her shoulders. For good measure, there were big brown eyes and flawless skin. I had *never* seen a zit on Zuzu. She had ended up with the best combination imaginable from her ethnically diverse parents.

I pulled up in front of her house and in deference to the hour, texted the news of my arrival. This was Palm Springs, not Los Angeles; somebody was sleeping nearby. I saw long legs in skinny jeans coming my way, and then the door was wrenched open by my favorite self-esteem killer.

"You didn't call me last night," she said, not bothering to greet me. "If you want forgiveness, you better plan on buying my first two martinis."

"First three," I said.

We hugged over the gearshift then Zuzu said, "Oh shit! I think I left something on. Watch my purse."

I watched her bolt back into the house. I wasn't sure why the purse needed watching since I was the only one in the car, but I remained vigilant. I saw lights in various windows go on and off again as she made the rounds. I knew she hadn't left anything on.

Zuzu believes in disaster. She is ever cautious of fires started by unattended appliances. Every shelf in her place is screwed to a wall. She keeps a fire extinguisher in every room and always buys organic. Thirty gallons of water and a month's rations wait in her garage for the big one to hit.

I prefer not to think about all the catastrophes

waiting to befall me. However, since everything I owned had disappeared inferno style, I had ceased ridiculing Zuzu's eccentricities.

I watched her step onto the porch, lock the door, take two steps toward me then turn around to double check the locks. Sometimes it amazed me that she ever got anything done.

"So," she said, after she settled into the passenger seat and belted in, "You said we're partying with a purpose. Fill me in."

I told her everything, starting with Jack's request and ending with the morning's activities. "I figure he must be working on a Saturday night," I finished.

"I'm guessing he wasn't listed?" Zuzu said.

"No. He might not even have a landline."

"True. Poor us, forced to go to the bar in person. I like it. We get to have a little fun and get a little info about Jack's girl. Why isn't Jack here?" I reminded her about Fred Fennell and the nine iron.

"That Jack. It's kind of sexy, him defending Leonie's honor like that."

"Yeah, she wouldn't have it any other way. How's work?" Zuzu was an E.R. nurse at Desert Regional.

"Good. There was an accident the other day with a school bus."

"Yeah, that sounds good."

"Good because, luckily, it was just the bus driver and a couple kids. Turns out, the kids caused the accident. They set off a smoke bomb in the bus. So the driver can't see a thing and runs right off the road, and the little brats have the nerve to cry about a couple bruises and a broken arm. They're lucky no one was killed. I'm never having kids. You accidentally give birth to some little monster and there goes your life."

I shared those concerns to the extent that I had

aso sworn off procreation. And now that I had sworn off men, not reproducing should be a snap. I brooded on that for awhile then mentally snapped to attention when I heard Zuzu say something about a russet potato and an unmentionable orifice.

"Wait. What did you just say?"

She repeated herself.

"Oh my god," I said. "That's disgusting. Who does that?"

"More people than you'd think."

I was completely disgusted, but laughing so hard I barely managed to pull into the Yacht Club without crashing or peeing my pants. My stomach ached and I was in dire need of that martini now. We trundled out of the car and headed for the club, me tall in my boots, Zuzu even taller.

I swung my ass up to the door where we presented our ID's to the bouncer. Our legality verified, we stepped from the cool night air into the sauna created by hundreds of bodies jammed together. The DJ was blasting a dance mix and the crowd was making the most of it.

"I love this song," Zuzu called back to me.

I watched guys watch Zuzu as she slithered through the crowd. Like me, she was wearing jeans, but she had paired hers with a backless halter-top. Sometimes I envy her more modest bosom; the grass is always greener without a bra.

I pushed past a tall, dark, and damp Casanova whose shirt was unbuttoned to expose chest hair denser than the weave of my sweater. I shuddered and hoped none of his sweat had rubbed off on me. Zuzu had melted into the crowd. I slogged through the dancing bodies toward the bar knowing she would head there.

I stepped around a statuesque brunette and Zuzu grabbed me. She bent down to shout in my ear. "Where'd you go? He's working in the VIP lounge."

The VIP lounge was a supposedly exclusive area in the club. The truth was, as long as you were female and gorgeous or male and loaded, you could sail straight into the inner sanctum. I signaled Zuzu to go ahead and do her bombshell duty, but she won't always let me get away with that.

"You look hot, girl. Go use your god-given boobies."

Since she shrieked this so loudly that even the breathtaking din was unable to keep her voice from the surrounding partiers, I approached the hulk controlling access to the VIP room with an embarrassed flush spreading from my face all the way down to the god-given boobies in question.

I put on my brave face and took a deep breath in preparation for charming the giant guarding the door, but before I could speak he looked down at me and said, "Evin?"

Behind me, I heard Zuzu scream, "Hugo!" and then she flew past me and landed in the arms of Hugo Staniky. Hugo had been our varsity quarterback.

He hugged Zuzu and grinned down at me.

"She hasn't even had a drink yet," I told him as he set Zuzu down and gave me a hug.

"She has no idea what she's talking about." Zuzu gave me a playful shot in the arm. "I pre-gamed." She turned back to Hugo and said, "What are you doing working here? I thought you were a sexy fireman."

"I am. We're building an addition to the house. I'm here for the extra cash. When did you get back in town?" Hugo said to me.

I told him I was fresh from the snow.

"Did you finally ditch that creep who peed in the

shower?"

"How did you know about that?" I said, turning an accusing look on Zuzu. She shrugged, all innocence and gave Hugo's arm a squeeze.

"Anyway, that was ages ago. I just ditched a different creep."

"That reminds me," Zuzu said. "Give Serena my love."

That was the last thing he would do if he were smart. Serena Staniky, nee Greenly would have a fit if she knew Zuzu, or even I, had been within breathing distance of Hugo. Serena and Hugo's had been a storybook high school romance, which evolved into a seemingly content marriage complete with five (seriously, five) picture perfect offspring.

After each birth Serena had bounced right back to head cheerleader fighting weight. It was too bad because she was a complete bitch to everyone but Hugo. All I had ever been able to say in her favor was that she had always seemed to adore Hugo and appreciate him for more than just his general hunkiness.

On the other hand, her adoration caused her to behave like a jealous shrew, unable to behave civilly toward even the most casual female acquaintance of Hugo's. Of course, Zuzu knew this as well as I did, but unlike the rest of our class, she had never tired of baiting Serena.

We spent a few minutes catching up before Hugo waved us past the velvet rope that separated the very important people from the average Joes and Janes. Zuzu blew Hugo a kiss goodbye then grabbed my hand and dragged me across the lounge in search of Rex Neuland. On the way, we snagged a small booth. It was vacant, but not clean. I left Zuzu gingerly arranging debris on one corner of the sticky little table while I fought my way through to the bar.

I stood on the brass rail and leaned over to check things out. Looking down the length of the bar, I saw arms waving twenties, an annoyed looking server loading her tray and two overworked bartenders, one of whom was Rex Neuland. Conversation seemed impossible. I hung in there long enough to order and finally emerged from the throng with a couple of filthy Bombay Sapphire martinis held high.

I huddled over drinks with Zuzu and we talked strategy.

"Just ask if you can take him out to breakfast when he gets off," Zuzu said.

"He'll think I'm trying to pick him up."

"So?"

True. I felt queasy though. It was bad enough waylaying Rex and asking him inappropriate questions at work, but luring him elsewhere to do so touched on a whole new level of inappropriate.

We spent the next little while indulging our martini habit. I had planned to limit myself to one, but after the first I realized that was an arbitrary restriction. After two, I realized my nervous stomach had settled and that the alcohol was actually helping. In between rounds, we hit the tiny dance floor. When our server informed us of last call, we ordered doubles.

Now there was a steady trickle of people heading out of the club. I swigged the last of my martini, settled my tab with the non-Rex bartender, and walked very carefully down the length of the bar with Zuzu right behind me. Staying upright had somehow become more complicated than usual, but I felt completely confident approaching Rex Neuland.

I clung to the bar and attempted to hoist my ass onto a stool. To my left was a girl. I took in her long hair jealously; there wasn't a wave in sight. She was boldly made up, heavily accessorized, without a costume jewel to be found. Perfect nose; looked done.

"Hi, you're Rex aren't you?" I said when he approached our stretch of bar, "I'm Evin Hart. What are you doing when you get off?"

Rex gave me an odd look, and glanced at the girl next to me. I hoped she wasn't a combative girlfriend. Without responding, he continued down the bar, gathering drained bottles and glasses smeared with lipstick. I didn't sweat it; I felt good and I figured he had to come back eventually.

I was looking at the girl now thinking she felt familiar, and she was looking right back. It took me a beat to realize I had seen her the night before at Dr. Bobby's house. I turned away, wondering what Bobby's bitchy girlfriend was doing hanging out at his son's bar.

It was then that she said, "What do you want with my brother?"

Anne Stinnett

Seven

I was unwell. I opened my eyes, was sorry I had, and shut them again. I only just remembered sloshing through the door last night. I coughed weakly, bile rising in the back of my throat, and bolted on wobbly legs to the bathroom, arriving without a moment to spare, to spew the remains of last night's good time.

Gulliver objected to the morning after sounds and used his big dog voice to let me know it. I shushed him, dragged myself into the shower and out again, brushed, gargled, threw up once more, and gargled again. I threw on something and shuffled out to the kitchen barefoot and aching. Jack was waiting with coffee.

"I'm dying," I told Jack, taking the coffee he had doctored to my liking. "And I'm definitely taking a break from alcohol."

"I know that feeling, but shouldn't you swear never to drink again?"

I snorted, then winced, "A break is more believable." The coffee was staying down. I took another sip. It stayed down too. "Jack, I'm sorry. I didn't find out anything from Rex. I'm not good at this whole finder of lost loves thing; even if you don't actually love her."

"At least you had a good time."

"I did meet the step twins."

"And?"

"Awful." I told Jack what I could remember about Rex's cold shoulder, Reina's haughty glares and the total lack of cooperation that had ended with Hugo apologetically hoisting me over his shoulder and removing me from the bar.

"She's kind of evil," I said now.

"Because she made a scene and embarrassed you?"

"Uh...yeah."

"People defend family."

"It's a bad family."

I threw caution to the wind and took a few vigorous gulps from my mug.

"Don't worry," Jack said. "We're getting help. You need to get dressed; we're meeting him in half an hour. I have a lesson after that, so we'll pick up your car on the way."

"You have a lesson? You're the one obsessed with finding this woman. And you're too busy to help?" I was screeching and it was bad, bad, bad for my head.

"Ev, I have to work. There's no reason you have to go, if you don't want. Harry can handle it."

"Actually you don't have to work, you have tons of money. Harry?"

"You remember Harry. We were just talking about him."

"We don't need him." I was trying not to scream, not out of concern for Jack's feelings, but for fear I might rupture something in my brain if I did.

"We need something."

"What's he still doing here anyway?"

"He lives here."

I huffed. I'd been overcome with the need to flee the desert. I hadn't hesitated to venture into the sunset in pursuit of my still elusive destiny; whatever that was. I found contentment in others annoying.

"You used to play with him."

"No." I wished Jack would stop making me talk; it hurt.

"You did. Ask your mother."

I searched my pickled, cranky brain and came up with, "He never washed his hair." I didn't want to talk about Harry Chalmers.

"You didn't wash your hair either when you were that age. He'd been working with Stella for years when she died."

"I don't think we need help."

"Evin, it's done. Don't worry, you'll like him."

I doubted it. Kiss or no, I never had.

"Fine. But didn't his mother take off when he was a baby? And then his dad died a few years later?"

"Yeah, so he grew up with Stella." Jack gave me a hard look. "But don't feel like you need to discuss all that with him. And I'm sure you didn't mean to insinuate that the loss of his parents diminishes his worth."

"Like I'm that insensitive," I snapped. "Where's my car?"

***

My car was at the Yacht Club. Zuzu, a responsible sort of party girl, probably thanks to the mangled DUI victims that paraded through the ER each Saturday night, had procured a cab to take first me, then herself, home.

We retrieved it, and then I followed Jack's Range Rover to the nearest Starbucks. As usual, it wasn't far. When we arrived, I spilled out of my car and went to meet Jack's detective.

I would not have recognized Harry Chalmers. I shook hands self-consciously, suddenly certain I was rumpled and smelly. I had showered this morning, but not since the last bout of vomiting. I frowned at Jack. He'd tricked me into expecting an adult version of the wiry, grubby kid I hardly remembered, not over six feet of solid magnificence. It was downright unacceptable.

"Are you okay?" Harry said, inspecting me with dark blue eyes. I didn't remember the hypnotic eyes, and unlike my own, they held not a tinge of red.

"What the hell did you tell him?" I scowled at Jack, making my headache worse.

"Just what Zuzu told me when I helped her get you inside last night."

I tried to form a suitably dismissive and witty retort, but everything that whizzed through my head was either ridiculous or too bitchy to say in front of someone who didn't really love me.

"He didn't say anything to make me think less of you."

"What does that mean?" I said.

"Forget it," Harry said.

"Fine. Let's just go."

"Did you bring the key to Maggie's house?" Harry asked Jack.

"Evin has it."

"Are you sure you feel up to this?" Harry asked me. "I can manage."

"I know what both places look like normally," I told him. "And I'd prefer to help."

***

We had dropped my car off at Leonie's. I was strapped into the passenger seat of Harry's shiny new Jeep Rubicon in Red Rock Crystal Pearl. I knew the color because I had briefly considered blowing my car insurance on one and had gone on a couple test drives. However, there was nothing wrong with the Thunderbird that a dedicated mechanic couldn't cure, and in deference to my lack of career prospects I was trying not to be financially impulsive.

"What?" Harry said. He'd caught me looking; I turned away and scowled over at the car next to me. The white haired motorist in the next lane looked startled.

Since there was no communication happening in the Rubicon, I dialed Zuzu, curious about how she was feeling.

"Hey Ev," she answered on the first ring. "Glad you didn't succumb to the alcohol poisoning."

"It was close."

"What are you doing now?"

I filled her in on the day's proposed events. Her focus was skewed, she began loudly interrogating me about my companion.

"What guy? Did you pick someone up last night when I wasn't looking?"

"No!"

"Well, who is he? Is he cute?"

I glanced at Harry; he winked at me. Who winks?

"No! He's a private investigator. He's not cute at all." A deep laugh sprang from Harry's throat, like Athena from Zeus's forehead.

"Evin, I know you're lying. He sounds cute. He sounds beautiful. Tell the truth."

"No. He's… I knew him when he was a kid. I don't remember if you ever met him. His aunt was a friend of Jack's."

"How old is that fine boy?" Zuzu shrieked.

"Why?" She needed to calm down. Now.

"I'm twenty-five," Harry said.

"See," Zuzu said, "That's not too young. That's only six years. You won't even be a cougar. You have to be forty to be a cougar. I say go for it with that fine boy."

"Man," Harry corrected.

Ugh! "Stop yelling Zuzu," I said. "He can hear you. I just wanted to see how you were feeling and make sure you got home ok," I said. "I have to go now."

"If you have to go, then go," Zuzu said, "But cheer the fuck up already. I'm feeling fine and so would you if you'd drink some water and take a couple aspirin before you pass out. Bye."

My phone went dead. It started vibrating before I could put it away. It was Zuzu. I answered reluctantly.

"By the way, it's sexy as hell that he's a detective. Like Magnum."

"Just because he's a detective-" I faced the window again as though that gave me privacy. "What about Nero Wolfe?"

"Archie Goodwin."

"He was just the assistant. Hercule Poiroit."

"Kojak."

"Kojak? You think Kojak was sexy? He was going to be *my* next example."

"Give it up Ev. I know he's good looking. I know he's so good looking that you can sit there telling me he's not right in front of him, without worrying about hurting his feelings. Plus, you already have a history with him. He's the one you kissed, isn't he?"

I felt justified in hanging up on her.

***

At Maggie's the yellow tape was down. It looked the same as it had on my first visit, but felt different. That may have just been me. Harry parked on the street and we scrunched across the gravel to the front door.

I produced the key and we stepped through the doorway. I took the gloves he offered and donned them.

"I thought this was legal," I said.

"I always prefer not to leave prints."

"I already left prints."

"Then don't wear them."

The house was cool. I heard the air conditioner humming away, but it hadn't made the house cold enough to prevent the remarkable stench of dead fish. I followed the smell to the kitchen. Make that dead crustacean.

Apparently, Maggie had been working on an appetizer tray to go with the bottle of California Chardonnay that was sitting uncorked on the counter. A dozen departed shrimp slumped gracelessly around the rim of a crystal bowl filled with cocktail sauce. A wedge of brie and a box of oyster crackers had been waiting to join the shrimp on a bamboo tray. I gagged.

Whatever its condition before the murder and subsequent searches; the kitchen was now in a state of complete chaos. Cupboards were ajar, drawers open, the trash bag removed from the can. Harry came in. I turned to him and said, "Would the cops have done all this?"

"Searching is messy."

I told him about the mess that had been in the living room before the cops even showed up.

"Let's have you take a look in there." We returned to the living room. The disarray was greater than I remembered.

"I'm not sure," I said. "They moved the books, those are different."

"Different how?"

"How they're stacked. They weren't on their sides before. They were upright, like they should be. All those books were pulled off the shelves." I could see Maggie's books were no longer in any coherent order, it was a literary free-for-all. I turned to the entertainment center.

"You know, it felt like forever before the cops got here, but it couldn't have been. It isn't that far from the police station and it's a good neighborhood." I took a breath and thought. "So," I said, "I don't think Maggie had much time for an impromptu search. I think she just looked where she would have hidden something."

"That makes sense, but it wouldn't necessarily have worked. The person that hid whatever it was could have had different ideas about a good spot."

"Isn't it just as likely they had similar ideas? For all we know, Maggie already found it. I mean if it was Maggie." We were moving steadily from one room to the next, Harry looking efficiently through the bedrooms and bathrooms. "How is this helping us find her?"

"Can't hurt. Could help. I'm interested."

"I'm not. I feel bad about all this, Hazel and Maggie, but mostly, it makes me sick. I just want to know Maggie is ok, and that she's not some wacko killer and forget about everything else."

"You don't have to do this. I can drop you off at home." His concerned tone kept me from snapping.

"I can't not help Jack."

On that happy note, I wandered back out into the living room.

The books were killing me. No matter the mayhem and death surrounding me, I was pained by good books treated badly. I started returning them to their proper orientation, blowing off dust as I worked. The lone Stephen King was still nestled in a stack of Hemingway's. I picked up the lot, pressing it together and rotated it onto the shelf.

Harry joined me. "Nothing interesting back there. I'm going to take a quick look at the pool."

"Do you think there's anything left to see?"

"Probably not. A lot of the job is going through the motions. I'm here. I look. Cheer up." He slid the glass door open and stepped onto the patio. The warm air oozing in from outside gave me a shiver.

"There's blood by the edge of the pool," Harry reported.

I was happy to take his word for it. "Yeah, I must have missed that the other night, I was distracted by the body." I tried not to dwell on that. The general misery of my hangover was giving way to frustration. "We haven't found anything new. We're supposed to be finding Maggie, not wallowing in a murder."

"Let's drop by Jack's. Maybe she's holed up there."

Anne Stinnett

Eight

Mystic Springs sprawled in the sun like a handful of jewels. Fairways of emerald green, deep pools of sapphire, and homes with floor to ceiling windows that sparkled like diamonds tempted the eye and conspired to empty the pocket. Polish, polish everywhere, the only things in the rough were the golf balls.

Potential residents could choose from condominiums or single-family homes. Although the traditional nuclear family didn't seem to exist here. I had never seen a bike left on a lawn, or a basketball hoop in a driveway. The houses were in sedate, pristine rows with too little space in between them, and the condominiums were grouped in small clusters surrounded by transplanted greenery.

I loved Jack's condominium. It was only two bedrooms and a den, but it was stacked four floors high.

My phone rang just as we pulled up. It was Jack. I handed the phone off to Harry and made a hasty exit from the Rubicon. I didn't have the heart to report our lack of progress.

I entered through the small foyer that led to the living room and kitchen. Everything smelled funky. I glanced into the kitchen to see if Jack had left something out to spoil. It was gleaming and unused. I hoped nothing had crawled into the walls and died.

I trotted down the stairs to Jack's study where he kept some unloved golf clubs and a partners desk that had been a gift from Leonie on a long past anniversary. No Maggie. Down a short hallway off the living room was a bathroom. The kitchen held a small laundry alcove that I doubled back to check. Both were empty. The bedrooms were upstairs, each on its own floor.

I headed up. On the second floor was an extra bedroom but like everything else in the world, it held no clue to Maggie's whereabouts. I checked the closet. Some are bursting with dark secrets, but this one was empty except for some spare golf shoes and a lone hanger. The room was furnished with a double bed and matching dresser and nightstands. I dropped to one knee and checked under the bed to be thorough. Not even a dust bunny. I heard Harry calling from below.

"Hang on," I yelled back. "I still have to check Jack's room." *Not that he ever used it.* I trudged up the remaining flight of stairs. The master suite was blindingly bright, sprinkled with windows and a skylight on top. The bedroom set was antique, mahogany and manly. The body on the bed was new, blonde and bloody. I dry heaved and backed out of the room. I didn't stop until I stumbled backward off the top step. I flung out an arm, managing to catch myself on the banister before I tumbled down the entire flight.

I called for Harry; but it came out like in a nightmare, soundless. Now that I knew what the smell was, I didn't want to inhale it. I pulled the top of my shirt over my mouth and nose, and forced a deep breath. Then another. I pulled myself up by the banister. I didn't scream, but I did run. I barreled into

Harry on the landing outside the spare bedroom.

"You ok?" He said.

"She's dead." I gagged. "Maggie's dead."

"Stay here. Don't touch anything else." Harry disappeared up the stairs. I took three more deep breaths to steady myself then disregarded the instruction to stay.

Harry was on the far side of the bed, peering down at Maggie's face. I looked away from the blood soaked form.

"Did you see her face?"

"No. And I don't-"

"How's your stomach?"

"Right now?"

"If you can take a look at her without throwing up, I think you should."

"Sadist."

"Yeah, but that's not why I want you to look. Jack sent me a picture of Maggie and I don't think this is her."

"I should have stayed downstairs," I said, moving warily around the bed.

"Well, maybe this will teach you."

"Teach me what? Never to help Jack? That's how all this started."

"I think it started before that. She's been dead for awhile."

"What's awhile?"

"Maybe two or three days."

"That's not that long."

"No. But Maggie was alive Tuesday night."

"Oh. Right." It was Thursday now.

I made it around the foot of the bed and edged my way closer to Harry and the dreadfully dead woman. The blood and other mess that had spilled from her saturated the bedding beneath. Even worse than the gore was the smell. I closed my eyes; deep breaths were out at this point. The air was tangy with blood and bad meat. I wasn't sure if it was worse because I knew the source or because I was in the room with it; at least last night's excesses had left me with nothing to vomit.

I opened my eyes at Harry's insistence and tried to examine her dispassionately. Her hair was blonde and beautifully highlighted like Maggie's. She had a ski slope nose with a pointy little tip. The nails on the ends of slightly chubby fingers were French tipped and manmade.

"It's not her," I said, and removed myself from the immediate vicinity. "Maggie's nails were natural, and the nose is wrong... different, I mean. What the fuck is going on?"

"I don't know, but here, put these on." Harry said, again producing gloves. I saw he was already wearing a pair.

"I'm not touching her," I said, and shoved them back.

"For this," he said, holding up an excessive shoulder bag. "Come on." We stepped back onto the landing where Harry bent and carefully upended the bag on the floor.

"Are you crazy? The cops are going to want that!"

"They're going to get it. After we have a look." He looked up at me. "The quicker you help, the sooner we call them."

"Fine. Then you're taking me home and I'm done. I'm sorry about Maggie if she didn't do this, but, she probably did and Jack will just-"

"Save that speech for Jack."

I looked down. I told myself that just because I

was in the perfect position to kick him in the face, didn't mean I should. He finished searching through the various zippered pockets of the bag in time to catch my expression before I'd gotten it completely under control.

"You are a scary little woman," he said. I quirked an eyebrow at him; I didn't think that was what one said to a woman one was actually scared of. I sighed and plopped down on the floor.

"Wallet?"

"No," Harry said.

A few stray pieces of paper had fallen out in the initial dumping. I examined each one and found nothing more interesting than a grocery list that looked like it had been knocking around the purse for months.

"Here's something." I said, holding up a cheap cell phone.

"Let me see."

I handed it over, the better not to be an accomplice to whatever crime was being committed.

"Nothing in the contacts. One number in the memory."

"So?" I said. "Call it."

Harry pulled out his own phone, input the number and hit the speaker feature to connect the call. I heard it go straight to voicemail. The voice that emanated from the phone managed an impressive level of sultry, in spite of the poor quality of Harry's speaker phone feature.

"Who's Candace?" I said.

Anne Stinnett

Nine

The cops came and did their thing, Detective Quick arriving in short order to goad them on. While they searched, photographed and catalogued, Harry and I were invited to the police station to assist with their inquiries. We were allowed to go in Harry's jeep, but two black and whites trailed behind us the entire way. I spent the drive over trying without success to reach Jack.

At the station Harry and I were separated, and eventually, questioned. I wasn't privy to Harry's session, but my interrogation was more ruthless than the last. Apparently finding two bodies in two days seems suspicious to some. I had to admit, if only to myself, that I might have had an easier time if I had not sarcastically informed Detective Quick that it was useless to separate Harry and I now, as we had already gotten our stories straight.

He kept me there for hours making me prove it.

I ignored three calls from Leonie, two while in the clutches of Quick, who may as well have been an amnesiac as far as our previous bonding was concerned. Her third call I rejected as I sat on the curb waiting for Harry, because I was absolutely disinclined to have a truthful conversation.

By the time Harry came out, I was bordering on frantic. I was still dialing Jack; still getting no response. My calls were going straight to voicemail and I was so strung up I wanted to do something violent. Unfortunately, there was no one deserving in my vicinity. I could have used a few minutes with my porn bound ex. I threw my head back and blew out a loaded sigh.

"It's not for everybody," Harry took his eyes off the road and assessed me, "this job, I mean."

"But it's for you?"

"Yeah. Not the bodies, but the rest."

"What is the rest?"

"Helping damsels, kittens and the elderly."

"I think we should drop this, leave everything to the police. And why the hell won't Jack answer his phone," I said, shaking mine under Harry's nose. "He's so irresponsible, he's barely a grown up."

It was getting dark, so I knew Jack wasn't still holding forth on the fine art of the backswing. We were cruising down Indian coming up on the turn that would deliver us to Leonie's, and bring an end to my inept and reluctant involvement.

"You passed it!" I snapped as we sailed by our street. I saw the muscles in Harry's forearm shift as he tightened his grip on the steering wheel.

"We do need to get you dropped off," he said, regarding me with those blue eyes, which were looking remarkably cold. "Do you want that to be at home?"

"Sorry." I caught myself in an eye roll. So did Harry. "No, I am. I'm just bad with death and uncertainty. And I'm worried about Jack."

"And Maggie?"

"Less and less."

Harry had made the next turn and was making

his way back toward Leonie's.

"Keep trying him. He'll answer eventually."

"Not that. I'm worried he's going to get hurt somehow because of Maggie. It's hard to think well of someone who disappears and leaves you with a body."

Ride of the Valkyries began to blast from my lap. I snatched up my phone, and pushed ignore.

"It's my mother," I said, in answer to Harry's querying eyebrow. "And don't judge me. Have you seen her since she started practicing Absolute Truth?"

"No. Is that what it sounds like?"

"Yes. She tells the truth. Always. No matter how much we beg her to stop."

"Sounds entertaining."

"It's not."

Leonie's was as cool and quiet as we had left it. Gulliver was thrilled to see us. Harry took Gulliver's kamikaze introduction in stride, bracing himself and scratching under my baby's chin until he was a puddle on the floor.

Of course. Gorgeous and an animal lover. Although, he'd already shown his snarky side. Leonie had recently informed me that I brought that out in people, using herself as an example.

I tried Jack again and swore when I got no answer.

I had just disconnected when the landline started ringing. I moved to the counter to scope out the caller ID. Unknown. The niggling in my stomach provoked a sense of urgency that wouldn't allow my customary screening.

I answered on the fourth ring.

Before I could utter my wary hello, Jack said, "Evin?"

"Damn it Jack, where have you been? I've been

calling you for hours. We just came from your condo. There's a woman there. I thought it was Maggie, but it wasn't and she's-"

"Evin, shut up!"

I shut up. Not because a firm masculine tone commands my obedience, but because it was so uncommon for Jack to snap at me that I was startled into silence.

"I'm in jail," Jack said. "They arrested me."

"Who arrested you?"

"The police, Evin."

"I know that. I meant why?"

"For murder. Two murders, of Hazel Neuland and Candace Brown."

"That's ridiculous. How could they do that?"

I had meant it rhetorically. Jack could only have been arrested (for murder that is) as the result of some egregious error, but he filled me in on the pertinent points anyway.

"Jack is in jail," I said to Harry. My voice came out squeaky and desperate. "They arrested him for murder. They're saying he killed Hazel and Candace Brown. The woman we found, her name is Candace Brown." I thought about it. "But that woman called Candace, so how could she be Candace?"

"Evin, are you there?" Jack said sharply in my ear, while Harry said, "Let me talk to him."

"I'm here. Hang on," I put the phone into speaker mode and set down the handset, "Harry's here too. Who the hell is Candace Brown?"

"I don't know. They arrested me right in the middle of a lesson." Jack sounded a little unhinged.

"You're upset about the timing?" I sounded a lot unhinged.

"I'm upset because a woman was killed in my

condo, apparently with a knife from my kitchen, which may be the knife they found in Hazel's body. Maggie is missing, and I have no alibi, because this morning was the first time I left Leonie's in a week. You have to find Maggie. She knows something."

"So they arrested you because the murder weapon may have come from your kitchen?" I said. "That's it?"

There was silence from the phone. I looked at Harry.

"Jack?" I said.

"I don't know, Ev."

"You're sure you don't know Candace Brown?" Harry asked Jack.

"I'm sure. And I didn't know Hazel either."

I told Jack everything would be ok. He disagreed, which I understood; I hadn't meant it anyway.

"I need a lawyer, Ev."

"I'll take care of it."

"You know a lawyer?"

"No. I'll just-" Leonie's ringtone blasted from my cell. Gulliver started barking and turning frantic circles. He knows.

"Hang on. Leonie's calling," I said to Jack. "I know she knows a lawyer." I grabbed my phone and pressed talk.

"Hi," I said, and braced myself.

"Evin Jaymes Hart, I did not raise you to ignore my calls."

Not on purpose.

Leonie raged on, "I have been trying to reach you all day, and I am furious. I turned the picture of you on the end table face down because I can't stand the sight of your face."

"Sorry. I couldn't talk."

"Is that, lacked the ability to talk, or found it

temporarily inconvenient to do so?"

I sighed. Loudly. Into the phone.

"I thought so. When I don't want to speak to someone, I have the decency to answer the phone and tell them so. I expect the same courtesy from you, Evin. You need to pick up the phone and share your uncensored thoughts. To do otherwise is dishonest, inconsiderate and not how I brought you up."

Actually, Leonie was a Johnny-come-lately to Absolute Truth having only been practicing for about eighteen months. Coincidentally, the advent of AT had come just before I had raised the avoidance of Leonie's calls to an art form.

I broke down and told her this. I practiced Absolute Truth only on Leonie and only in self-defense.

She laughed. "And didn't saying so feel marvelous? You're one of my favorite things, darling."

"I know."

"Now that I like you again, tell me why you're happy I called."

I told her about Maggie, the bodies, and Jack in the slammer.

"Again?" Leonie said, referring I assumed, to Jack being arrested, not the body count.

"It's not like what happened with Fred Fennell," I said. "He didn't do it this time."

"How could you not tell me?"

"I just found out. In fact, he's on the house line now."

"If you just found out, why have I been unable to reach you for hours?"

"Because, at first I was being questioned about the woman who was stabbed to death in Jack's condo, and after that I just didn't feel like talking to you." Self-defense.

"He should never have bought that place." I thought that was a ballsy statement considering Jack had only bought the damn thing when Leonie had insisted on the separation.

"Mother-"

"I'm coming down there."

This I didn't need. "It's going to be fi-"

"How is that darling? The current state of affairs is nowhere close to fine. I think you need me. I'm coming."

"We can handle it."

"No you can't. If you and Jack could handle things, he wouldn't have been arrested in the first place."

"How is it his fault? He didn't even know them."

"Obviously Maggie has somehow embroiled him in all this. If your stepfather hadn't goaded me into throwing him out he would never have met her. His refusal to live in his condo makes him culpable as well. If he had been in his proper place, his little girlfriend wouldn't have had free reign to strew bodies around. Your decision making process is suspect as well. You let Jack be arrested and you threw away five years of your life getting a Master's in Theater Arts. So you need my help."

"Mother, we all appreciate your quest for the truth-"

"*Absolute* Truth, darling, and I don't think you do."

"Fine, I don't. Nobody does. By the way, there was nothing wrong with my major. I need to find a lawyer so I'm hanging up." I drummed my fingers on the cool marble of the countertop and frowned at Harry. I didn't hang up.

"You don't know a lawyer. If you pick one out of the yellow pages, you have no idea what you're getting. I refuse to deal with whatever extreme reaction you would have to Jack's execution. I will handle his attorney."

I took that to be an Absolutely Truthful statement. Leonie was determined that the world should perform to her specifications, and it usually did.

"You," she said, with fearful calm, "find that woman."

I told her we were doing our best.

"Make it better than it's been so far," she said, and hung up.

Harry looked bemused. "Don't ask," I said, "If you hang around too much you'll get the full treatment eventually."

"Something to think about," he said.

"Jack, are you still there?"

He was.

"I don't know how much you heard, but Leonie's finding a lawyer."

"Don't you know any, Jack?" Harry asked.

"Just tax guys, or contract law."

I heard voices in the background from Jack's end.

"What's going on?" I said.

"I have to go." Jack sounded stressed. "They're getting ready to move me to Banning."

"Why Banning?"

"That's where the jail is. Tell Leonie. I'll call when I can."

I placed the handset back in the cradle, and looked at Harry. Before I could muster a word my cell phone went off again. It was Zuzu.

Instead of hello, she greeted me with, "By the way, what with your grouchiness earlier, I forgot to give you Rex Neuland's address."

Good news. It had been so long. "You are the best." I riffled madly through the junk drawer in search of pen and paper. I came up with a half pencil someone had filched from the library and an old receipt from Clark's.

"I am the best, but save your praise for when I've done something that wasn't diabolically easy." She read the address to me.

"He just gave you his address?"

"Phone number. We exchanged. I used that to get his address."

"Nice. He doesn't know about anything. Right?"

"I don't know what he knows or what he doesn't. He's expecting a buzz from me so I know he's going to be disappointed."

"Hey!" I said, although it was true.

"Not like that." Zuzu was laughing at me. "He's expecting me to call because I'm interested in him, but instead he's going to get you asking questions about his dead stepmother. See the difference, my fine bosomed friend?"

"Jeez, Zuzu. Ok. And thanks."

"Yup."

"Do you know when he'll be home?"

"Now you've ruined everything, by expecting too much. It's the story of your life Evin."

"Not true. I have virtually no expectations and I'm beyond thrilled to have Rex's address. I mean not thrilled, obviously, because Jack is in jail and some woman is dead in the condo, well, not in the condo anymore, they took her away."

"Who's dead in the condo? Jack is in jail? Who's with you? The hot guy from earlier?"

I checked my ear for blood. Zuzu could project. I confirmed Harry's presence, and then filled her in on Jack's arrest and the preceding events. "But Leonie is working on a lawyer for Jack, so he'll have a great one, some top of the class shark that will get him released right away, and probably get that damn Detective Quick fired too, so don't worry Zuzu..." I took a deep breath and sobbed it back out. My throat was clenched and painful; I did my best to clear it. Harry extended a box of Kleenex and averted his gaze. I accepted, grateful for the moment of tact. I blew my nose on the pale blue tissue then took another to dry my eyes.

"Sorry," I said, to the world in general.

Zuzu did her best to reassure me. "Jack will be ok Evin. They're going to find out who really did this."

"What if they don't? Jack can't prove where he was, because he's been here drinking and feeling sorry for himself for the past week. Even worse, the police think the murders were done with a knife from his kitchen." I was pacing back and forth, dodging Gulliver who was sprawled across the kitchen floor.

"If Jack doesn't know what she was doing there...he didn't know her did he?"

"No. He didn't even know Hazel. We don't know why she was there. We know Jack had the bad sense to give Maggie a key, so presumably, that's how she got in. None of us knows who she is. I think Maggie might have killed her, but I don't understand why she would do it at Jack's. The cops suggested that Jack was sleeping with Candace and stabbed her to death in a fit of rage. It's bad." I remembered Quick had made the same suggestion to Jack regarding Hazel. I sat down for a second then popped back up to pace some more. My stomach was roiling.

"Maybe Maggie set him up because she was jealous."

"No," Zuzu said. "That still wouldn't explain what happened to Hazel. Unless Jack was carrying on with her too."

"No way. He was barely carrying on with Maggie. He's team Leonie forever."

"When is she getting here?" Zuzu asked.

"She's not coming." She had said she was coming. I didn't want to believe it.

"You sure? She hates to miss out on anything exciting."

"Yeah." I refused to think about that right now. "Look Zuzu, we have to go, ok? I'll let you know what happens."

Anne Stinnett

Ten

Gulliver, Harry and I, were en route to Rex Neuland's. Gulliver was expressing his fascination with Harry by trying to force his way between the front seats and into Harry's lap. Harry had won this extreme show of affection by roughhousing with Gulliver in a way that I never did anymore, having too often ended up at the bottom of the dog pile, covered in drool and unable to breathe. In Harry, Gulliver had found his match. I guess boys do need a man in their life. I was in the passenger seat trying to dissuade Gulliver from climbing into Harry's lap. An accident wouldn't be the worst thing that had happened today, but still.

The next generation Neuland lived in a modest brown house in Palm Desert. Like Maggie's, it had region appropriate landscaping. Unlike Maggie's, it didn't look good. There were a few unhealthy looking aloe veras in orange clay pots dotting the otherwise naked sand. One had tipped over and spilled dark soil onto the pale ground. In the driveway sat a much-abused old Saab. It went well with the yard.

We approached the door, Harry looking sexy and competent in khakis and a striped button up. The shirt was shades of blue and the sleeves were rolled up showing strong forearms. I was sweaty and rumpled, but I tried to project an authoritative attitude while Gulliver frisked by my side. Maybe he should have stayed home. Maybe I should have.

Harry reached for the bell; I grabbed his arm. Since my discovery of Hazel's body, every action had been greeted with an equal and opposite calamity. I was frantic to find some answer that would lead to the real killer and free Jack, but I was nowhere near prepared for additional sinister revelations. Harry placed a hand over mine. It was large and reassuring, the kind of hand that could handle a crisis. I took a deep breath and nodded, then he used it to ring the doorbell.

The chimes had hardly faded when there was a thud from the other side of the door. Gulliver, perhaps mistaken about who was inside and who was out, started barking and strained forward, pulling me with him. Harry grabbed him by the collar and hefted him back. Not surprisingly, the door didn't open.

Harry rang again, nudging Gulliver and I out of the way to smile reassuringly at whoever was observing our little carnival through the peephole. It was a good smile, shiny-white and even. The door opened to reveal a pixie faced girl with shoulder-length cranberry hair waving away a cloud of aromatic smoke. A row of three silver hoops adorned her lower lip and a stud sparkled in her nose. She wore a battered Hello Kitty tee over black jeans. The inside of her lower left forearm sported a tattoo of a beetle with a yin yang symbol for a body.

"What does that mean?" I asked, socially intrusive questions being preferable to this misbegotten crusade.

She followed my gaze and answered, "Oh, that's just to remind me about balance and that there're two sides to everything, you know? I got it cuz my boyfriend and I used to fight all the time, I mean like crazy, you know? Stupid shit. Mostly, stupid shit he said, of course, right? But one day I realized, stupid or not, he can have his opinion. I mean for sex that good I can put up with a few stupid opinions, you know?"

I felt my eyes getting big. I glanced at Harry whose smile had widened. He nodded to her that he did know. Eeesh.

"So yeah, that's why I got it. To remind me that people can have stupid ideas and it's ok. It's balance, yin and yang, you know?" I guess we did. "Saved our relationship; completely prevented me from going nuts and committing some kind of murder-suicide pact. You know?"

"I don't think it's a pact if you do it *to* someone instead of with them," I said.

"Who are you anyway?" She said, giving me an unfriendly look.

I was someone who desperately wanted to be in bed, curled up with a book, far from reality. I was going to commit a murder-suicide pact on everyone in my immediate vicinity if this mess didn't come to an acceptable conclusion soon.

While I was contemplating that, Harry had been introducing me. My attention was pulled back to the conversation, such as it was, when the girl said, "You have freaky eyes, you know?" This from someone with a score of holes in her head and fluorescent hair. Not that I would judge based on appearance, when I had many, more valid, reasons.

"It's called Heterochromia iridium. Would you like me to spell it so you can go look it up?" I said politely. Harry gave me a look. I ignored it.

"What's your name?" she asked shifting her focus

to Harry. My lip curled. All on its own, you know?

"Harry. And yours?" He extended a hand her.

"I'm Trina." She giggled. Someone should tell her that Goth girls don't giggle. "Just so you know, we broke up anyway, my boyfriend and I, I mean. These things tend to work out for the best, you-"

"We know!" It slipped out.

Harry gave me another reproving look before rolling his bright, blue eyes at Trina. Gulliver whined softly and pressed his head against my leg. I scratched the top of his head and leaned down to tell him he was a good boy. I shifted irritably. The sun was beating down causing sweat to break out in a variety of uncomfortable places.

"We're looking for Rex Neuland," Harry was saying when I tuned back in, "This is his house, isn't it?" Finally, the point.

"He's my roommate." Trina said. "Well, I guess technically I'm his roommate since he owns the house and I rent from him." She looked right at me and said, "You know? He's not here now though."

"Do you know when he'll be back?" I said.

"No dude." She looked at Harry and added, "Sorry," and a smile.

"Maybe we can catch him at work," Harry said.

"I don't think he's at work, for once," Trina said. "All this stuff is going on with his stepmom. She was murdered. Actually murdered, I shit you not. Anyway, his family is fucked up generally, and now of course everybody's flipping out cuz of this, you know?"

"I met Rex and his sister last night." I said. "I think she was picking him up from work." I was actually a little fuzzy on that, but, whatever. You know?

"Yeah, she brought him home."

"That was nice, I guess."

Trina snorted. "She should drive everyone around. I mean she talked Dr. Neuland into getting her that Benz. It matches his. How gross is that?" It was pretty gross. "She might as well make herself useful."

"Rex didn't get a car?" I asked.

"No. He's big on doing shit for himself." Trina shrugged at the foolishness of self-sufficiency.

"This must be hard on him," Harry said.

"Yeah, it is, it really is. We talk a lot, you know? He works nights and so do I, even though I work from home, so usually when he gets back we blaze up and bullshit."

"Sounds like you two are close. I'm actually here about his stepmother's murder. I've been hired to make sure the investigation is thorough, and that the police don't get the wrong idea about anything."

"By Dr. Neuland? Yeah, that makes sense with the divorce and all." It did make sense. I was surprised it had occurred to her.

"Hey, Trina," I said, "Do you think we could come inside for just a minute. It's hot. And maybe Rex will come home in the meantime." I pulled my top out to blow down my cleavage hoping to dry the annoying trickle of sweat running between my D-cups.

"Hot? Dude, it's not even ninety today. Where are you from?" By the time I geared up to answer she had lost interest.

"He can't come in," she said abruptly, motioning to Gulliver with her chin, "I have a cat. But you can come in." She looked up at Harry from her petite barefoot height and flashed a smile as luminous as his, but marred by the array of hardware surrounding it.

I looked at Trina with her piercings and anti-social hair, and at Harry with his CK looks and style and thought that he probably wasn't her usual type. I guess gorgeous men are universal. Presumably, Harry was charming her in the interests of furthering operation Liberate Jack. Whatever.

Harry leaned forward and murmured something to the wretched Trina and then, with a flash of eyes and another nonconforming giggle, Trina escorted us through a gate on the side of the house. Shortly, we were in the backyard, butts in seats, the seats part of a rather shabby patio ensemble. Trina disappeared into a green and gold kitchen that looked like it had stood untouched since its construction in the fifties. To my surprise, she reappeared with a bowl of water for Gulliver.

From here, we could hear the music playing faintly inside. The playlist switched confoundingly from Nirvana's "All Apologies" to Frank Sinatra's "It Had to Be You."

"You have eclectic taste in music," I said.

"I know. Frank Sinatra's super old and dead right?"

Insightful. Right?

"But, I love this song, you know?" Trina said. "My dad used to listen to him all the time. He's dead now."

Now I felt like a bitch. I exhaled. "I'm sorry to hear that," I said, and it was absolutely true. I thought maybe I should mention that my dad was dead too, establish common ground, but no words came out. I took that as a sign that Trina and I would not be best friends forever. Or ever.

"It's ok. I was little." She turned definitively back to Harry, leaving me to assume share time was over.

"So, you know the whole family?" Harry said.

"Well yeah, you know. I went to high school with Rex and Reina. I mean, Rex and I have always been kind of tight, so I met the units in high school." She caught Harry's questioning look and added, "You know, parental units? It's from some movie I think."

It was originally from SNL. So, Harry wasn't a huge sketch comedy fan. So relevant. I yawned. The heat and the tedium of being relentlessly ignored had me all psyched up for a three hour nap. Gulliver had started his; he was sprawled beside my chair, head on my foot, gently drooling.

Trina was droning on, "Anyway, Dr. Neuland was ok, even though he's kind of scary when you talk to him. He never cared if we ditched class and had some beers by the pool. He has trouble keeping it in his pants though. I guess it sucks if your dad bonks everything around, you know? Rex hated it in high school, he thought it was embarrassing, but he would just drink and we would get high, que sera sera. Reina, his sister would really flip out. Then, Dr. Neuland would buy her something and that would be that. Hang on, k?"

Trina disappeared again through the patio door and returned with a dented Peppermint Bark tin, which turned out to contain several baggies of sticky looking greenery and the essential accoutrements.

"It's medicinal," Trina said, when she caught my look. "I have anxiety. I got a prescription from this great doc in Venice Beach. Besides, I have to do research for my job."

My brows shot up. I retrieved them, but not before Trina noticed.

"Dude, I'm a writer. For *Natural High*. You know, the magazine."

I didn't subscribe.

"Anxiety, that's tough," I said and flashed my shiniest smile when she looked at me doubtfully.

Trina's nimble fingers had already managed to assemble a fat, calming joint. Based on her speed and dexterity, I figured she'd suffered from anxiety for quite some time.

"So," Harry said, shifting in his flimsy chair. "The twins find their father's infidelities upsetting? I'm sure Rex is glad he has you to talk to."

"Yeah well, he just stays away from it now. When you grow up you don't have to deal with your parents shit so much." She paused to place the joint between her lips and inhaled.

Harry agreed that was a good lesson and had the gall to look at me when he said it.

"What about Reina?" Harry asked. "How is she coping with Hazel's death?"

"There was some drama lately, I guess. We didn't get into it much. Reina was pissed at Dr. Neuland. I think Rex is kinda protective of her, you know? Reina, I mean. But Mrs. Neuland was gonna be an ex anyway. I think Dr. Neuland was freaking out cuz of the money situation. The prenup and all, and it was trickling down. The property not the freak out."

She paused and sifted through the peppermint box pulling out a small clip with which she grasped the butt of the joint. "No, the other way, I mean. The freak out trickled down from Dr. Neuland. Not property."

What the hell is she talking about I thought, and said, "What property?"

"I don't know exactly. I think Dr. Neuland was going to help Reina out with some badass townhouse she wanted to buy up by Bob Hope's house."

"Did he help Rex buy this place?" Harry asked.

"Kind of. The story I got is Dr. Neuland helped by putting up the down payment, and that's it. Rex planned to pay Dr. Neuland back, you know, eventually. But like six months ago, Rex got a bug up his ass about it and started working all the time to pay back the down payment. He used to just work a few days a week and party the rest of the time, you know? Took lots of trips to Vegas. Totally perfect life. But like I told you, Rex has this thing about not taking stuff from his dad, cuz he doesn't like him that much. If it was me I'd take more if I didn't like someone, but whatever."

So much to admire in such a small package.

"So Bobby and Hazel were getting a divorce, right?" I said, leaning forward and tapping the smoked glass tabletop to get Trina's attention. "Was he seeing someone besides Hazel lately?"

"Uh, yeah. I think I said that already. Right?" Trina looked at Harry for support.

"We didn't quite get to that," he said, saving himself from getting kicked, "but no time like the present."

"Yeah, there was another one, that's what all the trouble was about, but I don't really keep track you know?" Trina took the last puff, and was wracked by a fit of coughing. When she recovered, she asked if anyone wanted a bottle of water.

"Yes." I said immediately. I could feel the sun burning my scalp. I shifted my chair a bit trying to bring my head under the protection of the umbrella sprouting from the center of the table. Trina returned with three deliciously cold bottles of water. I cracked mine open and downed half of it, my haste allowing trickles to run down my chin and neck. Harry took a more sedate sip and Trina set hers on the table where it remained untouched. I thought the cottonmouth would be killing her, but maybe she was immune.

In spite of the water, my patience, never

abundant, was waning. "So what were you saying before about the prenup?"

"I told you everything." She looked at me as though I was the idiot. I felt my temper surge. Gulliver lifted his head to assess the situation. He's very aware of my moods. I soothed him down, which had the collateral effect of enabling me to get a grip on my annoyance.

"Dr. Neuland had a prenup so Hazel couldn't, you know, take his money," Trina finally said. "But Rex told me it had some clause about cheating, so when he got caught, he was screwed."

"There really is no excuse for not cheating discreetly," I said. "I plan to be excruciatingly careful when I start cheating on my husband."

Trina nodded. "For sure, dude."

I don't know why I bothered.

"Do you know the name of Dr. Neuland's latest girlfriend?" Harry said.

"Oh, yeah. It's Candy. Can you imagine? I guess she's not even a stripper. Technically. Although, she did dance kind of naked. She was a showgirl in Vegas, which makes sense because of the name. It's no wonder Hazel took off. A fifty-six year old man sleeping with some slut named Candy."

"Candy what?" I managed.

"I dunno," Trina said. "I mean, it doesn't really matter now, right? No mistress, no wife, no divorce. Oh wait, Brown, it was Brown. I guess, Dr. Neuland wouldn't have had to dump the mistress if he knew the wife was gonna be dead right? Weird how it turned out."

"That is strange." Harry lifted his water out of the ring of condescension it had left on the table and took another sip. "Can you tell us anything about Verona

Neuland?" "The twin's mom?" Harry nodded. "Not much man. She had already taken off by the time I knew the twins, you know? She lives way the hell out in Palos Verdes."

Anne Stinnett

Eleven

"We have to call Detective Quick," I said. "We have to tell him about the affair. Bobby's wife and girlfriend are both dead. Both stabbed. I mean, it had to be him."

I pawed through my purse, frantically digging for the detective's card. "Jack never should have been arrested. This is ridiculous. What's wrong with this purse?"

Harry ignored my struggles with the errant bag and offered, "Quick probably knows about Candace and Bobby."

"Found it." I waved the besmirched card under Harry's nose.

"Maybe you should hold off."

"Shut up for a second. Please." I dialed Quick's cell. There was no answer. I wanted to leave a message, but both my courage and my brain deserted me.

"So what? Why shouldn't I have called?" I turned on Harry. "I want this behind us. Isn't cooperating with the police the best way to accomplish that? I want to get Jack out of jail. Then, I want to swim and sleep in the sun, which is what I came out here to do. I did not drive for two days in a small car with a large dog and the pitiful remnants of my belongings, just to get swept up in this clusterfuck. Which, by the way, I am not at all qualified to participate in, but because Jack needs saving, I don't really have a choice. Since you're the detective, if you have an opinion I guess that should count for something. But, feel free, in fact, feel obligated, to share your reasoning. Because I don't think Jack is paying you to screw with me and flirt with Drusilla Queen of the Damned back there."

"It's Pricilla, Queen of the Damned."

"No it's…" I paused for my brain to catch up with my mouth. "That's not the point."

"Jack isn't paying me. I've known the guy most of my life. My Aunt Stella adored him. And I'm sorry," he added before I could re-launch my mouth, "I know how tight you two are. This will be over soon, Evin. We know Jack didn't kill anybody. It's just a matter of how soon that's proven to the satisfaction of your detective."

"He's not my damn detective." I turned to look at him and Gulliver took the opportunity to kiss my cheek. This was no quick peck, but several hearty swipes of the tongue that engulfed the entire left half of my face. Between the two of them, I felt comforted.

Of course I fought it. "What about all the people who have been proven innocent after spending half their lives in jail? What if they never find out what really happened and just convict Jack?"

"Evin," Harry sighed and turned onto Leonie's street. "We won't let them."

He pulled up in front of the house. I hopped out and tried to persuade Gulliver to exit the vehicle without his beloved Harry. Finally, I stood hand on the door, looking in at Harry. "We still need to talk to Rex though, don't we?" I said.

"Yeah, you want to hit the Yacht Club again

tonight?" I'd never seen such an evil grin.

"How can you joke?" I snapped, turning away because the frequency of my public tears was getting ridiculous, and I could feel my eyes filling up again.

Harry reached over and put his hand on my cheek gently rotating my face towards his. "I can joke because I believe what I said about everything turning out ok."

I let my eyes meet his and he said, "Try it," before releasing me. The warmth from his hand lingered on my face, but I didn't notice.

"I'll call Leonie," I said. "Find out about the lawyer situation. Then, maybe I can see Jack."

"I'll check on Jack, but we can't see him tonight anyway. It's getting late." Gulliver was dancing on the sidewalk, tugging on his leash.

"Fine. Whatever. I'll make sure my mother got him a lawyer. And then..." I didn't know what.

"And then I'll pick you up in the morning. We'll drive down to Palos Verdes, chat with Verona."

As annoying as Trina was, at least she had been free with the information. Harry had Verona Neuland's address written on a Zig Zag in his pocket.

"Why not just call?" I said. "All I've done since I came back is go here, there, everywhere. I'm sick of it."

"It's better in person, easier to read people. Harder for them to refuse to talk."

"What if she's not home?"

"Then we'll have some time alone while we wait for her." He smiled. I tried to remember how annoying he had been throughout the day, but still my mouth went dry. I couldn't manage a retort, but I did pull together a disapproving look.

"You know you don't have to come."

"Yes, I do. You know I do." I was playing with the

end of Gulliver's leash.

"Yeah. So we'll talk in the morning."

"Call if you hear anything."

"Evin. What else would I do?"

I watched him drive away then I let Gulliver pull me inside.

I wanted to do something. Or rather, I felt like I should. My nerves were jangling from inaction, as though every second I didn't spend actively trying to help Jack brought him one step closer to a long life in the big house. I didn't know what to do, so instead of being a hero, I decided to take Gulliver for a walk.

It was nearly dark now, and the air was cooling quickly. I gathered Gulliver and his leash, reattached them and off we went.

Gulliver bounded along, sniffing and anointing choice landmarks. I followed behind trying to sink back into the comfort of Harry's assurances. It was almost impossible to believe Jack could be convicted of stabbing two women to death, more than impossible that he could have commited such violence. Unfortunately, what was impossible to me was possible to Detective Quick, even plausible. Therein lay the source of my dread, because my certainty of Jack's innocence would not save him from anything.

Who knew what a jury would see. What they could be led to believe. The Fred Fennell incident could come up. The sum of that incident was this: Jack took a few swipes at a few bottles during an after-hours poker game at the Yacht Club and then punched Fred Fennell once or twice, because Fred had been wondering aloud about various aspects of Leonie's anatomy. I thought Fred was beyond creepy, especially since he'd been carrying this particular torch since he and Leonie had been freshmen in high school. The prosecution though, would warp that tiny disagreement to color Jack as violent, dangerous.

I stopped because Gulliver had delivered a steaming pile to the Rasmussen lawn. I struggled to produce a bag from the depths of my pocket. Before I could, I heard the shuffle-shuffle-thud of Mrs. Rasmussen's slippered feet and rubber tipped aluminum cane. I cringed.

"I hope you're planning on picking up that animal's number two!" I sighed because I couldn't stand the scowling biddy addressing me; I did it under my breath because I was raised right.

"I always pick it up," I said turning and pulling Gulliver away to keep him from greeting the dread Mrs. Rasmussen. All I needed was to have to deal with the aftermath of my dog-hating, decrepit neighbor taking a nose to the crotch.

"She's a liar!" Mrs. Rasmussen shouted. I had no idea who comprised the invisible audience she was playing to, but I knew they wouldn't be sympathetic to me. "And don't think I didn't see you just leave it on the ground earlier."

"That wasn't on your lawn."

"Ha! She admits it." I looked around again for the person being addressed. Maybe Mr. Rasmussen was peering out from behind the curtains, grateful that for once, he wasn't the one being reprimanded.

"Mrs. Rasmussen," I said. "I forgot a bag last time, but I went back and picked it up. Both piles." I held in a scream.

"I don't like-"

"Come on Gulliver," I said, and sprang into action, action being a rapid jog away from Mrs. Rasmussen. "Bye now," I called over my shoulder. I didn't feel any obligation to hear what she didn't like; especially when it was something about me. I guess I wasn't raised right, only right adjacent.

We made it out of earshot and slowed to a stroll. There were houses along the entire street, but there was a feeling of privacy on the block. The yards were fenced, front and back, and shielded by healthy trees. Houses here were sanctuaries, holding the world at bay with brick or wood or iron.

We paused at the end of the street and debated whether to go on or go home. Gulliver wanted to go on. I was inclined to return home, but it didn't look good for my side. Finally, a half crumbled cookie and great heights of coaxing convinced Gulliver to head back. I was ready to dispose of my fragrant sack. The cute little paw prints that covered it failed to make the contents any more adorable. I held it casually away from my side, pinched between my forefinger and thumb to prevent it to splating against my leg. This was the one unpleasant facet of life with a dog. Just like babies with diapers. And spitting up. Babies also screamed in the night. They screamed during the day too, and had noses that never stopped running. Maybe a bag of poop now and then wasn't so bad.

We ditched our burden in the garbage and headed into the house. Gulliver raced to his bowls and sat at attention, motionless except for the Pavlovian string of drool. I mixed a can with his dry food and delivered it.

There was nothing decent to eat, but I wasn't hungry. I snatched my cell phone off the counter as I went past and saw that I had missed nine calls. All from my mother. I felt my Leonie headache kick in.

There were no messages. I pushed call. On the other end of the line was Leonie's voicemail. In my ear, smooth as glass her recorded voice said, "Tell me something true."

"Mother, you called nine times. You cannot call nine times and not leave a message. You want truth. This is the truth. You are making me crazy. If you call nine times with no explanation, it makes people worry because nine calls imply some kind of urgent situation, maybe even a disaster, and if you don't have the decency to leave a message someone might begin to frantically wonder what possible catastrophe necessitated the making of nine goddamn calls!"

Gulliver jumped up from his after dinner doze and started to bark. I realized I had gone to the far side of shrill and hung up.

I paced around the house. I took deep breaths. I eyed the liquor cabinet. I needed comfort. After last night, it should be non-alcoholic comfort. I had Gulliver, who in most situations was the epitome of comforting, but for now, I wanted words. I needed to be talked down from my mental ledge. Harry didn't need to know the extent of my crazy. Even though I was off men for now, he was too gorgeous and new to see me figuratively foaming at the mouth. I called Zuzu.

Twenty minutes later, the doorbell rang.

Anne Stinnett

Twelve

Even without the benefit of details, Zuzu had heard the distress in my voice and come prepared.

I was still a wreck. I had spent the time waiting for Zuzu making repeated calls to Leonie and Maggie, all of which had gone unanswered. I accepted the family size bottle of Bombay and the jar of olives and headed for the kitchen. Zuzu hopped her True Religion clad ass up on the counter and Gulliver plopped at her feet. I tended bar. There were some tense moments when we couldn't crack the olives open; but in the end, after some sharp blows to the lid, followed by the fortuitous discovery and clever application of a wide rubber band, we prevailed.

"So what's happening now?" Zuzu sipped daintily and nibbled an olive as we talked.

"I have no idea."

"How's that?"

"Leonie won't answer her phone."

"Well, she's probably punishing you for not picking up when she called you. Maggie is hiding out. Why don't you call Harry? I thought it was his thing to check on Jack? And you can't expect that cop to call you back if you didn't leave a message."

"If Leonie was punishing me, she'd leave a

message telling me so. As for the cops, Harry thinks they already know about Candace. He says they're bound to find the connection between her and Bobby when they start going through her life. And I don't need to call Harry. I'll just talk to him in the morning. He's coming to pick me up." I finished my martini, popped an olive in my mouth.

"You're being shy with Harry, aren't you? Don't shake your head at me. I know you are. Well, shit."

"Shut up, Zuzu, I am not. He's kind of an asshole, is the actual problem. And he would have called, if he had any news."

"Sounds considerate for an asshole."

"Zuzu..." Gulliver thumped his tail on the floor. "See," I said motioning at my beloved canine, "he doesn't like you giving me shit."

"Oh, so in this house a tail-wagging dog is a pissed off dog. Got it. He is fine though, right? The man I mean."

"Not really. I mean, he's not that bad, but looks don't matter." I meant it. I wanted to anyway.

Zuzu laughed. "Ok, then. We can't call Harry because he's a fine asshole, or whatever. So, what can we do instead?"

"Drink. I wasn't going to since it didn't work out so well last night, but-"

"We're already drinking. What else? Oh, I know. Let's call that cop again."

"Zuzu, it isn't a game."

"Believe me Ev, I know." She polished off her drink and waggled her glass at me. I went to work on refills for us both.

"Just call him again. Leave a message. Do you want him to know or what?"

"Yeah, ok. It can't hurt. It can't, right?"

"Just call. Jack could be getting shanked with a toothbrush right now."

"You're supposed to be helping me feel better." I found the number in my cell and hit the talk button. "It's his voicemail again," I hissed at Zuzu who made a hand motion that I took as encouragement to leave a message.

I thought of Jack in a cement cell with a metal toilet and I talked. I was two drinks in, having downed my second for courage. Still, I remained concise and focused while relaying the information that the dead women were the wife and mistress respectively, of Dr. Robert Neuland, who for some reason was still running around free as a bird while decent, law-abiding stepfathers were being locked away left and right. I had just started to pontificate on the I.Q. level required to be a detective for the Palm Springs police when Zuzu snatched the phone from my hand and hung up.

"Holy crap!"

"What?" I said. "It's fine."

"You shouldn't have called." Zuzu almost fell off the counter she was laughing so hard.

"You made me."

"I know, but shit, Evin. You shouldn't have left a message."

"You told me to. You waved your hand."

"If he comes to arrest you, my story will be that I tried to stop you from dialing that number."

"I said my name, right?"

"Yep. You and your damn liquid courage need a keeper."

"That was supposed to be your job."

"I'm fired. Here." She refilled my glass and said, "Let's go be comfortable at least." She sauntered into the family room where she plopped onto Leonie's white Naugahyde couch.

"Besides, you were morally obligated to leave a message. You just reamed your own mother for not leaving a message, didn't you? You were just being the change you want to see in the world."

"I don't think that's quite what Gandhi had in mind, but I'll go with it," I said.

"Speaking of going with," she said, her aggressively casual tone setting off alarms in my head, "What exactly happened with that Cory guy?"

"Nothing. He was a jerk." Cory had been the jerk prior to Jason, the would-be porn king.

"They're always jerks," Zuzu said. "You know perfectly well I'm looking for details."

"It's no big deal. And they're not always jerks." I had dated several nice guys. They tended to object to something in me. Zuzu didn't know about that. As much as I loved her, there was no escaping the fact that she was 5'9" and rejected cute doctors on a regular basis. She had no frame of reference.

"Nevermind," I said.

"You know what I'm going to say about that." She looked me in the eye. I had no emotional privacy.

Zuzu was nattering on, "We'll do everything we can to help Jack tomorrow, but now is the time to let off some steam. Start fresh in the morning."

"Maybe."

"And I'm staying long enough to meet Harry. So spill it. Why no more lawyer boy?"

"You can know if you guess." I smirked at her.

"Come on. Ok. If you tell me what happened, I'll tell you about the toe guy."

"Eewww!" I shrieked. "Don't you dare. I'll tell you if you keep the details about the toe guy to yourself."

"Are you sure? We were on our way back from the McCallum and he just pulled over on Monterey, by that hill where we used to go ice blocking and then-"

"Stop. Stop or I'll scream." Gulliver, raised his big head, assessed the situation and let it flop down again.

"Ok, then spill it." Zuzu grabbed a pillow and nestled into the couch after placing her drink on the end table with exaggerated care.

"It really wasn't that big a deal," I said. "You know, you date, you have sex, someone's apartment burns down so you decide to live together, and then suddenly you're stuck with someone who leaves their socks on the floor and whines about annoying allergies they somehow forgot to mention on the first twenty dates."

"He was allergic to Gulliver?"

"No. He said he was allergic."

"You didn't believe him?"

"It seemed like it would have come up. It wasn't until we'd been living together for a couple weeks that he even thought to mention it."

"Hmmm. Any hives? Sneezing? Watery eyes?"

"Nope. Even when Gulliver would spend all day sleeping on his pillow, he never itched a bit."

"You let Gulliver sleep on his pillow?"

"I didn't let him. It was just hard to stop him when it fell on the floor."

"Evin!" Zuzu was laughing again, "How often did that happen?" She said, reaching down to give the beast in question a scratch behind the ear.

"Every day for a week."

"Oh my god, Ev."

"He was faking allergies hoping I'd get rid of Gulliver," I said. "I stand by my choice."

"I'm not saying you're wrong. This dog is adorable,

for sure." Gulliver had rolled over onto his back and was gazing lovingly at Zuzu. Adorable yes. Loyal, not so much.

I was almost finished with my drink and feeling the lure of sleep, but Zuzu wasn't finished gossiping. "So you got revenge on him for lying about his allergies and then dumped his dog-hating ass?"

"It was more like we had a fight and I busted him on not having allergies, but to do that, I had to confess to the pillow thing and it escalated pretty quickly after that. I guess you could call it mutual."

"Well, you can't trust a man that hates dogs. What about the other one? That you met like six months ago at Trader Joe's?"

"He was a musician."

"Oh. Everything they say?"

"Worse. His idea of birth control was to do it anally."

Zuzu laughed. Cackled really. I pressed my lips together and watched her flop around on the couch clutching her stomach.

"Did you?"

"No! We never did it at all."

"You have the worst taste in men. I mean seriously, I'm surprised you never picked up John Wayne Gacy."

"I don't think he liked girls," I said. "As for my bad taste, I'm aware. That's why I gave up men."

"You could never."

"Fine. Call it a sabbatical."

"That's ridiculous; date Harry. He's gorgeous and smart and he likes your dog. Plus, you already kissed."

"We were kids. You haven't even met him."

"I know, but you have such bad instincts, that if they're telling you 'no' he's probably the one."

"I'm going to bed."

"Ok, but sleep on your side or your stomach in case you throw up. I went to school with a guy that choked to death on his own vomit."

"Everybody did," I said. "But I'm fine. You should sleep in the guest room if you can't drive."

"Is there still a TV in there? I want to see if 'I Didn't Know I Was Pregnant' is on."

"Do you have any idea how much it frightens me that it's a series? I don't know how you can watch that crap."

"I started to feel guilty for watching 'Springer'. I felt like I was contributing to the exploitation of people too stupid to know the world is laughing at them."

"As opposed to all the Mensa members who couldn't figure out there was another person inside them."

"It's work related."

I shook my head at her. "So you'll be informed enough to accost people on the street and accuse them of being pregnant, and not knowing it? I'm never going out in public with you again."

"Yes you are. I'm going with you and Harry tomorrow. I want some adventure too."

"You have adventure every day," I said. "People and things, and people with things in them..."

"Entertaining yes, but believe me, the spirit of adventure is dead by the time they get to us."

"Should you really be laughing at your patients?"

"I don't laugh at most of them. But if you come in with a self-inflicted vegetable you get what you get."

I had to concede the point.

"Besides," Zuzu said. "I want to meet Harry. If you don't want him, maybe I do. I'm so done with the toe guy, even if he is a surgeon."

I had nothing to say to that so I headed off to bed. I didn't worry about playing hostess for Zuzu, she'd been here a million times. I stopped to let Gulliver dip briefly out the patio door. I toyed with the idea of trying to ditch Zuzu in the morning, but it was probably hopeless. Then finally, we were in my room, snug in bed, one girl under the covers, one dog on top of them.

Thirteen

Zuzu did not get left behind. In fact, she was the first one up. It was the crack of 7:30, when my eyes snapped open and I shrieked at the sight of a figure looming over me. I struggled to sitting before I realized who it was. Zuzu looked fresh and clean in an all white ensemble consisting of shorts, halter-top, and wedge heeled sandals. Long brown limbs stuck out everywhere. I pulled the covers over my face and hated her.

"So," Zuzu said, yanking the bedclothes from my grasp. "I was right. Harry Chalmers is gorgeous."

I grunted.

"Harry R. Chalmers, but he won't tell me what the R. is for." Zuzu smiled wolfishly. "Seriously Evin, yum. Why'd you lie?"

"I didn't lie. I have my own opinion. What are you wearing?" I said, after I pulled the covers off my face. "Did you go home?"

"I keep a change in the car."

"You had *that* in the car?"

"I did. I took your dog for a walk too, but I don't do the dog shit thing, so your neighbor was pretty pissed."

"Which neighbor?"

"The one that used to come over and yell at your

mom when we camped out in the backyard. That looks like Mr. Magoo and has chin hairs."

"Mrs. Rasmussen?"

"Yep."

"Zuzu." I sighed. "Thanks. For walking him. I guess. I smell coffee."

"Here." She thrust a full, steaming and heavily doctored mug under my nose and I remembered why I loved her.

"Where is it? I'm going to have to go pick it up."

"The poop? Harry got it. He even looked good doing that."

Maybe I could get tips.

Gulliver bounded into the room and launched himself at me, undoing all the painful progress I had made towards getting my ass out of bed. Zuzu redeemed herself for setting me up to get reamed by the neighborhood waste watch by plucking the mug out of my hand the instant before Gulliver struck, sparing me, if not a scalding, some severe cleanup.

Behind Gulliver came Harry. "I thought you said she was almost ready," Harry said. Zuzu shrugged.

"I am."

They both eyed me doubtfully. I leaned over and peered around Gulliver's rump, which was corrupting my line of sight to the mirror. For my vanity, Gulliver's monstrous wagging tail thwacked me in the eye. I shoved his backside with all my might and he took the hint, jumping, gracefully for once, off the bed. I blinked, took a hard look at myself and said, "Ok, give me twenty minutes."

***

I made it on time. Showered, shaved and all. I

paired jeans with a white tank top under a thin grey hoodie. I added my pink Chuck Taylor's to boost my mood. I took a minute to call Leonie, then Maggie, again without success.

Harry drove again, but today Gulliver stayed home. Zuzu had dished up his breakfast while I showered, so all that was left was to set him up with fresh water and a peanut butter filled Kong. Gulliver settled, we were on our way. Zuzu called shotgun. This disturbed me since she kept giving me surreptitious nudges and nodding in Harry's direction. I figured her sudden maneuvering for conversational proximity to him did not bode well for me.

However, maybe there were no embarrassing matchmaking attempts on my horizon. If Zuzu had set her own sights on Harry, she was welcome. They would be two ridiculously attractive people riding off into the sunset. I kicked a rock and sent it skittering across the street. I watched it bounce off the opposite curb and jumped into the back of the Rubicon.

In spite of my disgruntlement, by the time we hit the freeway, I was dozing. When I woke up, we were in the thick of L.A. traffic. I commented on the stifling trickle of cars.

"You're lucky you slept through the accident," Harry said. "It took us two and a half hours to get from Corona to Anaheim."

"What happened?"

"Don't know. When we went by, there was nothing but a crumpled Chevy sitting on the back of a tow truck."

Zuzu chimed in, "With everyone else rubbernecking like mad, you know how people do. It didn't look that serious though. I bet everyone walked away. Not like that pile-up a few years ago on the 10.

That poor guy lost the head of his-"

"Zuzu," I screamed, drowning her out, but not slowing her down.

"And they looked for it, of course, but the gas tank was leaking so there was an explosion and then everything burned up after that. It was before I started working the emergency room, so I didn't get to see it, but you just cannot imagine the pictures. It looked like something you'd see at a cheap German buffet, like some kind of horrible raw bratwurst. I mean even more unappetizing than most-"

"Zuzu," I tried again. "What about patient confidentiality?"

"It's ok. No names," she said.

"His name was David Gregson, it was all over the news."

"Well that's not my fault."

"Zuzu. I am begging you. Stop."

She turned to face me, grabbing the back of her seat to steady herself. "You just found two dead bodies. One bloated, one bloody. What's the problem?"

"No one was bloated," I said.

"She wasn't in the pool long," Harry said.

We whizzed down the road at a steady forty-five miles an hour with Harry and Zuzu cheerily exchanging tales of gore. I sat back, my ponytail whipping around behind me, captive of the wind. I hoped we were almost there.

***

Verona Neuland's house was raunchy with architectural features. During the course of our journey, we had left the sun behind. Here the sky was low and grey, enhancing the medieval feel of the property. Turrets, pillars, stained glass and statuary fought for attention. Everything that money could buy; nothing that good taste would consider. All it was missing was the moat. Instead of protection against the aqua-phobic, the house featured a low decorative stone wall, which would deter no one who stood taller than three feet. Behind the short wall were tall hedges, thick and luscious, working hard to protect their home from my prying gaze. Harry shut off the Jeep and the three of us sat for a moment gazing across the street in awe.

"Wow," Zuzu said, climbing out of the passenger seat and gazing up. "Can I please divorce Bobby Neuland? I mean, the columns aren't for me, and I could live without the stained glass, but I'd love a shot at the raw materials."

"You mean the cash?" Harry said.

"I do indeed. You can come along with Evin when she visits."

"I'm sorry we let *you* come along today," I told her. My phone started emitting Leonie's ring, I answered immediately.

"Mother what the-," was all I managed before she cut me off.

"Evin, I hope you weren't about to swear, profanity indicates a lack of thought."

"It's not meant to express thought Mother, it's meant to express emotion."

"Darling, just listen. I've been clever and I want someone to know. I can't have an entire conversation, an overweight flight attendant is drunk with power, and about to confiscate my phone. I thought she would be grateful to receive a discreet heads up about her overpowering breath, but people will surprise you. I wanted to let you know that everything is fine. I found a perfect lawyer for your stepfather and I'm insisting he act immediately to have Jack moved to protective custody. See you soon."

And she was gone. I gaped at my phone as if it might snap to attention and elucidate. Leonie was on the move. While Harry and Zuzu were putting the top on the Rubicon, I gave them the gist of Leonie's monologue.

"By perfect does she mean vicious and morally flexible?" Harry asked.

"Wouldn't it be a better trick finding a lawyer that wasn't?" Zuzu said. "How did she manage protective custody?"

I shrugged. Leonie always had her ways. I crossed the street and approached a sturdy iron gate. Inside the yard, I heard the fall of a fountain. I worked one of my sneakers between the bars and stood on the lowest rail like a kid. I perched on my toes and craned my neck, attempting to improve the view. From this position, I could see not a fountain, but an actual waterfall, an overwrought monstrosity that spilled down the gullet of a man made pond.

"Do you like it?" said a voice from my left.

I shrieked and jumped backward off the gate. I slammed into something hard and realized I had launched myself ass first into Harry. I tried to disengage from him, while still putting distance between whoever was behind the gate and me. Instead of the organized retreat I was trying for, I sprawled, in what felt like several directions at once. My butt hit the ground. Before I could settle in down there, Harry grabbed my developed yet feminine bicep and snatched me back to my feet. He didn't return my arm.

The voice spoke again. "Can I help you?" I cleverly deduced it was coming from the woman standing before us. She was about my height, but notably thinner. Her little arms and legs were like twigs, but her physical frailty hadn't made her timid. She opened the gate and stepped out to confront us.

Harry smiled. It seemed to be his go-to weapon.

She smiled back. It lit up her serious face and made her look younger, though it deepened the lines around her eyes and mouth. She wore her silver hair long and loose. I love silver in other people's hair. The few strands I grow of my own, I pluck aggressively.

I looked up at Harry. Not a strand that wasn't glossy black and shiny.

"Hi," he said. "You must be Verona Neuland."

Anne Stinnett

Fourteen

"I'm Verona. Who are you?" She said it pleasantly, but firmly. She was expecting to dismiss us shortly. I thought she might be holding a grudge about the snooping and the fall.

"I'm Harry Chalmers, and this is Evin Hart." I got a bit of the smile, and found myself not minding so much that he was still holding onto me. "We need to talk to you about your ex-husband."

"What about him?

As if she didn't-

"His wife's murder, to start."

"I don't see how I can help you," Verona said. "What happened to Hazel is terrible, but I'm not involved in Bobby's life anymore. I haven't been for a long time. You told me your names, but not why you're asking me about this."

"I'm an investigator," Harry said, producing his wallet and flipping it open with one hand to expose something to Verona's gaze.

"Not a badge?"

"No badge. The licensing board likes to be sure no one is confused about the extent of our authority. I promise to be brief."

Verona Neuland showed her manners by agreeing.

"I have a little time. You should come in. This probably won't be a conversation to have in front of the neighbors." She turned and led us through the gate.

I was a little amazed. I would have told inquisitive strangers lurking around my house to go to hell. Maybe it was the opportunity to trash her ex that was motivating her cooperation. I thought about a couple of my choice exes and saw the appeal.

I tried casually to extricate my arm from Harry, but didn't succeed. I let him keep it instead of making a scene. Far be it from me to disrupt our united front. Except a third of our front was MIA. I craned my head around for a glimpse of Zuzu.

"She's fine," the blue-eyed brute said in my ear. "She's waiting in the car. I was worried too many of us would make the wrong impression. Luckily-"

"Oh shut up," I said quietly. "Anyone could have fallen off that gate." I smiled my own brilliant smile through clenched teeth at Verona when she turned to assess our progress. She looked at me doubtfully.

"I hope you don't mind dogs," Verona said. "I have two."

"I love dogs." Harry flashed a sardonic grin and added, "but Evin is a little nervous around animals."

"Oh, well I can-"

"It's ok. Don't put yourself out. She can handle it. Right Evin?" I nodded and smiled again, not as brightly since the last one hadn't gone over so well.

When Verona stepped inside, I had time to stick my tongue out at Harry behind her back. He motioned me inside, finally releasing my arm. Two little balls of fluff were bouncing around my ankles like overgrown tribbles. I had never been afraid of a dog in my life, let alone one that probably rode in its mistress's purse, but I plastered on a concerned expression like I'd seen on the faces of dog hating cowards confronted with Gulliver. For verisimilitude, I refrained from any and all tribble petting.

We all filed through the house into Verona's living room. The dogs romped ahead followed by Verona, me, then Harry.

It was a large room, clean, and uncluttered compared to the opressive abundance outside of the house. All things being relative, uncluttered in Verona Neuland's living room meant only one marble cupid lounging by the fireplace. Like Leonie, Verona had dared a white couch. Unlike Leonie's, this one was less than immaculate. There were two especially worn and grubby patches on the cushions. I watched with my detecting eyes and sure enough, moppets one and two flung themselves onto the unfortunate construct, scratched, circled, and burrowed snugly into their accustomed spots.

I left the couch to the dogs and Verona. I sat myself down on the loveseat opposite with the coffee table between us. My plan was to sit smack in the middle of it to create a buffer from Harry, but he somehow maneuvered so we were side by side across from Bobby Neuland's ex-wife.

It was stiflingly warm. I looked up to see a vent directly overhead. I could feel heat rippling down like lava. To my right was a table cluttered with music boxes. The coffee table contained a display case in its center that was busy showcasing a fantastic array of glass and ceramic swans. The pictures on the walls were art, not family.

When we were all settled, Verona reiterated, pleasantly enough, that she didn't know anything that could help us.

"If it isn't too hard, would you tell us something

about your ex-husband?"

"Too hard." Verona harrumphed. "No, it isn't too hard. Like I said, it was a long time ago. I was sorry to hear about Hazel, but..." she shrugged.

"Why were you sorry?" I said. "I wouldn't have anything good to say about a woman that had an affair with my husband. And ended up marrying him."

"Well, you've never been married to Bobby Neuland. Better her than me." She patted her lap and one of the dogs obediently relocated itself. She stroked the silky looking hair, which seemed to comfort her. "And your information is wrong. Bobby didn't cheat on me with Hazel. It was with some anonymous little tramp. Multiple tramps actually. Hazel came by him honestly, after the divorce was final."

Yikes.

"At least you did well in the divorce, right?" I said. Harry's leg nudged mine. I nudged him back in agreement; that had been a grossly inappropriate thing to ask.

"Financially. Yes."

I tried my hardest not to look at the cupid, but couldn't quite manage it.

"I know it's awful, but I've grown fond of it. At the time, I wanted the most expensive things my architect and decorator could envision. I wanted to gouge my lecherous husband. And since you're so curious about my financials, I still get alimony."

"How much?"

"Enough to hurt Bobby. But I wish it had been more. Then maybe the kids wouldn't have been so spoiled. Houses, cars, it's too much."

I thought this was a little pot and kettle, but then Verona had probably taken a lot more shit from Bobby than their kids had.

"Did you have proof of infidelity?" There was Harry, staying faithfully on point.

"Yes. I had ample, irrefutable, embarrassing proof of infidelity and a prenup that paid me by the unauthorized bonk."

Bobby Neuland's prenuptial agreements had left him worse off than California's community property laws would have.

"He said you had him followed," I said. I was no detective, but I figured lying was permissible.

Harry moved closer. I don't know what he thought he was going to do. Grabbing my arm wouldn't shut me up, and I was sure he wouldn't go so far as to cover my mouth. I was a little distracted by the warmth of his thigh now pressed more firmly against my own. I gave him a look that said, *knock it off, why can't I help, do we not want this kind of information?* It was really more a quick string of bizarre facial maneuvers, and I had no idea what Harry made of it all, but he smiled, just a quick one. And I skipped only the shortest of breaths. Harry's focus returned to Verona so, all business, I put mine there too.

When she spoke, her eyes were hard and her voice was soft. "Bobby was paranoid. I never had him followed; I never needed to. When we were married, he was never discreet with his affairs. I never knew if he assumed I would put up with it, or thought that I was too stupid to notice. That was the worst of it, that he didn't even care enough to exercise a little discretion. There were witnesses all over town. There was proof on our joint credit cards. Now, I'm sure, he knows better."

"Let me ask you, Mrs. Neuland-"

"Verona is fine."

Harry continued. "Were there any other problems

when you were married to Bobby? Was he ever physically threatening?"

"I'm sure you've seen what he's like. All the bluster in the world, wrapped in that big oafish package. However, he never hit me, or even threatened to. Although, it was a long time ago, and I have no idea what he's like now. Still unpleasant, I imagine."

"Was there anything else," Harry said, "that contributed to your leaving your husband?"

"Besides him sticking his unimpressive dick in anything that could be had? Pardon my French. Besides having to deal with his ridiculous temper? Besides being generally miserable? No, nothing."
Speaking of miserable.

Harry told Verona how courageous she had been to leave. I thought leaving Bobby Neuland showed a resurgence of common sense more than courage. In fact, I couldn't imagine the circumstances that would result in a seemingly intelligent woman agreeing to legally bind herself to Bobby. Of course, no one asked me.

"How well did you know Hazel?"

"We only met once. Rex liked her, I think. She made an effort to be good to my children, and I appreciated that."

"So you had joint custody?" I was a little confused as to why the twins had been with Bobby at all. He wasn't an influence I'd want around my hypothetical kid. I shifted on the loveseat, which felt more like an upholstered slab of rock every second.

"The twins stayed with their father when I left. Reina wanted to stay and Rex stayed with her. Their school and their friends were all in the desert."

"It must have been hard to leave them." Harry said.

Verona's eyes were suddenly shiny. "Well sometimes things are so bad you'll give up anything to just get away. Even your own child. Children." Harry plucked several tissues from a porcelain box on the coffee table and rose to press them gently into Verona's hand.

Verona blew her nose. Yuck.

"Reina and Bobby are close." Verona said, patting her eyes dry. "That's the main reason she wouldn't leave. She's a daddy's girl. He spoils her. I want different things for them than Bobby does. Rex understands the importance of working, of making something of your life, a lesson I hope Reina learns. Bobby buys her everything she wants, buys her love. Part of me thinks my disapproval encourages him, but I may be overestimating how much he factors my feelings into his decisions."

"We heard they didn't get along with Hazel," I said. "The twins, I mean."

"The twins?" She let out a high-pitched laugh. "No. Who told you that?"

"Someone who knew them in high school."

"There was a period of adjustment, but that's normal, in blended families. It didn't last long. Rex was such a good boy, he was always there for his sister. Let me show you something." She pushed herself off the couch, dislodging the fur ball in her lap and disappeared.

I turned to Harry, who said quietly, "You're quite an irritant. It's working though. Keep it up. You're a great bad cop."

I decided I was offended and opened my mouth to say so, but Verona reappeared clutching a green leather photo album with an ornately embossed cover.

"I'll join you over here so we can all see," she said,

and wedged herself in next to Harry on the loveseat.
This prompted a freakish chain reaction, which left me
wedged against the incredibly solid arm of the damned
thing. The heat was still blasting down and Harry was
warm. Too warm. He smelled...ahhh yum.

"Did you just smell me?" he whispered out of the
corner of his mouth.

Shit. "No," I said.

The album had all the typical family shots: cute
babies in the tub, first birthday cakes, and bikes,
menorahs and Christmas trees. The best of both
worlds. The twins had been dark haired imps, showing
off gaps in their teeth in the early pictures and braces
in the later.

In the last image, Verona and Bobby stood with
the twins between them. Bobby in the picture was
younger and leaner, but just as grim. Verona was
smiling at Rex, her arm around his shoulders. Reina
was standing behind, on what appeared to be a bench,
leaning forward on her father's shoulders. The twins
were middle school awkward, but with underlying
promise, like in spite of the pimples and the hair they
didn't know how to deal with, they'd end up beautiful.
And they had. But I'd been right about Reina's nose.

"He really likes the blondes," I said.

Verona gave me a dirty look. "No, I mean, you.
You were a blonde. In the picture. There." I pointed as
though there was some chance she couldn't figure out
to which picture I was referring. "Natural I'm sure.
Like you are now." I laughed. At what I didn't know. "I
just mean you look natural. In a good way. Not a
sloppy way." Why the hell was I still talking? Harry
should shut me up. He didn't. "I only mean that all the
women we know about Bobby being with are blonde.
Or were blond, I guess, because two of them are dead

and you're not blonde anymore." *Fuck!* "But it looks good, I like silver hair, I was thinking I liked your hair when we first saw you."

I finally managed to reign in my mouth, not because I had run out of ghastly things to say, but because Verona's face had gone from pissed to shocked.

"Two of them?" she said.

Now my flood of words had truly dried.

Harry explained.

"I knew about Hazel, Rex told me, but not about Candace. Candace Brown? He didn't tell me." She was crying again, clutching Harry's knee for support. He harvested more tissue from the box on the table and patted her on the back while she dabbed and blew. Ugh. For the moment, it was good to be me.

I peeked around Harry's shoulder, to see Verona nestled in his chest, clutching his shirt. The formerly pristine white button up was now awash in mascara and tears. Harry was bestowing calming pats and seemed unconcerned that he was covered with moisture from the body of a stranger. My reaction would have been to run screaming for the nearest shower, but Harry with his sterner stuff, disregarded the salty wetness and said, "Did you know Candace?"

Verona pulled herself together and apologized for the shirt. "No. I just can't believe... I can't believe someone else was killed." I knew that feeling. The tribbles had finally caught on to the histrionics of their mistress and were hoisting themselves into her lap.

"Look, if you've asked me everything, I think I might like to lie down for awhile," she said.

I felt bad about that. We had just shown up at this woman's home and wrecked her day. She looked like she had a Gladys Kravitz sick headache.

"We'll get out of your hair then," Harry said,

disengaging from Verona to stand. "By the way, were you here on Tuesday?"

"Was I here? Do you mean where was I when two murders took place a hundred and fifty miles away?"

That summed it up nicely.

"What is wrong with you people? I give you all the help I'm able to, including answering invasive personal questions and you ask me what I was doing?" Verona leaped to her feet and was gaining volume with every word.

"Just get out! I don't have to put up with your accusations. You want to accuse my ex-husband, fine. But not me. Not my children. Don't come back here. Don't call. I won't help you anymore." Verona had worked herself up to flushed and panting by the end of her speech. Harry looked a bit taken aback. He shot me a look I couldn't interpret.

I hoped I wasn't expected to smooth this over. Nope. No time. Verona was hustling us out of the house.

We were thrust through the door, over the welcome mat, which most certainly did not apply to us anymore, and all the way back to the vine covered gate. I was leading by a nose, so I yanked it open and was pushed though, the force of Verona's wrath backed up by a few surprisingly powerful shoves.

She never yelled, "And stay out!"

But I thought it was implied.

Fifteen

We looked across the street to where the Jeep had been.

Harry looked at me; I felt guilty by association.

"She doesn't usually steal," I said. I was casting around for something helpful to add when something wet struck my cheek. The good news: it was rain, not bird poop. The bad news: there was more where that came from.

In seconds, we were being pelted with chilly drops. I flipped up the hood on my sweatshirt, but it was scanty protection. There was no going back to Verona's for shelter. Harry looked like a sexy drenched rat. I felt the same, except I thought I might be missing the sexy. I was scanning the street for shelter when Harry tugged my arm. I turned and saw headlights hurtling toward us. It was Zuzu to the rescue.

She screeched to a stop six inches before our drenched state would have become irrelevant. Harry yanked open the rear door and boosted me in, then jumped in front and slammed the door shut. Zuzu took out someone's recycle bin in the course of her inept three-point turn. "Do you want to pick that up for me?" she asked Harry.

"No," he said. And we were off.

"Could you turn up the heat?" I was freezing.

"Yup. So how'd it go?"

"It went. Too bad our ride took off."

"Sorry. Needed caffeine."

I pushed my hood back, leaned forward and stuck my head between the front seats. My hair was as wet as the rest of me; nothing I was wearing had done anything to protect me from the elements. I let Harry fill in the majority of our visit for Zuzu. I added detail when the spirit moved me. By the time we had gone over everything we were back on the freeway, halfway to Riverside.

"She sounds miserable," Zuzu said. "I shouldn't be shocked I guess, but I always am, when I hear about mothers giving up their kids."

"You haven't met Bobby Neuland. I'd do anything to get away from him too," I said.

"Would you leave Gulliver?"

"No. Besides, she didn't exactly give them up. It's not like she never saw them again. And she's certainly protective of them."

"Hmm." She didn't sound convinced. "Speaking of the Neuland kids, we're meeting Rex tonight."

"Who's meeting Rex tonight?" It sounded like there was a temper under Harry's sunny exterior.

"Well, I'm going to," Zuzu said.

"By yourself?" Harry said. "That's not smart."

"Not by myself. I figured I can get away with bringing Ev, because sometimes girls can bring a friend."

"Girls can bring a friend?" Still with the tone.

"For safety," Zuzu said. "And moral support."

"What if for safety, you two don't go out to meet some guy who could be involved in two murders," Harry said. "And girls don't bring a friend to go out with me."

No. A girl wouldn't want a chaperone when she was with Harry. "Do we really think Rex is involved?" I said aloud.

"We don't know he's not," Harry said.

"Hey, did I mention Reina lives with Bobby?" Zuzu turned to look at me.

"She was there the night Jack and I went looking for Hazel," I said. "But how do you know she's living there?"

"How do you think?" she said. "Rex mentioned it. She just came back."

"From?"

"School, she got home a few months ago. She's staying with their dad while she house hunts."

"It's Palm Springs, not New York. How long does it take to find a place?" I said.

"You don't have a place." Harry said. "Maybe she's discerning. Maybe she's broke. Besides, it takes longer to buy a place than to rent."

I had seen the familial manors, and I wasn't buying the broke theory.

Traffic backed up suddenly, forcing Zuzu to slam on the brakes. The tires produced an almighty screech and we laid a trail of rubber an inch deep behind us. The Rubicon fishtailed. I closed my eyes.

Zuzu brought us to a smoking halt a foot shy of disaster. I felt the cessation of movement, but no impact. I looked around for outraged commuters, but everything was business as usual.

SoCal drivers are hard to surprise.

"You ok back there?" It was Harry asking.

"I'll be better if you don't let her drive anymore."

"Good call."

The rest of the ride was uneventful, but my ass was sore again by the time the windmills came into view. I wanted my dog, dinner and a bath. Not together.

"So what's the plan?" Zuzu said. "Am I on my own for tonight? I'm supposed to meet him at 8:30."

It was almost 5:00.

"Is she bluffing?" Harry asked.

I looked up to find his eyes on mine in the rearview   mirror.

"Probably not," I said.

"That's right, I'm not bluffing. I'm there for Jack Dekker whether you all are or not."

"I think it's more that she's enjoying the excitement," I said to Harry. "But that doesn't mean she won't do it." I wanted silence and a dark room, not this endless scheming and debate. "It seems like he was pretty open on the phone, maybe we don't have to ambush him."

"Yeah, but that was him talking to a hot girl he met at the bar, not him answering pointed questions about his family for strangers," Zuzu said. "Get into the spirit of things. Don't you remember when Jack-"

"Yes. Whatever it is. I remember it. I'm trying. This isn't fun for everybody, Zuzu. I hate traipsing around intruding on strangers, murderous or not. Obviously, I'm going to do whatever I have to do to save Jack. If it's ok with you, I'd rather do it without a lecture."

Now I had silence. It was strained, but it lasted all the way home.

When we turned onto Leonie's street, I could see right away that the gate was open. Either Leonie was back or we were being burgled in broad daylight. With Gulliver's safety in mind, I rooted for the former.

Harry pulled to the curb in front of the house and parked. I'd expected we would go our separate ways, at least for a few peaceful hours, but Zuzu wanted to see Leonie, and Harry tagged along for whatever nefarious reason. I brought up the rear, unready as always.

I heard Gulliver's voice booming through the kitchen window. Zuzu opened the front door and disappeared into the house. Harry paused to let me catch up. When I got to the door, he made a sweeping gesture for me to precede him inside. I flashed him a cheek dimple and went on by.

Gulliver bounded to greet us. He deposited a slurpy kiss on my chin and raced back to the kitchen, nearly bowling Zuzu over. Behind me, Harry laughed. It was very masculine, deep and throaty. I let myself smile in response. He couldn't see my face.

In the kitchen, Leonie and Zuzu embraced and exchanged a double cheek kiss. It looked rehearsed, but I knew it was just some kind of unholy harmony.

"Zuzu. You look wonderful. You always had such a sense of style. Not like Evin. I don't think they should make those shoes in adult sizes."

I looked down at my Chuck Taylors.

"Evin darling, you look just like you did in high school," Leonie said.

"Thanks," I said.

"No darling, that wasn't a compliment."

From anyone else it would have been.

"I think you look cute," Harry said in my ear. *Be still my...hmmm.* I glanced back and smiled before I could stop myself. To make up for it, I gave myself a stern mental lecture on the dangers of romantic entanglement.

"Who bought steak?" Leonie said. "I would like to know who I'm angry with."

"Who do you think?" I said.

"Oh. Well, I gave it to the dog."

"All of it?"

"Not to begin with, but he kept begging for more. I thought you forgot to feed him."

"No. I didn't forget to feed him."

"If he gets sick, it will be your fault Evin."

This should be good.

"You've always been so forgetful, what else could I think?"

"That dogs like steak?" Harry suggested.

"Mother, he'll eat as much as you give him. I mean, would you give a kid all the candy they wanted?"

"Well, certainly not after that Halloween when you were E.T." We had all learned some hard lessons that year. One of them was that at seven years old, I had the uncanny ability to regurgitate twice the volume of candy corn ingested.

"Just remember that if anything goes horribly wrong with Gulliver's stomach, you primed the pump."

"I don't appreciate the tone, Evin. And if anything does go 'horribly wrong,' deal with it before I find out."

Speaking of horribly wrong, Gulliver chose that moment to reacquaint himself with Harry. In an instant, he snapped from supine on the floor to all fours and launched his attack. I heard doggy toenails scrabbling for purchase on the tile. In my mind, I took this opportunity to step in and gently but firmly contain my slightly unruly canine companion. In reality, I hadn't even moved when Gulliver's paws caught traction, and then it was too late.

Gulliver leaped and a series of nightmareish images flashed through my head: Harry sprawled injured or dead, everything of value, both cash and sentimental, transformed into one big pile of rubble, the lawsuit brought by Harry's next of kin against

Gulliver and me. I managed to blurt, "Hey!" which had no effect on anyone. Then somehow, Harry had plucked Gulliver out of midair and deposited him neatly on the floor before giving the naughty beast a few solid pats to the rump. He was rewarded with a volley of cheerful thumps from Gulliver's tail.

My first thought was that there must be an impressive set of muscles lurking under that mascara stained shirt for Harry to have been able to stop a hundred and a half pounds of airborne dog without tearing something vital. My second was that we needed obedience training. Soon.

Leonie sighed and said, "I'm cooking. I'm also annoyed no one has taken the time to notice my effort."

"It smells great," Zuzu said.

"Well Zuzu, I appreciate the effort, meager as it was, but I know it smells great. I don't need my culinary skills validated; I just want to be appreciated for my hard work. And I do not mean silent appreciation."

Zuzu and I exchanged quick glances; we didn't want to risk being chastised for bestowing a sub-par compliment.

Harry gave it a shot. "You're a doll to cook for all of us. Did I mention, you look gorgeous doing it? Most women get sweaty in the kitchen."

"What a lovely compliment. I hope I don't have to solicit the next one. Evin, set the table. Harry, I'm waiting for you to greet me properly. It's been a long time."

Harry kissed the cheek Leonie offered and told her (again) how great she was looking.

"Yes," she agreed. I rolled my eyes.

"You don't think so, darling? Be truthful. Take a good look."

Eeeessshh. For the record, she is stunning, but I would have died before saying it just then. I eyed her size six frame. She was tallish, with smooth, clear skin over great bones. Perfect nose; wasn't done.

"I don't like this game," I said. "If you have to be the center of attention, why don't you tell us what's going on with Jack?"

"Certainly darling, although it sounds as if Jack will be the center of attention, in absentia. Here Evin, taste this. It's Orange Roughy."

"Yuck. No." I threw up a hand to defend myself from the fish laden utensil.

"Evin is one of those, 'no food with a face' people," Leonie explained to Harry. "I agree about the real animals, but fish? Fish don't have feelings."

"I'm not sure that's accurate," Harry said. "I thought you were dedicated to complete accuracy."

"Not accuracy, Harry darling. Truth. Absolute Truth. It's a common fallacy to think Truth is about the facts. Truth is about expressing your uncensored feelings and thoughts. Think of it as a colonic for the soul."

Zuzu and I went dead still; I could see Harry fighting a smile.

Before anybody lost it, Leonie decided she would taste the fish herself. The look on her face when she did made me glad the fish wasn't for me.

"It's actually terrible, darlings," she said. "I'm sorry. Unfortunately, it would be rude not to partake, as I put so much time into the preparation. Don't worry Evin, you can eat everything else." She looked so happy that I had to smile. No one else did.

"We could order in," Harry said.

"Absolutely not, everything is almost ready, and I hate waste. Think of the starving children, darlings. It doesn't taste good, but it won't kill you."

I smirked at Harry and Zuzu.

"Here darling, I'd like you to finish the potatoes while I pour some wine." I took the masher and went to work while Leonie assembled glasses, corkscrew, and bottle. I was determined that one dish would be edible. Leonie poured and passed until all the humans present were in possession of a chilly glass of Riesling.

"Zuzu, would you mind just chopping these... thank you. And Harry if you could set these on the table..." She pointed out the appropriate dinnerware to Harry. "And the silverware is there in that drawer. Now I told you about protective custody?"

I stirred and nodded.

"How did you do that anyway?" Zuzu said, busy chopping a cucumber into not so symmetrical bits.

"Please darlings, give the credit to the attorney.," Leonie said.

This was suspiciously modest. I caught Zuzu's eye. She shrugged.

"I got Matthew Kellar. Evin, do you remember him? He's a friend of mine." I didn't, but there were so many. Leonie defined "friend," as anyone who might eventually be of use.

"So," Harry said, "Matthew Kellar had Jack placed in protective custody?"

"But how?" Zuzu asked again. She rolled her eyes at me, "Didn't he have to give a reason?"

"Obviously," Leonie said, "I don't know the mechanics of how a jail works, Zuzu."

I glanced up from the potatoes again. Leonie had for some reason, gone lobster red.

Oh my god. "Did you lie?" I said gleefully.

"I practice Absolute Truth Evin, as you well know. I give myself and others the courtesy of-"

"She made him lie," I said.

"Evin your determination to paint me as a hypocrite is disgusting. If you say one more word, I will douse you with the sink hose." Motherly love. "I told him to get Jack into protective custody. I did not dictate to him how to do his job, and I remain Absolutely Truthful. I have no idea what Matthew told the authorities at the jail, but since he is an attorney, he is not likely to become a disciple of Absolute Truth anyway. The worst that can be said is that I failed to lead him in the right direction, but I didn't corrupt him."

She polished off her Riesling. I followed suit, smiling into my glass.

"How he managed is moot, because Jack refused to go. It seems he's bonding and making friends with the general populace as though it's happy hour at the clubhouse. Harry darling, would you mind popping open another bottle? Right there in the fridge. Thanks."

Harry topped us all off, except for Zuzu who waved him away. "I've been drinking too much lately. Evin is a bad influence."

I blew her a raspberry.

"I used to wonder if I drank too much," Leonie announced. "I enjoy a before dinner drink, and of course wine with dinner, and an after dinner drink, or two, which I admit sounds like a lot. But, when I began to practice Absolute Truth, I was able to admit that I don't care."

I dragged the subject back around to Jack and the lawyer.

Leonie deigned to participate in a conversation that was not about her. "According to Matthew, the trouble is the knife. They think both of those wretched women were killed by the same one, and it came from the set in Jack's kitchen."

"And Evin darling, I hate to be cruel," Leonie said, which was a sure sign she was about to be. "But in the interests of motivating you, I need to let you know that you are somewhat culpable in Jack's arrest."

I could see Harry was about to object, but I shook my head at him and said, "How so?"

"You shared information with him about the body you found in the pool, which you were instructed by the police to keep to yourself. Instead you chose to gossip with your stepfather about it."

"It wasn't gossip." My tone was on the savage side.

"My point is," Leonie said, "He let information slip that he should have had no way of knowing."

"Fine," I said. "I'll just tell the cops that I told him everything."

"Don't," Harry said, "It wouldn't do much at this point besides get you in trouble."

"And it's not your fault, at all," Zuzu said.

"Darling, I know this makes you feel bad, but-"

"Forget it. Just spare me any future motivation." I clenched my jaw shut and took deep breaths until the desire to fling something at Leonie receded. I dumped the mashed, seasoned potatoes listlessly into a bowl. I pictured them hitting my stomach and felt sick.

"Did the lawyer know anything else about Candace Brown?" Harry said. "When exactly she was killed or what she was doing there?" We knew it was the same day, because we had been questioned, but Quick had been cagey with specifics.

"No. Matthew says they know, but that horrible detective is balking at disclosing anything until he gets the official report. If we would all simply practice the Truth..."

She trailed off winsomely, leading me to ponder the fallout of rampant A.T. I shook it off quickly. This was no time to subscribe to Leonie's lunacy.

"I think everything is ready." I topped off my glass and headed for the table, taking the bottle with me. "Let's make this the 'with dinner' round."

Sixteen

The mashed potatoes and salad were excellent. The fish was washed down with quantities of wine. Leonie nibbled on salad and left her orange roughy untouched. She excused herself immediately after dinner, saying we wouldn't mind tidying up the kitchen since she had cooked. I didn't think that version of events was Absolutely Truthful, but I was well past my Leonie quota for the day, so I was glad to see her go. Instead of after dinner drinks, Harry, Zuzu and I had dessert while we hashed out our options.

Harry was firmly against anyone showing up to meet Rex under false pretences.

"I thought you private detective types were all about the subterfuge," I said, forking in a mouthful of apple pie cheesecake. It was heaven. The one domesticity at which Leonie excelled was baking.

"Neither of you is a private detective type," Harry said. "If you go in there trying to be sneaky you'll just blow it and piss him off."

"Maybe he would want to help. Maybe it bothers him that every woman his father sleeps with ends up sliced to ribbons."

Harry gave me a look.

"Sorry, I don't know where all that optimism came

from," I said. "It's probably the alcohol. And sugar."

"He could be the one slicing them to ribbons. Remember, nothing has happened to Verona. Maybe he has a problem with any woman trying to take her place."

"Or maybe he peeped at them in the shower and then had to kill them when they caught him," Zuzu chimed in.

"Or maybe, you two aren't taking this seriously enough." Harry was vexed.

"We are. It's just a quick conversation in a public place. I don't think it's that dangerous. But I was thinking, I don't really know what I said to him that first night in the bar. We kind of made it martini night," I said to Harry.

"I saw you the morning after, remember?"

Oh. "Yeah."

"What about Leonie?" Zuzu said.

"You can't take Leonie. She's practicing Absolute Truth."

Zuzu considered. "Can she just not talk?"

I knew this one. "The truth does not censor." There was no chance Leonie would not talk.

"Well someone has to go," Zuzu said. "So I don't end up in a ditch."

"Do we have ditches?" I wondered.

"Maybe on the date farms. Although, I'm not sure he'll bother to drive her body all the way out to Indio," Harry said.

Zuzu smacked him on the shoulder. "It's not funny, Harry. People get killed and left places all the time."

"If you think you're going to end up in a ditch, you shouldn't go."

"I promise you won't end up in a ditch," I told her.

"At least not tonight."

We finally settled on a course of action. We (we being Harry and Zuzu and *not* me) would keep Zuzu's date with Rex. They were going to play it straight. The best-case scenario was that honest and helpful conversation would ensue. The smart money was on almost anything else.

Although we didn't know for sure what sort of impression I had made on Rex, it was safe to assume it hadn't been good, so although I was allowed to go, I was relegated to discreetly lurking. In disguise.

It wasn't much of a disguise. I wasn't going to be right in his face or anything. Leonie provided an old pair of reading glasses, which I did my best to look over rather than through so I wouldn't get a headache. In addition to the glasses, I donned a blue tracksuit with a hood. I figured in a pinch I could pretty much cover my entire face.

Harry leered at my dowdy outfit, but in so charming a way I found myself laughing rather than contemplating violence or a restraining order.

"I'm too old for you," I said primly.

"Ok."

Well, that was unflatteringly easy. Still. Good.

Zuzu wanted to borrow something to wear. Her outfit was rumpled from the day in a car, and the bit of fish she'd mishandled showed plainly on her white top.

There was too much of a height disparity for her to wear my pants so we put her in a skirt that was knee length on me and sexy on her. I rummaged briefly and came up with a sweater to go with it.

While we were at it we restrained my hair as well as we could and pinned it up. It looked as different as it could from the night I'd met Rex, when it had been wild with sweat and dancing. I reconsidered and pulled a few strands down to frame my face, because I was having trouble reconciling my vanity with the Robert Palmer girl look.

We wrapped up the primping when Harry threatened to leave without us.

I brought Gulliver in from the yard where he'd been lounging and digesting his dinner. "Love you, be good," I told him and bounced his tennis ball down the hallway toward Leonie's lair. He bounded off after it and the rest of us slipped out the door.

***

The day's sun had gone, leaving the air cool and slightly damp. Dry as a desert didn't always apply in the valley. The tourists were carefree in tee shirts and sandals, the locals had bundled themselves in hoodies and knit caps to brave the sixty-degree evening.

We were en route to Las Casuelas, where Zuzu had arranged to meet Rex Neuland for margaritas.

"I don't think we should be meeting him here. What if something goes wrong and we can never come back for chips and drinks?"

In response, I was informed that under no circumstances should I order a margarita of my very own, or for that matter, any tequila based beverage.

As a precaution, Harry dropped me off around the corner. I would walk in separately and try to procure a seat from which I could observe the proceedings without being recognized. At the last minute, Harry produced an old Palm Springs Angel's baseball cap and placed it on my head, pulling the bill down low.

"We'll see you inside." Zuzu gave me an excited wave and they were off. I walked slowly to give them time to get in ahead of me.

There were still quite a few people out walking: couples of various composition, dogs with their people, a pack of teenagers. Me. I lurked down the street, looking, I hoped, more normal than I felt. Five minutes after Harry had dropped me off, I slipped through the restaurant door.

Rex was nowhere to be seen. Zuzu was stalking around a table in the lounge. Harry waved me over.

"He cancelled," Harry said quietly.

"I can't believe it." Zuzu climbed on a barstool and crossed her endless legs, drawing stares from around the lounge.

"What happened? Did he know we were ambushing him?"

"He got called in to work."

I reached over to pat her arm.

"We'll go talk to him at the bar," Harry said, earning a venomous look from Zuzu. My venomous looks are often ignored (frequency desensitizes), but Zuzu's were rare and potent. Harry drew back.

"He was supposed to meet me ten minutes ago and he just calls now?" Zuzu snapped.

"He's a jerk."

"Obviously."

"It wasn't a real date," Harry said. Zuzu and I gave him level stares. "You tricked him into meeting you here so we could question him."

"That's not the point, Harry," I said.

Harry looked confused. "You remember he might be a murderer, right?"

"So you're saying, it's ok to get rejected by a murderer?" Zuzu's arms were crossed and her eyes were narrow.

"Yes," Harry said carefully. He clearly thought we were unhinged.

"Would you guys mind dropping me off?"

"No. But are you sure?" I said.

"I'm sure."

We dropped Zuzu off. As we drove away, Harry asked for clarification.

"What are you talking about?" I said. "He pretty much stood her up."

"It wasn't a real date."

"He didn't know that."

"Is she interested in him?"

"Of course not. It's just inconsiderate. Hasn't anyone ever stood you up at the last minute?"

"I feel like it's in my best interests to say yes."

"It was, but now I won't believe you."

"So her feelings are hurt?"

"Yes." I had no idea what was so incomprehensible. "She's also embarrassed because we were there."

"You know that's a little crazy, right?"

"It's not crazy. I'm sure she'll be fine tomorrow, but of course it's upsetting." It was upsetting to me. My own love life was enough of a wasteland. If men were standing Zuzu up, what hope was there for those of us who were shorter and surlier?

Harry sighed. I imagined it was at the foibles of women. We were quiet for awhile, before he said, "We'll root for him to be the killer, then."

***

There was a problem getting into the club. Proprietor Fred Fennell, Leonie's greasy admirer, was at the door and he wasn't pleased to see me.

Fred Fennell was not technically short, but he looked it next to Harry. He'd done a pre-emptive shave on his head, but you could see that if he hadn't taken action, nature would have.

"There's a dress code," he said curling his lip at my outfit. Harry looked casually but devastatingly put together, as always.

"Oh come on-" I started before he cut me off.

"If that wasn't keeping you out, it would be what you did in here the other night. So forget it."

"What did I do?"

"You know."

I didn't. And I didn't much care. My focus was on getting inside and putting the figurative screws to Rex Neuland. I couldn't explain our agenda. Fred would not be on board with helping Jack.

Harry tried reasonableness. I could have told him that would be a no-go.

"Fine." I snapped. There's nothing creepier than a guy who's obsessed with your mother, but I could make it work. "How about, if you won't let us in, I tell Leonie you grabbed my ass."

Fennell looked put-upon. Harry smiled.

"How about I let you in and you tell her something nice about me?"

"She's not that gullible."

I could tell he wanted to say something unpleasant, but was wary of a bad report going to the object of his affections.

"Go on then. But if you make trouble, don't think I won't call the cops on you."

I saluted smartly and we stepped inside.

"What's that back-story?" Harry asked.

"It's awful. He went to high school with Leonie; he practically stalked her. Even now, he's excessively interested and not shy about saying so. That's why Jack got in that fight with him. He's repulsive."

"Don't women think undying devotion is sweet?"

"To someone you actually have a relationship with, yes. He should try being devoted to his wife."

"Who married him?"

"Her name is Elaine. She's sweet and mousy." She was a member of Leonie's book club. She came to the house every few months bearing various delicacies encased in deliciously crusty homemade sourdough. "Makes great sandwiches."

We skimmed through the club and found Rex was at the back bar again. I didn't see Hugo tonight. We approached Rex, who for whatever reason, did not look thrilled to set eyes on me. Wearing the expression he was, he looked eerily like his father.

Still, like a good bartender with not a lot going on, he listened.

Then he told us to get lost.

"Look," I said, not budging. "We need to find out what happened. If your father didn't kill Candace and Hazel, then you should be interested in helping us find out who did."

Rex threw Harry a look of disgust. "I don't care who killed them. If my father did it, let him go to jail. Same goes for yours."

"Your stepmother was murdered," I snapped. It was good that the bar was nearly empty. "How do you not care? Unless you killed her."

"I didn't kill anyone." Rex let loose a nasty laugh. "I feel bad about Hazel, but Candace was a gold-digging bitch. She ruined everything, and she got what she deserved."

Harry tried to reason with him, with similar results. Rex Neuland was raging on and gaining volume. I'd heard about discretion's relationship to valor so I took my valiant self and started inching towards the exit.

"You bring this crazy bitch to my work to ask me about another crazy bitch?" He was yelling at Harry but waving his hand at me.

Right in front of Harry? Even though my current policy was hands off the cute boys, I didn't want Harry with his bright eyes and beautiful strong hands thinking I was crazy. Rex was cute too, in an angry, brooding way that would normally have had me panting to understand his tortured soul. But just now I thought he was a dick.

"I'm not crazy," I said.

"Yeah, that's why you threw up all over my bar and talked your much hotter friend into helping you stalk me."

"You knew about that?" Zuzu would be happy to hear that her charms hadn't failed her.

"Yeah. You idiots didn't think my roommate or my mother would tell me you were sneaking around asking questions?"

Good point.

"We didn't sneak," I said. "And so what if I threw up? It's a bar. Everyone has thrown up in a bar. Your father is probably a murderer. We're going to do something about Candace and Hazel and Maggie too, if you've done anything to her." I found myself straining against Harry's arm, which had come to be wrapped around my waist. My eyes had welled up from sheer fury. I heard my voice tremble and felt my nose start to run. I am not a sexy crier. "And there's no way Jack is going to jail for murder."

"From what I hear, he's halfway to never seeing daylight again. Stay away from my family. Stay away from my house unless you want to get hurt."

Security was converging. Harry was tugging me

along. I apologized profusely to a three hundred pound no-neck in hopes that when he heaved me out the door, he would do it gently. I hid under my baseball cap to avoid meeting the eyes of staff and patrons alike.

***

"I think maybe he's scared," Harry said.

"Really? Did you miss the swearing and the threats?"

Harry grinned. "Exactly. Why do you think he's so mad?"

"I'm supposed to think it's because he's scared of getting caught and spending the rest of his life in prison?" I said.

"I don't know, he just seemed scared in general."

I thought about coming home, about the future, about my lack of plans and general ambition. I thought about the possibility of Jack never getting out of jail, and of living with Leonie for the rest of my life. I sighed. "I'm scared in general too."

"You mean like E. coli, and wars, and end of the world panic? Earthquakes?" Harry said.

"No. But thanks for that."

"No problem."

"So that's what you think his deal is?" I asked Harry. We were sitting in the Jeep, outside Leonie's, top on but windows down, enjoying the night air. "You really think he's scared?"

"Very possibly."

"He didn't seem scared to me. I think it's something else."

"Like?"

"Like jealousy maybe; Of Candace taking his father away, breaking up the family." Although, apparently he hadn't had that reaction when Bobby and Verona split which would have been more natural. "We should call the police and tell them how much Rex hated Candace."

"I still don't think we should go running to the cops every five minutes."

"Why not? How do we know what will end up convincing them? What if we're sitting on information that would exonerate Jack?"

"We're not."

"How the hell do you know? Rex clearly hated Candace. He says he got along with Hazel, but we don't know that. Maybe he and Bobby did it together."

"How about you lose the tone?"

I narrowed my eyes, but considered the tone and finally dredged up a, "Sorry."

We sat in silence for awhile, but that was leading to a lot of bad thoughts.

"So, then what?" I said. "If you're going to outlaw knee-jerk, gut reactions what do we go on?" I rolled my head from side to side trying to loosen the knots that were reaching up to provoke throbbing in my temples. I took a deep breath of cool, damp night air and let it out slowly.

"Keep looking. Keep questioning."

"We haven't found anything, and no one wants to answer questions. Look at Rex," I said. "We know nothing."

"We know he's pissed off at his father and Candace. That's far from nothing."

"But we don't know why. According to you, we don't even know anything worth mentioning to Quick."

"I want us to have credibility when we do find something significant."

"What if that never happens?"

"It will. You should go to bed. We'll start again tomorrow, if you're still in."

"What else would I be?" I fumbled in the dark with the unfamiliar door latch until Harry reached over to put his hand on mine. He still smelled good, but I refrained from an obvious whiff. He turned to look at me, his face inches from mine.

"I know this isn't the time…" he paused. I couldn't breathe which was just as well, because I couldn't swear I was in a state of minty freshness.

"Goodnight Evin." What was that, six inches of space between our lips? Four? This was not good. Except it probably would be really good. Which was not good. I needed to find out what was wrong with Harry before I hit the point of no return. I gathered myself and frantically pawed through my head for a subject that could save me from my hormones.

"Hugo," I breathed.

"I'm Harry." Four inches became twenty-four in a hurry.

"No. I know. I was just thinking, I should call Hugo in the morning. He might know something about Rex. They work together. I'm sure they've talked. Everybody likes Hugo."

"Yeah, he sounds great."

"We've been friends since high school. He'll help us if he knows anything."

"Ok. I'll pick you up. Noon."

"Noon? I thought you were all about the worm."

"I have some work to do on another case. I have a mortgage."

"What kind of case?" Maybe Zuzu was right. Harry might be dateable. He was hardworking.

"It's just a routine, infidelity case."

"Sounds depressing."

"Those always are, a bit," he said. Sensitive.

"So, you have a mortgage?" I said. Stable.

"Yeah. And a leaky roof."

"Jack will pay you."

"I don't want Jack's money."

"Because you're friends? Such good friends you can't let him pay you? It's not like you went to war together."

He looked me in the eyes and said, "Does it really matter?"

"Maybe." *What were we talking about?*

"I think what matters, is why you're still sitting here," he said.

"We're talking."

"We're done talking."

"Then I'm going."

He came around to open my door and put his hand on my cheek. My insides were rioting. I felt his thumb stroke my lower lip. It was a soft touch, barely felt, but the inner effect was scandalous. I leaned forward and he kissed me. There was a warm, soft brush of his lips on mine and then it was over.

"And I thought the last one was good," Harry said.

I jumped out of the jeep fast. It was either that or jump on Harry. I didn't want to be caught engaging in amomaxia for the second time. It had been embarrassing enough when I was sixteen. I said a hasty goodnight and fled into Leonie's.

Anne Stinnett

Seventeen

I stood in the foyer, the door shut and locked behind me. Gulliver's bark rang out from the master suite. I heard Leonie object to the noise.

When Gulliver bounced into the room I gave him his due greeting and let him lead me back to Leonie.

"Hello darling, how was the sleuthing? Gulliver and I had a lovely night. Nat Geo ran a Koala Kingdom marathon. He seemed quite interested. I wouldn't have thought a dog would pay attention to television."

"Yeah, I usually leave Animal Planet on for him when he has to stay home alone."

"I'm tired of talking darling. Goodnight. Before I forget, you have things to attend to in the yard. Tomorrow?"

"First thing."

I retreated down the hallway to my own room, Gulliver frisking ahead. The air conditioner was silent, the slight chill in the house was seeping in from outside. My bed was unkempt. Gulliver didn't mind. He jumped up and sprawled out, tongue lolling happily from the side of his mouth. I tried to coax him down so I could return the bedding to a smoother, more comfortable state, but he would not be persuaded.

Gulliver is not a dog that has to be bribed with a biscuit to perform every little sit or stay, but love of me was not budging him.

"Come on," I whined. I am thoroughly against such behavior in theory, but I was tired and frustrated. In general, not sexually. I sighed. Not just sexually. I tried some A.T.

"Gulliver you are being selfish. There is room for both of us, if you let me straighten everything. But you can't sleep in the middle."

He was unimpressed. I tried to push him off the bed. I tried to pull the covers out from under him. I decided that my next dog was going to be a tribble.

Perhaps something in the kitchen could be the irresistible force to shift immovable Gulliver. I foraged in the refrigerator and came back with a chunk of Brie. Lest anyone think my dog is spoiled, it was not heated. Gulliver snapped to attention. A string of drool eased from his jowls; it stretched all the way down to the bed, to my relief missing my pillow.

I waved the cheese. Gulliver charged and I tossed it out the bedroom door and shut it smartly behind him. I made the bed, and didn't let him back in until I'd washed my face and brushed my teeth. We finally settled equitably, and comfortably.

I fell asleep with the kiss playing over and over in my head. I didn't embellish once.

***

I had lied to Leonie about picking up the yard first thing. I had to walk Gulliver who woke bursting with energy. Then there was coffee. Two cups. It was third thing in the morning that I went out to the yard and had my anti-treasure hunt. It was my secret though, because Leonie had been gone when I woke up. She had left behind a faint whiff of Chanel No. 5, because Leonie likes the classics, and half a pot of coffee, for which I was grateful.

After dealing with the yard, I had a shower. Clean and caffeinated, I felt as good as I was going to, so I called Leonie to see where she'd gone. The call went straight to voicemail. I looked up Hugo's number.

It rang five times before Serena answered.

"Is Hugo there?" I said.

"Who's calling?"

"Hi Serena." I tried to let my sigh out quietly. "It's Evin Hart."

"Evin. Fabulous. Hugo is busy."

"It will just take a second." I was giving her my best perky. It wasn't so great.

She huffed and called Hugo to the phone. I waited. Serena and I didn't speak but I knew she was still there from her breathing. I heard a small clatter as Hugo picked up another extension.

"Hello?" he said.

"Hugo, it's Evin."

"Hey, Evin."

"It was great talking to you Serena," I said, when she didn't hang up.

"Anything you have to say to my husband, you can say to me," she said.

Ick.

"Serena it's nothing personal," I said. "I just need to talk to Hugo about someone he works with."

"What's up, Evin?" Hugo said.

I gave him a quick sketch of the murders and Jack's predicament.

"I read about that," Serena said. "Your stepfather always was a little shady."

"Jack isn't shady."

"He's not a paragon either, is he? Hugo, make it quick, I need you," she said and slammed down the phone.

"Sorry, about that."

"No worries," I said. "I wanted to see if you knew anything about Rex that might be helpful."

"I don't know much, Rex mostly keeps to himself. Everyone knows he doesn't get along with his father, but I have no idea why."

"What about Hazel? Do you think he might have had some wicked stepmother grudge going?"

"As far as I knew he got along with her. If you're thinking along those lines, I would think his sister would be more likely."

"Why?"

"She's kind of possessive of their father and... she can be kind of a bitch." This was from the guy who'd been with Serena Greenly for half his life.

I agreed. I wouldn't mind if it was Reina. It was too bad that when Hazel was killed she had been with Eddie Daigle, fulfilling his high school fantasies.

Well, maybe not all of them.

I told Hugo about last night's scene at the Yacht Club.

"He is kind of an angry guy," Hugo said. "It might not be anything more than that."

"Angry about what?"

"Life, I guess."

"Yeah, having rich overly indulgent parents and good looks would piss me off too," I said.

"Uh...Ev-"

"Hugo, I said I needed you." Serena was back on the line.

"Alright babe, I'm coming," he said. "Sorry I couldn't be more help Evin."

To annoy Serena, I told him in my sweetest voice that he had been nothing less than invaluable, added that I hoped to see him soon, and hung up.

It was 10:00 a.m. Jack was in jail, Leonie was absent, Zuzu was at the hospital, and Harry was working on a sad infidelity case. I wondered who had the energy to cheat so early in the morning. We were out of bed and I was dressed. Gulliver was all charged up for something. We decided to hit the dog park.

I retrieved Gulliver's leash, generating a certain degree of canine excitement, but it wasn't until I grabbed the car keys that things really got hectic. Gulliver barked frantically and spun in excited circles. I finally flung open the door allowing him to charge into the courtyard where he sat quivering by the Thunderbird. I managed to fasten his leash once we were in the car, and I counted that a victory.

The dog park was decently populated. Various spaniels, retrievers and shepherds cavorted across the wasted grass, chased balls and splashed in the wading pool. The morning was bright and warm, perfect park weather.

We passed the little dog area, the chain link preventing rank and sundry adorable beasts from swarming all over us, and through the double gate. Inside, I released Gulliver who immediately took off in pursuit of a cute little boxer in a pink rhinestone collar. I kept a weather eye out lest he become involved in an altercation (which was unlikely), or excrete anything that needed picking up (which wasn't).

Door number two was a bingo.

That unpleasantness behind me, I snagged a plastic chair and parked it and myself under a tree. It wasn't long before Gulliver trotted over to drop a ball at my feet. I scooped it up and threw it across the park. Instead of bounding joyously after it as a dog should, he looked at me reproachfully.

When we go to the park, Gulliver likes to collect a pile of tennis balls, and any other toys he can snatch from the unwary or weak. Once, I had to spend twenty minutes tracking down the rightful owner of a fancy purloined Kong. Instead of being lauded for my conscientiousness, I was publicly scolded for rearing a thief.

Gulliver ambled off, I assumed to have another go at pirating tennis balls.

I felt eyes on me and shifted in my chair to check it out. A few feet back and to my left stood a man. He was young and trim, maybe six feet, maybe less, with dark hair cut short and piercing brown eyes. I knew about the piercing part, because they were currently focused on me. Suddenly I was freakishly uncomfortable, like I was standing in a spotlight braless. In spite of the intense self-consciousness he was causing, he seemed familiar.

I had just turned away when it hit me. He was one of the cops that had responded to Maggie's house. Officer De la Cruz. I took another peek to make sure. Yup. He was in street clothes and seemed far less friendly and reassuring than when I'd seen him last. I guess he had heard about the second body. I couldn't tell if his gaze was hostile or assessing, and I didn't much care. I was in no mood for another run in with the long arm.

I turned back around and scanned the park to see where Gulliver had taken himself. I finally located him in the corner, opposite the gate we'd come in.

There was a bit of a frenzy taking place around a woman wearing head to toe pink. She was decked out: pink sandals, pink corduroys, pink bejeweled tee shirt.

Her sunhat was actually white, but it was adorned with an ostentatious bouquet of what looked to be pink mums. She was trying to shoo dogs away. I figured the least I could do was go retrieve mine.

I had taken two steps when the woman started to shriek. I could see her waving around a bag of Pupperonies. I had once made the mistake of bringing food to the dog park. However, I had not shrieked. I broke into a run. De la Cruz and his harsh brown eyes arrived at the melee just as I did.

"No, no, no, no, no, no, no, no!" I could make out words now. "Naughty dogs." She was trying to stuff the bag into her pocket, which would do no good even if she managed it; they would still be able to smell the damn treats. She didn't manage. She fumbled and dropped the bag. It hit the ground, a brawl broke out, and Pinky started shrieking in earnest.

It was all over in seconds but I think it went something like this: I waded into the pack intending to grab Gulliver, but I saw that wasn't the highest priority. There was a whirlwind going on practically under the pink woman's feet. It was composed of Gulliver's cute boxer friend and a little dachshund, who was getting the worst of it. I thunked the boxer on the shoulder to get her attention, when she released the smaller dog's throat, I hauled her out of there.

She bit my hand.

"Oh my god, I'm so sorry."

Strong, steady hands took the boxer from my own shaking ones, which was good, because I needed mine to manage my own dog who had taken umbrage at the attack. I looked up into the face of Officer De la Cruz, which was disconcerting since the voice I heard was feminine.

"I'm really, so sorry," the voice said again, and of

course, it was the woman with too much pink and too little sense who was talking.

She produced a leash and secured the boxer, who was still showing fang to the doxi. The hot dog, outclassed in size, but not attitude, had been picked up by De la Cruz and was snarling back from the arms of the officer. I held on to Gulliver's collar with my good hand and examined the tooth shaped dents in the other. By now, all the dogs who had been involved in the treat fiasco had been claimed by their people and were drifting away.

The woman was babbling on, "Like I said, she's a rescue. I've only had her about four months and I wanted to do a little training. We're working with a behaviorist and she said that I should practice with Princess Grace in a busy environment so she learns to listen to me in any situation. That's why-"

"I find it hard to believe a trainer told you to do this here and bring treats," I interrupted. "Didn't you realize they'd all want one?"

"I'm sorry, I really am, are you sure your dog is ok?" she asked for what must have been the fifth time.

"She'll be ok, I think," De la Cruz said rubbing the little dog's head. I could see from her little bone shaped nametag that her name was Roxy.

"What about your hand? Are you going to sue me?"

"No, I'm not going to sue you." At least not for the bite. Maybe for stealing ten minutes of my life with this inane conversation. "It's fine. I'll be fine, you should take your dog home. She looks upset." Actually, Princess Grace looked happy as a clam, I was upset. "But good for you for adopting," I added, because I thought it was, and also, she seemed nice in spite of everything and I was starting to feel bad for being so bitchy. Unfortunately, my benevolence encouraged more conversation.

Just before I started to scream, Pinky wrapped it up and left.

Then there were two. I nodded to De la Cruz and started to move off.

"Thanks," he said behind me, and I turned.

"No problem. She's ok?" I nodded at Roxy.

"She's fine. She lost some fur is all, and knowing her, she started it anyway. So..." He shrugged. "I'll run her by the vet to be sure. Look, I didn't mean to make you uncomfortable before, if I was staring. I was just thinking about things."

"Things like two dead women and a third that's missing?" I said. "Yeah, me too. I'm probably not supposed to ask, but are you guys making any progress? Is Detective Quick still in charge?" I wanted the answer to be negative. In spite of my first impression, which had been ok, I worried now that Quick wouldn't be motivated to look beyond his bird in the hand.

"Yeah."

Perfect.

"Can you tell me anything? I don't want to get you in trouble, but I know Jack, so there has to be another explanation." *And I just saved your dog's life, incurring grievous bodily injury in the process.* I didn't say that part out loud, because saying it would make me an asshole, but the thought hung in the air between us. I brought my swelling hand up to my face for examination.

He sighed. "There's an APB out for Margaret Conner."

Maggie. "Because she's a suspect?"

"Because, officially, she's a person of interest."

"Ok. Unofficially?"

"Leaving the scene of a crime is bad." The brown eyes were sympathetic now. "But so is having a body discovered in your house." As Jack could attest.

We watched a couple of dogs racing for a tennis ball. I looked around for Gulliver and saw him splashing in the wading pool, for the moment staying out of trouble.

"You guys know that Candace Brown was Bobby Neuland's mistress, right?"

De la Cruz nodded.

"So how is he not under arrest? His wife, who was divorcing him by the way, and his mistress are both stabbed to death and he's not under arrest? Not to mention the rest of the family who are all acting sketchy as hell." I was trying to keep my volume down, but it was a struggle. "And instead you arrest a guy who had no relationship with either of them?"

"I didn't arrest him," De la Cruz said. I didn't know whether to take that as a statement of fact or something more. "I know you must be frustrated, but Dr. Neuland has given us a detailed account of his time on the day of the murders. On the other hand Mr. Dekker claims he was alone at his ex-wife's house for the entire week."

"Which means no alibi," I said.

De la Cruz nodded.

"And if, as you say," he went on, "Mr. Dekker had no connection to Candace Brown, why did she end up dead in his condominium? The preliminary findings suggest those two women were killed with the same knife. There's a connection. There's another one between Jack Dekker's girlfriend and Hazel Neuland."

"She wasn't his girlfriend."

"You're right about the husband being an obvious suspect. The trouble for you is, we have two other people to look at. They are possibly a couple, one has fled, one is in custody, and they each had a murder victim in their residence. You say there's no connection, but from our point of view, there has to be."

My eyes were welling up again. I felt like I'd been crying every day for weeks. I tipped my head back and blinked furiously until the blurred images cavorting before my eyes resolved into dogs, cavorting before my eyes. Sometimes you gotta have cavorting.

"Look," he said, his voice kind, "When something like this happens there are always family members who can't believe it. Even murderers belong to someone."

There was no point, in arguing with him about the impossibility of Jack stabbing two women. Instead, I said, "Do you know when they were killed? I mean I already know approximately."

He hesitated, and I added, "If Jack has no alibi for an entire week, and he is guilty, then it doesn't make a difference if you tell me that. If it was someone else it could make all the difference in the world. Please."

"Candace Brown died approximately an hour before Hazel Neuland. Preliminary reports indicate both women were killed between 11:00 a.m. and 1:00 p.m." He considered me and added, "You shouldn't get involved in this. If you're right it's dangerous. If not, you'll be screwed anyway because Detective Quick won't be happy to find you interfering in his investigation. Everyone knows he's a sarcastic son of a bitch, but his closure record is solid and that's what matters. We take our jobs seriously, and being a fan of Sherlock doesn't make you more qualified than the police."

No, but I was a step ahead since I could eliminate

Jack as a suspect. De la Cruz checked his watch. My golden opportunity was reverting to lead.

"What about Maggie's house being searched? Do you guys have any ideas about who? Or what?"

He shook his head, "It could have been anything."

It couldn't have been anything. It had to have been something relatively small, to fit in the drawers and cupboards that had been searched. Something maybe the size of a shoebox or a book. Or...oh. My breath caught.

"Thank you," I said to Officer De la Cruz. *You're an idiot,* I said to myself.

"Don't mention it. To anyone. Ever," he said. "Good luck."

"Can I get your number, just in case?" I asked.

He looked wary. "Look, you kept Roxy from getting her head ripped off, but we're even."

"What if we find something out? You wouldn't want to know about it?"

I got a dubious look, but it was followed by a number. I plugged it into my phone and patted Roxy's little head in farewell. I bellowed for Gulliver and he came running to meet me at the gate. We were out of there.

Eighteen

I tried to call Harry. I heard five rings and then Harry's deep voice telling me I knew what to do.

"Hey Harry, it's Evin. Uh, I was at the park..." He wouldn't care that I was at the park. The point. I should get to it. Ugh. "I thought of something. I think. I think I thought of something. Well, I did think of something. Just whether or not it's a helpful something is the question." Crap. "Just call me back. Or don't. If you're busy. I'll just see you at noon." It was a smidge after eleven now. I hung up and looked at Gulliver who was lounging in the passenger seat. He sat up and licked my face.

"Thanks for not judging," I told him.

***

Twenty minutes later, I pulled up in front of Maggie's house. I had dropped Gulliver off at home. Before going in, I speed dialed Leonie. She didn't pick up. I left her a message detailing my whereabouts and ETA. No way was I going to be one of those idiots who vanished never to be seen again because they neglected to inform anyone of their destination.

Precautions taken, I tossed my phone on the seat and locked the car.

It was spooky inside. A few days ago, Hazel Neuland had been out back being knifed to death. My nerves were quivering with anxiety at the thought of being discovered. Knifed myself. Thrown in the pool for my blood to mix with Hazel's. I avoided looking through the patio door.

I was standing in the living room, looking at a picture of Maggie on the tram. I wanted to punch her in the face. I didn't know what the hell was happening, but I knew she was to blame for some of it. At least for the part where Jack and I got involved. I could go back even further and blame Leonie for leaving. If Jack hadn't been jettisoned and left to his own devices he would never have met the disastrous Maggie. Who would have thought a broken home could wreck your life after thirty? Thirty-one. Whatever.

I crossed the room to what I'd come for. My breath was shallow. I needed to be right. We had to have more information or we would never be able to help Jack. The thought that I was too late sent my stomach spiraling in on itself.

I stood in front of the bookshelf and neatly plucked The Stand from the ranks. When I opened it, I found the unabridged version, a thousand pages more or less of apocalypse, just as the cover promised.

I was undone. My best prospect a wash. I was suddenly furious. I pulled books off the shelf one after another; yanking each open without thought or care and discarding them roughly.

I tore through Crichton, Dickens and Wambaugh, flinging disappointment after disappointment to the floor and snatching up the next. I was over halfway through the collection with nothing to show for my furor. I discarded *Lonesome Dove* and picked up an unwieldy hardback copy of *Atlas Shrugged*. I tried to flip the pages and couldn't. Right fucking *on.*

There was a neat little compartment in the middle, identical to the one in Jack's copy of Watership Down, and just like before, I found something good. Only this time it wasn't Patron.

I hadn't understood why both Hazel and Candace had been killed. If Candace had been pressuring Bobby to leave Hazel he could have killed her to preserve his marriage and bank account. Conversely, if Bobby had wanted to be rid of his wife, without the massive financial loss another divorce would entail, a quick efficient blade for Hazel may have seemed the perfect solution. However, both didn't fit any scenario that I had come up with.

I inspected my find. There were two letters, a cell phone with charger, and a memory card. I sank breathlessly into the nearest chair and unfolded the first letter.

It was headed, "To Mrs. Hazel Neuland," and it had been signed in a neatly looping hand, Candace Brown. In between salutation and signature was more of a list than a letter, detailing the dates, places and activities that had comprised Candace Brown's relationship with Dr. Bobby Neuland. They had met at a charity concert at the McCallum. Cute. Cuter if he hadn't been married.

The other letter was a short scrawl also addressed to Hazel. I raised my eyebrows, expressing my surprise for a nonexistent audience and wondered how it had gone over. I knew how it would have gone over me.

The phone was a little pink Palm.

I pressed the button to turn it on, but the phone refused to function, citing low battery and turned itself right back off.

Crap. I took a deep breath. The memory card

looked like the one in my little digital camera, but then they all looked alike to me. Still, I was betting on pictures, rather than random computer data. Assuming memory cards were capable of storing computer data. I had no idea, really. I abandoned that useless train of thought.

I shoved the memory card into the lipstick pocket of my jeans. The letters I folded down as close to nothing as I could and tucked them deep in my bra. The phone and charger were distributed to back pockets.

I put Ayn Rand's empty classic back on the shelf, and started flipping through the remaining books just in case. To be thorough is not always a good thing.

I was halfway through the last shelf; had found nothing else along the way. My fingers were grubby and my nose itched. I brushed the hair out of my face with my forearm.

I froze. Completely. My arm was at my forehead. Body, breath and bowels all clenched into one tense unmoving knot in response to the sound I had heard behind me. It was a sound I knew, and I didn't know it any less surely for having only heard it previously in onscreen entertainments. It was the sound of a gun being cocked.

I wanted to run. Disappear. If I had covers, I would have had them pulled over my head faster than a heartbeat. And my heart had never beat faster.

A gun would be better though, than a knife. I didn't want to end up like Candace, sliced and bloody. Like Hazel pierced and bleeding in a swimming pool. Shot would be better than stabbed. Maybe. But it wasn't good.

"Come to borrow a book?" The question was drawled in that maddening accent I still couldn't identify.

A chill ran down my spine. Slowly, I turned around.

"There you are," I said. "We've been wondering what happened to you." Wondering if she needed to be helped or hunted. I was currently thinking hunted.

Maggie looked as different from the day I met her as she could. Her hair was brown now, and pulled back in a half-assed ponytail. Wisps were escaping everywhere and her face was unarmed. Cosmetically speaking.

The hand that held the gun revealed none of the trembles that wracked my own body.

"Give me everything," she said.

I didn't want to. It seemed unlikely we would find her if she disappeared again. This time with evidence we needed.

"I didn't find anything," I said. "I just started. You go ahead and look. I'll just-"

"Evin, shut up. I don't want to hurt you. And I'm sorry about Jack. But, I can't fix his life, or yours. I have to save my own."

I rolled my eyes around hoping to spot a handy bulletproof shield waiting to be snatched up. None, nada, zilch. Fuck.

"Maggie, we can help you," I said.

"Help me by handing over the phone in your back pocket. The letters too, and the SD card. Now."

"That's my phone."

"No it's not. You left yours in that piece of shit car. I saw it out front. Stop screwing around."

"It's a classic." That wasn't the issue. "Look, for all I know you killed two women and you'll kill me the second I hand over anything."

"I can kill you first then search your body at my

leisure."

That had occurred to her pretty quickly. "What about Jack? He's in jail for murder and if you didn't do it, I know you know who did. I thought you cared about him."

"I feel bad about Jack, but he'll be fine. He's always fine."

That was true. Jack *was* always fine. So why was I here, about to take a bullet to one of my favorite places? And they were all my favorite places. There wasn't a single body part that I wouldn't hate for her to shoot.

Maggie moved closer, and I saw that her gun hand was starting to tremble. So now, if she didn't shoot me on purpose, she might do it accidentally.

"So, was it you?" I asked because Maggie was terrified. Scared in a way that I didn't think the killer could be. Of course, it wasn't easy to give her the benefit of the doubt when all I could see was the little hole in the barrel of her gun.

"It wasn't me." She was speaking softly, the venom gone from her tone. "I was helping a friend. Or trying to. It worked out about as well for me as it did for you."

What gave her the right to bitch? No one was pointing a gun at her favorite parts.

"Why was Candace at Jack's?" I said.

"She needed a place to stay, why do you think? Hazel wouldn't put up with her being here. Jack wasn't using it. He was always whining about how he hated going back to that huge luxurious condo. You people and what pass for your problems are ridiculous."

I thought my current problem was rather significant. But now wasn't the time to get into that.

"Maggie, please. We need to get out of here. We

can get you somewhere safe. You know who killed them, don't you? Just tell me."

My eyes were all about the gun, but I could see Maggie was starting to disintegrate. Unfortunately, only in the emotional sense.

"Don't be stupid," she said, "I don't know anything except that I have to get out of here, and you're holding me up."

"I told you-"

"I'm telling you. My life means more to me than yours does. Are you going to make me prove it?"

She was visibly pulling herself together. The gun was a steady menace and the eyes of the woman holding it were hard.

"Ok." I reached back into my pockets and came up with the phone and charger. She held out her hand. I imagined myself seizing her by the wrist, pulling her off balance, disarming her. Instead, I placed the Palm and its charger gently in her grasp. If I got out of here alive I would learn self-defense. Better yet, I would embrace my inner hermit and avoid crazy ladies with guns.

Especially guns aimed right at my face. Fuck. *Really?* Not only was she willing to kill me, she was going to doom me to a closed casket.

I looked at the gun. It was pretty, for a gun. A little silver barrel with a pearl handle. It looked small. I guess that's why she was aiming at my head. Too easy to survive a flesh wound from that glorified pellet gun. What happened to not wanting to hurt me?

I'd zoned in so hard on the gun that I missed something Maggie said to me. I looked up at her face just as a shot rang out. I was surprised not to feel anything. The patio door had shattered and come raining down, the first casualty.

When Maggie crumpled to the ground, I didn't know what to make of that. My face and chest were sticky wet. I raised my grubby hand to investigate. There was blood. Tissue. Bits. Of Maggie. She had fallen and flopped backwards. I looked down. I could see that there was a great hole, slightly off-center, below her breasts. Her eyes were still open. I looked away.

Too late, it occurred to me that I should move. When the second shot rang out, I was tripping over my feet, trying to flee. There was a god-awful crack, felt or heard, when I smacked face first into Maggie's coffee table.

I dragged my eyes open. It took everything I had. My head ached dully; a more piercing misery afflicted my temple. I tried to focus, but everything went dark beneath my eyelids.

Nineteen

Two hours later, I had been poked, prodded and diagnosed with a mild concussion.

It didn't feel mild.

The gash on my head had been sewn shut with two stitches. I would rather have had ten. Two stitches were vaguely embarrassing. Proof I'd been inept enough to require professional attention, without the romantic pathos of a serious injury.

I was waiting with Harry and Leonie for the doctor's verdict. Zuzu was working and popped in sporadically.

"You're sure Gulliver is ok?"

"Yes darling, your dog is fine. He's been out in the yard doing who knows what and I gave him food and water, so he'll be all loaded up to do it again later."

Harry laughed. I did too, but briefly because it hurt quite a bit.

"My head hurts."

"Of course it does, darling. That's what happens when you get a concussion. I thought you understood you were supposed to extract your stepfather from trouble, not embroil yourself. Now here I am, nauseous from the reek of antiseptic."

"You don't find it reassuring?" Harry said. "All this

blatant cleanliness?"

"No. If that much disinfectant is needed, something is obviously wrong. They're trying to cover up the stench of death." Leonie looked fiercely at the nurse who'd been futzing around me. She was adorable, freckled and fresh. The smile she offered Leonie reminded me of a dog showing its belly.

When the nurse had gone, I asked Leonie to get me a Pepsi. Harry chimed in for coffee, and she went with no trouble.

Leonie was replaced, by my doctor. She was conservatively dressed in tan slacks and a beige sweater set under her white coat. The only sour note was her footwear. They were Crocs. And they were blue.

I hoped the doctor made herself scarce before Leonie returned. None of us would feel better for having heard Leonie's absolutely truthful opinion of Crocs. Dr. Barrett-Smith subjected me to some gentle probing and an offensive light before telling me I could go home in the morning.

"It doesn't hurt that much," I said. "Can't I just go home now?"

"No. You can be more adequately monitored here. If you had really wanted to go home tonight, you shouldn't have come in with insurance." Harry and I exchanged a look while the doctor chuckled over the state of the system. She controlled her mirth long enough to tell me someone would be coming shortly to move me upstairs. I figured that meant another hour or so.

Then it was just Harry and me.

I was folding the sheet into precise little rows, an activity that demanded so much of my attention that I could only offhandedly say, "Thanks."

"Thank Leonie," Harry said. I had. She had made me.

"I still can't believe she used the words, 'back-up'," I said.

"I still can't believe you fainted in my arms."

"I didn't faint, I lost consciousness for about three seconds. From the concussion."

"Mild concussion. I think subconsciously you were seizing the day."

"By grabbing the opportunity to be lugged out like a side of beef?"

"Lugged out in my arms."

I had been too freaked out to enjoy that part. I shook my head at him. Regretted it.

"It's a theory."

"You ruin everything," I said.

"I heard you have to spend the night." Zuzu had slipped through the curtain to join us. "See, that's why you can't be running around by yourself. There's no one to keep you from tipping over." Zuzu was wearing Batman Beyond scrubs and sneakers designed to improve her already enviable ass. She perched on the foot of my bed and frowned pointedly at Harry before addressing me.

"What were you doing there alone?"

"I didn't know where she was," Harry said. "I got a message, but..."

Oh. The message. *Damn.*

"You should answer your phone, Harry. She could have been killed, and it would have been all your fault."

"All?"

"That's right."

"Leave him alone, Zuzu," I said. "It wasn't his fault I was there alone. Besides, he did come find me.

At least I didn't get shot too."

"In the head," Zuzu agreed. "Or the face."

"My face is part of my head. Didn't they teach you that in nursing school?"

"You should be nice, Evin. I can make sure your dinner gets lost. Where's Leonie?"

"She went to get us stuff to drink. Coffee. Pepsi. Absinthe."

"Cool. So tell me already. What the hell went on this morning?"

"If you feel up to talking," Harry said. That was nice.

"She's ok," Zuzu said. Much less nice.

I sighed and told her about my morning, starting with De la Cruz, the dog fight, Pinky and my daring rescue of little Roxy. "So anyway, I kind of saved the cop's little dog so he was marginally forthcoming. But not if anyone asks."

"What all did he tell you?" Harry said.

I took a deep breath. "It wasn't much. Mostly, he said, that Jack is still their focus. He has no alibi for anything. Even if the times of death are a little different when the official report comes back, Jack would still have no chance at an alibi because he was in a funk all week and stayed at home drinking. At Leonie's drinking, anyway. They're looking for Maggie, or they were, but the gist of it was that Jack and Maggie knew each other and two murdered women turned up in their respective homes. So according to De la Cruz, the cops are sure there's a connection even if they don't know exactly what it is yet. Now that Maggie is dead, I'm even more worried about Jack. I was really starting to hope she was the killer. She could have been Bobby Neuland's new extremely jealous girlfriend."

"What reason do they think Jack had to kill them?" Zuzu asked.

"I don't know."

"They don't absolutely need motive," Harry said. "The fact that there was a woman stabbed with Jack's knife in his residence is plenty for them."

"It's impossible that Jack did any of this." Leonie had sailed back into my little cubby. "Honestly. Do not go around repeating every filthy lie you hear, Evin. This is exactly why the truth is so important and why we should practice it absolutely." She kept going, but I wasn't paying attention to her words anymore so caught up was I in the fact that two perfect trails of tears were running down Leonie's cheeks.

"Maybe you should go home for awhile," I told her.

"You're right, darling. If you and Harry don't get Jack out of jail soon I will make your lives miserable. I mean it. This has gone on long enough. How am I ever supposed to feel peaceful when everyone is running around up to who knows what?"

How she put up with us...

"Sorry?" I offered, going for pacification, but she had already swept out. I really wanted a nice big glass of wine to mellow me out and make me sleepy, but I knew the chances of that were nil.

"She is the prettiest crier," Zuzu said.

"I know. It's riduculous."

Harry looked at us like we were crazy, and said, "So, as of this morning, Detective Quick was satisfied with his arrest of Jack. But Maggie's death changes things. I hope he'll reevaluate his evidence in light of that. If not we'll continue on our own."

We sounded dashing. I was getting sleepy in spite of the dearth of wine. Harry suggested I finish my recap of the morning's momentous events. I yawned and told them the rest.

"When I asked if they had any idea what the object of the search was the night I found Hazel, he said it could be anything. That got me thinking about how it couldn't actually be anything, it had to be something that was a certain size. At least, no bigger than a certain size, and I remembered the *Watership Down* book safe we have at home, and that reminded me of *The Stand* because it was out of place on the shelves and I thought maybe it was a book safe, or that something was hidden in the pages of one of the books. They were all pulled off the shelves, like someone had looked behind them, but not through them. Not thoroughly at least. So I went to check it out."

I ran through my arrival at Maggie's. I told them about everything I saw and found, about Maggie's untimely arrival and the aftermath.

"You left your phone in the car?" Zuzu scolded me.

"That's what you took away from everything I just told you? It's not like I would have had a chance to use it anyway."

"Yeah, but still, girl. You can't just leave your phone behind. Anything could happen."

I sighed.

"Don't sigh at me. Who do you think is going to be stuck giving your eulogy, because we won't be able to trust your mother to get up there and give it. We can't have Leonie telling the Absolute Truth about you at your funeral."

Talk about true.

"Do you two always need a referee?" Harry said. He had his chair tipped back against the only solid wall and his feet up on the end of my bed. "So who hid the stuff at Maggie's house? We know it wasn't Maggie."

"We know that how?" Zuzu asked.

"Because," I said, "she knew what was there, but not where it was. She got the phone. I guess the cops took..." I trailed off because Harry was shaking his head. "No?"

"How do you know?" Zuzu said.

"I looked before they got there. Not for the phone specifically, I didn't know about that, but I looked for anything helpful. There was no phone."

"You searched her body?" I said.

Zuzu and I took a moment to digest that harsh bit of reality. Zuzu finished first.

"It's ok Harry," she said. "You did what you had to do, is all."

"Thanks."

"Then that bastard has the phone." That pissed me off. I found the damn thing. I got concussed. I deserved that phone. Even if I didn't know why it was important. It was completely unfair. It was like being tried for the same crime twice. It was like having to pay a fee to shop at Trashy Lingerie. Yeah, it's only a couple bucks, but if I'm going to pay sixty bucks for a push-up bra, I don't want to pay an extra two to get in the door. My head hurt. I wanted to cry, but I wanted to cry romantically and beautifully like Leonie. I wanted tears to well gently out of my mismatched eyes and spill romantically down my dewy, lightly flushed cheeks where they would be kissed gently away by my hero. Since when I cry it usually results in hiccupping and snot, I fought to hold myself together.

"Are you ok? Evin?" I looked up to see Harry looking back at me with a concerned expression. "Do you need a nurse?"

"Hey! I'm a nurse." Zuzu jumped up and started fussing with and around me.

"I'm ok, Zuzu," I said. She didn't even pause. When she was fluffing my pillow for the third time, I said loudly, "Ow."

"Ok. Sorry."

"So, how did he get the phone off Maggie if I was there? I didn't see anyone. I mean, I was just a few feet away from her."

"You were awake when I got there, but still pretty out of it. It would have only taken a few seconds for someone to dash in from the backyard and grab the phone, especially if they'd been watching and knew where it was."

"At least we have the memory card," Zuzu said. "It was in your pocket."

"Where is my stuff anyway?"

Zuzu produced what there was of my belongings. My clothes were absent except for my shoes and underwear which she pulled out with no regard for Harry's presence. Luckily, I'd been wearing good underwear; they were black and lacy and cut exactly right to make my butt look good. I don't think I dwell on my appearance, but I like to know what's going on behind me.

"Where are my jeans?" I asked Zuzu.

"Thrown out."

"I loved those jeans."

"Not anymore. Trust me," she said, and shook the memory card out of my shoe with a ta-da! sort of flourish. "But what about the letters?"

"Umm." Harry looked embarrassed.

"I tucked them in my bra." I said sternly, giving Harry an interrogatory eye.

"It's not like I was just patting you down for fun, although under different circumstances..." He paused to grin at me; I glared in return. It was too bad my cheeks chose that moment to start a slow burn that spread all the way down my neck.

"Don't worry." He was still smiling. "I didn't fondle you and I didn't see much. I just wanted to make sure we got a look at everything before it was confiscated. We can turn it over to the cops tomorrow after we make copies. We're lucky nothing else disappeared along with the phone."

"Why didn't he find the letter? The killer?"

"I don't think there was time."

"Why not shoot me?"

"I don't know," Harry said. "Maybe he thought he had. You were prone and bloody."

We were all quiet for a minute. I don't know what Zuzu and Harry were thinking about, but I was pretty stuck on what would have happened if Harry hadn't tracked me down.

Finally, I said, "Where are they?"

Harry produced the letters from a pocket. Zuzu crowded up beside me so she could read along.

"You already read it didn't you?" I accused Harry, who was conspicuous by his disinterest. "You went down my top and you read the damn letters without me. See?" I said to Zuzu, "I have horrible taste in men."

"That sounds promising," Harry said.

I grunted in a most well mannered way and turned my attention to the missive I was holding.

I knew the gist of what was written, but I'd only skimmed earlier, and I was glad to have the chance to read them more thoroughly.

"Hmmm," Zuzu said.

Yup.

I was surprised anew that the good doctor was a supporter of charity, but it was as likely to be business machination as genuine do-gooding. The letter referred to the evidence of the affair and concluded with:

> *Here's the proof I promised. I'm including the phone and charger just in case. Good luck with the camera. About the videos, you should probably just pass them along to your lawyer and don't look at them first. Don't worry I made copies just in case. So goodbye, I'm off now to your friends place, well your friend's, friend's place. I'll call like we agreed.*
>
> *Sincerely yours,*
> *Candace Brown*

"So what?" Zuzu said. "Candace is handing over proof of her affair with Bobby Neuland to his wife?"

"And telling her where to get more, while she's at it."

The other letter was dated February 11th, and was far more personal. Zuzu and I read it together, each clutching a side of the page.

Dear Hazel,   0211

I'm writing to say just how sorry I am. I do want you to know that I thought Bobby loved me, that I believed we had a future. I know I helped ruin your marriage, but I lost two relationships . We've both been hurt, you and I but I hope you can see, like I can, that Bobby is to blame. I'm getting what he owes me for ruining my life and I hope I'm able to give you the chance you need to do the same. I'm sure the videos and the messages on the phone will be enough to prove he violated your prenup. (and the letter of course) I am sorry. I'm sorry you had to know. I hope you forgive me. But if not, I'll be ok.

Yours truly,
Candace

"Wow. I would have kicked her ass, before I let her help me," Zuzu said.

"Stop crumpling it," Harry said. "We have to give that to the police."

"Jeez," I said.

"What do you think?" Harry asked me.

"If Hazel hadn't died that same morning I'd be convinced she killed Candace."

"But she did."

"So it was Bobby."

"What other relationship is she talking about?" Zuzu said.

"No idea," I told her. "But the guy she dumped for Bobby probably doesn't care at this point."

"Evin is right about the quality of the motive. If everything went according to the plan laid out here, Candace blackmailed Bobby with their relationship, then turned proof of the affair over to Hazel anyway."

"Bye-bye prenup," I said. "That's half of everything gone, plus whatever Candace got for herself."

"But everything didn't go according to plan," Zuzu said, then took herself away through the curtain in answer to a page.

True. "We don't know if he even paid the blackmail."

"He wouldn't, if he was planning to kill her."

"What if it was unplanned?"

"Take it back after," Harry said. "I might be able to check for a withdrawal."

"There wasn't any money at Jack's when we were there," I focused on Harry. "So we have a dead blackmailer, and a wife who was prepared, in every way, to take half of what was left."

"Not to mention a sleazy husband with an expensive life and a couple of greedy kids to support."

"And Verona," I added.

"And Verona."

"See," I said, although there was nothing to feel triumphant about since we were agreeing. "How could it be anybody else? Bobby obviously did it."

"The police don't think so."

"Because he has an alibi."

"We need to know what exactly the alibi is. So we can check it ourselves."

"I'm supposed to give a statement tomorrow, maybe I can find out from Quick."

"Find out what?" Zuzu had popped in again.

"What about the dog park cop?" she said, after I told her.

"He's not the dog park cop. He's just a cop, with a dog that he took to the park. He made it pretty clear he was done helping me."

"If you don't ask, you won't get."

"That's not true. I never asked to get mono in the eighth grade from Jerry Abbott, and I didn't ask for my apartment to burn down, or to suck at relationships, or even for unruly hair. And for your information, Pollyanna, I also didn't ask to get shot at."

Zuzu was unfazed by my litany. "You kind of did, by going over there alone when there's a murderer running around. Besides," she went on, raising her voice to drown out my objections, "because your house burned down and you can't keep a relationship going, you ended up here to help Jack when he needed you. And yeah, you got shot at and that sucks, but it wasn't anywhere near as bad as it could have been. You do realize all the bullets missed you, and now you're real close to being able to save Jack," she paused. "But I don't know what to tell you about the mono."

"So everything happens for a reason?" I rolled my

eyes, which caused a severe head twinge. "Is that what you think too?" I asked Harry.

"No. And I don't think-"

Zuzu cut him off. "That's not even what I'm saying. All I'm saying is that sometimes, and don't you worry Eeyore, I don't mean all the time, but sometimes, things work out. Sometimes, they even work out for the best. Honestly, girl. You better hope they're wrong about a positive attitude being good for recovery."

"Since none of us believe in fate," Harry said. "Let's make something happen."

Twenty

Nothing happened. There was limited discussion of the letter, a futile attempt to view the contents of the memory card on our own phones, and a bit of planning, with the whole shebang brought to an end when I produced an uncontrollable series of yawns that had both my visitors apologizing and making tracks for the door.

That was right before a nurse arrived to roll me upstairs.

Zuzu said she'd be back early for her shift and would see me then. Harry said he'd pick me up around ten and not to go anywhere without letting him know. I lacked a witty retort.

I had assumed Leonie would pick me up, but she had left a voicemail shortly before Harry and Zuzu left, to say goodnight and make her excuses.

I had listened to it once myself, then played it again on speaker, "Darling, I thought about it, and I have decided not to pick you up from the hospital. If there was something only I could do I would come in a minute, but I think it would be more convenient for everyone if Harry were to retrieve you instead. After all, the two of you have work to do. I know, I should be much more involved, I feel very ashamed of myself, but

I absolutely do not feel up to it. I'm in need of emotional sustenance, which I will be taking in the morning. I'm sure you would prefer not to deal with whatever energy I may put out when I am not quite up to par, so I do this to spare us both. I hope someday to be a better person, able to put others first more often, but never always, because that leads to resentment. If you feel you must judge me, go right ahead, darling. I'm a terrible parent for putting myself first. Although, you are in your thirties now, so I shouldn't need to coddle you."

Absolute Truth came in handy for the fiendishly selfish.

As the nurse absconded with me, I wondered if Leonie's emotional sustenance would be coming out in her soul's colonic.

***

So, it was Harry who came to collect me the next morning, showing up soon after Dr. Barrett–Smith had come by to declare that I was free to go, but still obligated to follow the slew of orders a nurse, older and more solemn than Zuzu, brought on neat printed pages.

Because Leonie was taking an emotional health day, and Harry being a man, didn't think of it, I had nothing to wear when it was time to leave the hospital. Zuzu was working again, but too busy with the aftermath of a three-car pileup to assist in outfitting me, so what I got was a tracksuit from the gift shop with *Palm Springs* emblazoned in glitter across a background of palm trees, pools and sun. It was lime green. I was mortified.

I would rather have made a break for it in my

bloody jeans and hospital gown, but I was summarily overruled. The tracksuit zipped up the front, and I had to wear yesterday's under-things. Although the gift shop at Desert Hospital sells books, stuffed animals, hideous clothing, flowers and knick-knacks, it does not sell lingerie.

Harry took me home. I craved a mental health day of my own, but I wasn't unabashedly selfish enough to pull it off. I got to see Gulliver, shower and put on real clothes. Jeans and a cardigan had never felt so good. Somehow, my Chucks had survived unscathed; I laced them back up.

Leonie was off somewhere. Doing something. For herself.

We headed to the police department. I hadn't called ahead. I was employing the same strategy I used when returning Leonie's phone calls. I was hoping Detective Quick would be out making someone else's life hell and I would get credit for stopping by to give my statement without the aggravation of having to give it. Of course, he was there.

The P.S.P.D. was a block away from the dog park; the vibe was worlds away. No puppies frolicked here. Which was just as well. Jail is no place for a dog.

We didn't even get a chance to ask for him, or sign in, or change our minds and run away, before he came strolling up. He was like the eye of a tornado; he wreaked havoc all around while remaining untouched in the middle of it all. He nodded to Harry and they shook hands. I was pierced by the grey eyes.

"Don't worry," Quick said, leading us into what looked painfully like an interrogation room. "You're just giving a statement. We're only going in here for the quiet."

"Got it. No psychological warfare intended," I said,

not believing it for a second. Both men smiled.

Inside the interview room there was a feeling of grunginess. My delicate posterior did not want to follow in the footsteps (per se) of the scores of hardened criminals that had gone before. I didn't want a life of crime to rub off on me. The detective motioned us to one side of the table and took his place opposite. I did my best to sit on the chair Quick had indicated without actually touching it. No go. I wondered if anyone was watching though the one-way glass. I felt watched, but I also felt like I was covered in bugs. My skin had started crawling the moment I walked in the room.

When we were all seated comfortably or otherwise, the detective parked his gaze on my face and said, "What are you waiting for? Take me through it."

I told my story. I left out the park and De la Cruz. When I finished, Quick took me through it again, harping on the five W's. I toyed with the idea of making a false confession, to break the monotony, but decided that would actually extend the process.

Finally, I interrupted myself to say, "You can't still think Jack did this."

"I don't think he did this." He gestured at my head. The stitches were holding it together. Quick was in shirtsleeves, rolled up, and a Charlie Brown tie that could only have been a gift from his kids. I did my best to ignore that humanizing aspect.

"Look, it's obvious that Jack wouldn't shoot at me. Even if he wanted to, he couldn't because you've locked him up and thrown away the key. And now Maggie is dead, and how you can't see that all of this is connected-"

"Evin?" It was Harry and he was shaking his head at me.

"Look Miss Hart," Quick said. "The problem I'm having with all of this is the timeliness of the shooting. Maggie Connor was a person of interest in the crime your stepfather has been charged with and now she's dead. I'm sure you can see how convenient that is for Mr. Dekker, if she had information concerning the murders of Candace Brown and Hazel Neuland."

"It's not convenient. Because any information she had would have helped Jack. Also, what about me? Do you really think I cracked myself on the head to make it look like...I don't even know what you think it looks like."

"It looks like someone wanted Ms. Connor dead. There are multiple possibilities as to why."

"How about because she was friends with Hazel Neuland and knew Hazel was killed by her husband? Maybe Hazel wasn't so innocent herself. She could have killed Candace and then Bobby killed her in revenge. Instead of looking into a scenario that actually makes a little sense, you decide to believe that I killed Maggie so she couldn't incriminate Jack, who killed everyone else, even though he had absolutely no motive."

"Speaking of motive, why did you go to Margaret Connor's house?" Quick said.

"What?"

Harry had been silent, he tapped the table now to get my attention and stirred himself to say, "Evin was checking that the house was secure in the absence of its owner."

"How conscientious of her," Quick said, and made a note. I hated when he made notes. "It's so unfortunate that the house wasn't secure. How's the head?"

"The head hurts," I said.

"How many stitches did you get?"

"Two." I knew I wanted more.

"It's amazing that an attempt on your life resulted in nothing more than two stitches."

"Well that's easy to say, if you didn't spend all last night being prodded awake by relentless nurses."

The detective leaned back stretching his legs under the table. At least someone was at ease. "I'm not saying that the minor nature of your ah, wound, is conclusive, just notable."

Harry nudged my foot and frowned at me. I frowned back. All the talk about my head was making it hurt more. I belonged in bed.

"What is Bobby Neuland's alibi?" I said.

"It's none of your concern," Quick said. "What is your concern, is that the next time you're at one of my crime scenes you will be arrested. Unless, of course, you're the body."

Harry stood up and took my arm. "We're done now, right?"

"Are you her lawyer, too?"

"No," I said. I definitely felt wretched. My head had yet to stop aching and now my stomach was in revolt as well. "He's a friend. He's helping me find out who really killed three women. Think of him as your complete opposite."

Harry yanked my arm and I flew out of my seat. I shook him off and exited the interview room, feeling a presence on my heels. I hoped it wasn't Quick. I was sure it would be far more satisfying to stalk out of the interview if I wasn't arrested immediately afterwards.

"Miss Hart." It was Quick. I was screwed. I turned my head and there he was. Was it too late to grovel? What was pride compared to freedom and my own sheets?

"We need you to sign your statement," he said.

***

"He wouldn't tell us about Neuland's alibi." I said, when we finally exited the station.

"What did you expect?" Harry said. "We're going to call your little cop friend from the dog park."

"He's not little," I said. "He's big. Not too big. Not obese either, if that was your next question. Strapping. A strapping guy, who likes dogs. With a gun. You don't have a gun."

"Maybe you need some food. And I have a gun."

"Food sounds good," I said leaning against the jeep. Harry helped me in, and shut the door when I was settled.

Harry got me home as fast as he could. I figured he would ditch me on grounds of my general unpleasantness, but he boldly stayed where no man... Anyway, I made sandwiches for both of us. They bulged with hummus, avocado, tomato and lettuce. I was still hungry when I finished that, so I nuked some Amy's soup. By then, I was much perkier if still headachy.

I had cuddled up on the couch with Gulliver, wishing I had nothing to do for the rest of the day but lie around watching sappy movies on the nothing-ever-goes-right-for-women network.

Harry inquired after my state of being. "Much better," I said.

"Then let's take a look at that memory card. Where's your computer?"

"Mine is in my room and Leonie has a laptop somewhere, but we can't use those.

"Why can't we?"

"I'm not putting it in my computer and we can't put it in Leonie's."

"Because...?"

"What if there's something awful on it? Like a video of the murders. A snuff film. I can't be responsible for something like that ending up on my mother's hard drive. She would kill me."

Harry argued against the possibility of snuff material, saying we knew from the letters what we would find, as well as rightly pointing out that if we had any real suspicions in that milieu we should not have passed GO on our way to turn them over to the police.

"Or there could be a virus. Porn stuff always has viruses."

"How do you know?"

Jason was how I knew. Big into the research. I should have run screaming. Sooner.

"Nevermind."

"It's homemade. Should be fine."

I had to agree with his reasoning. Then again, what chance did reason ever have against neurosis? We bickered awhile longer then hopped back in the jeep and cruised across town to Harry's house. To Gulliver's delight, he was invited.

***

Harry's place was two blocks away from Demuth Park and C-school. Just like Leonie's, the roof was straight, low, and almost flat. The house sat behind a rich green lawn and some unruly Bougainvillea.

We whisked ourselves in and through to the office without taking the tour or basking in the feng shui. I had an impression of lots of home entertainment equipment and large comfortable furniture.

The office was crammed with file cabinets, bookcases and computer stuff. Two desktop computers with, as far as I could tell, every possible accoutrement, perched side by side on a long table. I moved a laptop that was on the extra chair so I could sit down.

As we suspected, barring the snuff film possibility, what I had ferreted out was a relentlessly detailed visual diary of the affair between Candace and Bobby. I think we both expected photos, but what we got was a series of videos. Alive, Candace had been an all-American looking girl. Except for the tousled blonde drapes and super-sized boobs, she looked naturally young and athletic.

The former phenomenon of hot young women hooking up with older more, uh, established men, is now just a commonplace ick. But, looking at Bobby Neuland's hairy, naked ass I couldn't imagine a bank account big enough. Nothing else looked big enough either.

There were multiple videos. In every one, the illicit couple cavorted on or around a large and heavy looking bed. No surprise, Bobby Neuland hadn't been a fan of putting his lady first. Not one encounter was more than three minutes and done. The one point of variation from tryst to tryst was the array of colorfully patterned socks that Bobby wouldn't (or couldn't) perform without.

"What the hell," I said after we had identified six unique pairs. "Do you think he has extra toes? We're in the desert for god's sake. His feet can't be that cold. I hope you take your socks off before you..." *Shut up shut up shut up*. I shut up.

"Good to know." Harry's voice was low and warm. I

had an un-sharable response.

Harry was navigating back through what we'd already seen. I commented on the encore, and was told to pay attention. I could see now that the woman currently being subjected to the tired Neuland moves was not Candace Brown.

"There are two of them," I said.

Harry nodded. "Most of them are of Bobby and Candace, which we expected, but the last one is of him with Hazel."

"Hazel? Are you sure?" I nudged him a little to the left to get a better view. "You're right. Shit. So Maggie had sex tapes of Bobby with both his mistress and his wife? Why?"

Harry swiveled his chair to face me. "According to the letter, Hazel is the one who got the camera and card from Bobby. Maggie never actually had it. It looks like Candace didn't either."

"Right, it was only hidden in Maggie's house. By Hazel." At the moment, I didn't really care about who had put what where. I went back to what was worrying me. "I mean the wife might want videos of him with the mistress, well not want, exactly, but..."

"But, then we have the recordings of Bobby with Hazel."

"On the same camera."

"Taken after the ones of him with Candace."

"Right. This had to have happened before she knew about the affair." I said this with certainty. It's not like I thought Harry was untouched, look at him, but I didn't want him touched further. At least I wouldn't, if I intended to let anything happen between us. The last thing I'd do would be to put on sexy matching undies and frolic with him in front of a camera right after he'd cheated on me.

No need for an actual relationship when you're crazy enough to have a saga that rivals The Thornbirds constantly looping through your fevered brain. The upside was, when I screwed up my imaginary romance only I would know.

I was rolling my eyes at my idiocy, when Harry said, "What did I do?"

"Nothing. Just thinking."

"It must be interesting in your head."

Interesting. "Yeah. Change the subject."

"Ok," Harry said. "The time stamp on the one with Hazel is a week ago today."

"So?"

"So," Harry said, "Didn't you say Bobby told you that Hazel hadn't been living in their house for, what? Over two weeks now?"

I thought back, and agreed that I had said that.

The dynamic on the screen changed. I directed Harry's attention back to the computer. We had muted the sound after an uncontrollable fit of laughter. Now he turned it back up. Instead of passionate whispers and moans, the thing I heard from the speakers was Hazel saying, "Motherfucker!"

"What happened?"

Harry took the video back. Hazel's eyes were not closed in passionate abandon. Bobby was too self-absorbed to notice his wife's indifference, but he did take the occasional moment to look gloatingly into the camera. We saw Hazel follow Bobby's gaze; saw her focus on the camera. At which point, she started raining hell on her soon to be ex. We watched the initial scream of fury again. It got uglier after that. Bobby sprang off the bed, treating us to an extremely unfortunate full frontal experience while he spewed every epithet I'd ever heard at Hazel. She came back like a champ, and went him one further, swooping up ammunition from an elegant bedside table. She flung two remote controls, a framed photo and a clock before Bobby surrendered his position and scuttled from the room, his too pale butt bouncing behind him. When he was gone, Hazel went straight to the camera and picked it up. The video ended on a shot of enhanced cleavage.

"So she went back a week ago to find the camera," I said.

"Looks like."

"I don't think it would be worth it no matter what was up for grabs."

"It's not like she'd never done it before," Harry pointed out.

I huffed.

Harry expelled the finished disc and the memory card. "Let me copy the letters and then we'll turn all this over to the cops."

"This makes no sense."

"Sure it does." Harry was fiddling around with the copier, inserting paper, pushing buttons, smacking it. I figured the smacks for bad news. "Candace gave the phone to Hazel to use against Bobby, right?"

"That's the party line."

"And we thought Candace gave her the memory card too."

"Which is what doesn't make sense."

"What are you talking about?"

"They're disgusting." Wasn't that obvious? "And because it would take a really potent combination of balls and shamelessness to turn over footage of yourself doing the naked limbo with someone else's husband to the someone else in question."

"All true, but I don't think Candace had the

videos. I think Bobby had possession of them. Look at this."

I looked. He was indicating the portion of Candace's letter to Hazel that read, "Good luck with the camera."

"You think that means 'good luck getting it', as opposed to here it is, 'good luck using the videos to take your slimy husband for all he's worth now that I've gotten mine.'"

"Exactly."

"Because if he had the videos, either Candace didn't know where they were, or else, by the time she decided to let Hazel in on their existence she had lost access to them because she and Bobby were kaput."

"Do you concur?"

I did. I also thought Candace had lost access when Bobby dumped her to mollify his scorned wife. No matter what the circumstances, I couldn't imagine sharing naked videos of myself boinking some guy with his wife.

Before I could comment, Harry said, "He did withdraw the money."

"Really?"

"Look."

I looked.

"How did you do that?" I said. Bobby had cashed out a C.D. for five hundred thousand dollars and change. I watched Harry scroll through more financial records. I was starting to see how Hazel had managed to stomach dealing with Candace. Half of Bobby's net worth was well into the millions and that didn't include property.

"Now we know he paid. Or intended to," Harry said.

"I'm changing my pin and password."

Harry grinned and told me it wouldn't help. Then he hustled Gulliver and I out of the house to the waiting jeep. I felt like I had spent the last year having my body nudged, pulled and otherwise manipulated by Harry. And still, we hadn't gotten to the good part.

"Where are we going?" He was bigger; I might as well go with no trouble.

"Kinko's. My printer is rebelling. How's your head?"

"It hasn't turned gangrenous. Yet."

"I don't think a concussion can cause gangrene."

"You're not a doctor."

Harry laughed and I cracked a smile. Optimists are the worst.

Twenty-one

I was holding my hair out of my face with minimal success; the wind whipping through the Rubicon was turning my curls from bouncy chic to a snarled mass.

"Why do you think Hazel stayed at Maggie's if she didn't trust her?" I said.

"I think she was protecting Maggie. You'd be amazed at the stuff I don't tell you."

I gave him my special finger. "I don't need protecting." I suspected I really needed protecting. We pulled into the Kinko's parking lot and I clambered out of the jeep. Again.

"Nice hair," Harry said when I got out. "No really," he said when he saw my look. It felt, I'm sorry to say, like the look of someone about to burst into tears. "It's sexy. Like a wild...forget it. Do you want to wait here?"

I shook my head grabbed Gulliver's leash and marched on in, making a point not to hold the door for Harry. Wild what? Boar? Gibbon? Wild Lilith with the flesh of children between my teeth?

I wrenched open the lid of the first copier I came to, belatedly realizing I had nothing to copy. I swore. Someday, I would pick the perfect moment to storm off. This attempt didn't even rank as high as half-assed.

Harry joined me, graciously pretending I had been acting like a grown-up. He inserted a credit card into the copier's greedy maw and spread the letters in succession, over the glass. By the time a lank haired teenager approached to tell us Gulliver wasn't welcome, we had finished.

When we were back outside, blinking in the sun, I said, "De la Cruz?"

"Yeah."

I puffed out my cheeks and scrolled through my contacts until I came to the magic number. I looked at Harry, who grinned showing those gorgeous white teeth and smile lines around his eyes. Maybe I could just make out with him a little. Completely unprofessional? Absolutely. Except, I didn't actually work with Harry. I was just doing a stepdad a favor. Besides, Harry wasn't even working. He was helping an old family friend. Making out wouldn't violate any professional ethic. Getting naked, ripping someone's clothes off, no way that was unprofessional if you weren't technically working.

I was biting my lower lip and starting to breathe a little more ardently than usual, when Harry said, "You should stop doing that with your mouth."

"What?" It sounded breathy. I tried again. "Stop doing what?"

"Chewing on your lip, like that." He rubbed his thumb across my lower lip, in case I had forgotten where it was, I guess. I had nearly forgotten where I was. I stopped myself from doing anything inappropriate to his lingering digit. I felt like I should be wearing a ripped bodice, bosom heaving, hair flowing, virtue in danger. Instead, I was standing in the sun oozing sweat, I had wild hair and I'd been missing my virtue since I was sixteen.

I drew a semi-ragged breath and stepped away taking my tingling lower lip with me. *I will not fornicate on the sidewalk in front of Kinko's.*

I pushed talk. De la Cruz answered on the third ring.

I told him what I wanted to know.

"Forget it."

"We have information to trade."

Silence. I was getting the feeling De la Cruz regretted his outing to the park.

Eventually, he said, "I told you yesterday, we're even. You should quit while you're alive and well."

I wasn't doing that well; I still had a headache.

"But wouldn't it make you look really good if you came up with some great new evidence? Wouldn't you get a promotion or commendation or something?"

He laughed. "You're assuming no one would find out how I got the evidence. That I wouldn't be fired and maybe prosecuted on top of that. Maybe I should arrest you for withholding evidence. That way, I'm clean on how I came across whatever it is you think is so important."

"How am I withholding?" I said, moving back towards Harry for moral support. This was not the conversation I had imagined. I never got to have the conversations I imagined. "I'm trying to turn it over to you. The police. The official authorities. I just happened to have your number on me. I thought you wanted to hear if I found something."

"Not after you've kept it for a day."

"Barely. Look, please. Just blurt it out and then it will all be over and you won't have to think about it anymore."

"You mean my career?"

"It's not like you wouldn't have plausible

deniability. You guys had to find out from somewhere. For all Quick would know I found out from the same place."

"Then go do that."

"We just need to know what the official version is," I said. "Why Quick is so convinced that Bobby Neuland, who has by far the most obvious motive, tons of cash, didn't do it."

"I don't feel comfortable having this conversation over the phone."

I smiled.

***

We agreed to meet at the parking lot at the bottom of the tram.

The official version of events was that I was extremely fuzzy on the details of how the evidence had come to be in my possession thanks to my traumatic head injury. This also explained why I had neglected to mention said evidence while giving my statement that morning. De la Cruz gave me the alibis, although he held back some key details like the names of the patients Dr. Bobby was supposedly checking on. I objected, to no avail. I gave up, gave him what we had and he was out of there.

This arrangement left me vulnerable, but we had time to think of a story to appease Quick.

Harry said if it came down to it, he would say he'd been back to Maggie's this morning and found everything then. I worried that the second round of crime scene tape was still up and a cruise by the house confirmed it. Harry pulled up behind my car, which was at the curb patiently waiting.

I had an idea so I called Zuzu, expecting to leave a

message, but I got lucky and caught her on a break. After a few minutes of scheming, we had our version of the truth. It was this: When I had been taken to the hospital, Zuzu had taken charge of my possessions, not realizing the significance of any of the items on my person. After all, she was a nurse, not a detective, and as far as the police knew, not so close to either Jack or I that she would feel the need to become unwisely ensnared in our troubles.

Furthermore, in my befuddled state, I'd completely forgotten about the evidence that I'd fully intended to turn over immediately to the authorities. Many well-laid plans have been derailed by a vicious head trauma.

Luckily, on this bright momentous morn, I had called Zuzu, and arranged to swing by to pick up my things. The aforementioned things happened to include two letters and a little chip from who knows what. My memory refreshed, my duty clear, I made immediate efforts to get these evidential items into the proper hands. Whew.

When we had gotten this settled I told Zuzu I would talk to her later and hung up.

"That was sexy as hell," Harry said. "You're a natural."

"You like a woman who lies?"

Harry tucked a curl behind my ear, "I like a woman who does what's necessary. Who's sexy without trying to be. Who looks as good when she rolls out of bed as when she got dressed up the night before. Who stalks around on the same gorgeous legs she had when she was sixteen."

"You shouldn't be looking at a sixteen year old girl's legs."

"I was eleven."

"Well, you've never seen me roll out of bed." Oh. He had. "Fine, but it doesn't count if you didn't spend the night. And you've never seen me dressed up."

"Soon." I gave him a look. "Soon, I'll take you somewhere nice to celebrate."

"Shouldn't Jack get to celebrate?"

"You'll have more fun with just me."

Well, that was a given. A presumptuous given. But I'd rather see us undressed than dressed up. I didn't say that, there was no point in being openly slutty. Or desperate. I wondered how badly it would end if I gave in to my hormones. Maybe menopause would strike and they would go away. I was already thirty-one.

"The point is, you did well. And it was fun to watch you do it."

"I don't know," I said, dragging my stubborn mind from sex to murder. "That was a hell of an effort to find out Bobby Neuland's every minute was accounted for." According to De la Cruz, the doctor had been at work all day, except for a long lunch at his favorite restaurant.

"Not if the next thing we find out is that every minute wasn't."

"Besides, he said Reina was there too, and a secretary. It's not like he was all alone like Jack."

"It's ok."

"How?"

"Reina and the secretary, Julia Duane are his alibi. His daughter and an employee. Either or both could be lying."

"What about the patients?"

"He saw them in the morning. The last one was before eleven."

"Ok. Then why would the secretary care enough to lie? So she doesn't have to look for another job?"

"She could be schtupping him."

"Yuck. Everybody can't be schtupping him."

"Some people aren't choosy about whom they schtup."

"Well, I am." Choosy, in this sense, meant quantity control of my schtuppees, rather than quality control. Not that I didn't try, but on occasion I have been swept away by a shiny surface that rendered me oblivious to the lack of substance beneath.

"What are your criteria?"

"I don't need criteria."

"Why? Celibate? Lesbian? Bad relationship?"

"Two of those."

"There are lots of good relationships."

"So I hear. The trouble is I have bad judgment. I suck."

"That should help."

It took a few beats for that to sink in, at which point I hauled off and slugged Harry right in the stomach as hard as I could. He saw it coming and flexed. I nearly broke my hand.

"Are you being a jerk so I'll like you better?" I was trying to rub the pain away. "Because I told you-"

"No. But I'm all for you liking me better," he said. "I'll do whatever you want if you'll forgive me."

His eyes were still blue damn it, and glinting at me from under those dark eyebrows. I suspected mockery, but was currently unable to prove it.

"Whatever I want?"

"Whatever. For you. To you."

I used my haughty voice and said, "I'll let you know."

"Friends?" he said. I took his extended hand and nodded. I told myself there would be no benefits.

Harry threw the Rubicon in gear. I reminded him

about my car, alone and scared, waiting by the curb. We decided to drop it off at Leonie's.

I left the T-bird in the driveway, a note on the counter and off we went to reunite Robert Neuland with Mary Hart. Fun for the whole dysfunctional family.

Twenty-two

The offices of Dr. Robert L. Neuland were tucked away in a two-story Spanish style building behind Palm Canyon. Sequestered as it was behind elegant ivy covered walls, we drove past it three times, goading me to Google the damn place.

I was feeling good about the fact that we were close to the hospital in case mayhem ensued. I wondered if that had been the reasoning behind Bobby's procurement of that particular office space. Although, to be fair, I had no reason to suspect him of being a terrible surgeon, only a terrible person, husband, and father.

Across the street was a liquor store and across from that a law office. Instead of asking offensive questions; maybe I could get drunk and have Dr. Bobby reduce my boobs, or give me some lipo. If it didn't work out, I could retain a lawyer on the way home.

The space inside was larger than I'd expected for a one-man operation. I had expected schmancy and it was. The tile floors were nearly hidden with expensive rugs, exotic plants flanked leather club chairs, and top of the line plasmas punctuated the corners. A quiet door marked V.I.P. stood firmly shut on the far wall.

Only two people were waiting; side by side, absorbed in glossy magazines.

Beyond the waiting area was a partition. Behind the glass was a long built-in desk equipped with the usual office business: computers, charts, pen cup, personal photos. A discrete brass nameplate read Julia Duane. Despite the abundance of objects living on the desk, everything was tidy, including Julia. She had perfect posture and a buttoned up demeanor until she caught sight of Gulliver.

"Oh my gosh, he's adorable," she said, and disappeared from her protective cocoon to emerge and fondle Gulliver's ears. "Is he friendly?" she asked, about five seconds after her throat would have been torn out if he'd been channeling Cujo. I didn't judge. When faced with a dog in need of petting, I was also prone to that particular error in timing.

"How can I help you?" she said after a few more ear scratches.

Harry expressed our need for a quick word with Bobby or any other Neulands that were handy. She looked regretfully past her desk towards the back offices and told us that both Dr. and Miss Neuland were currently unavailable. Once it had been established that we had no appointment, looks of chagrin were exchanged all around. Ms. Duane asked if there was anything she could help us with in the meantime.

"There is," Harry said. "I'm sure you've heard they made an arrest in the murder of Mrs. Neuland."

Julia Duane stepped closer.

"The suspect's defense team is trying to disprove Dr. Neuland's alibi." Harry quirked an eyebrow at the gall of the defense and Ms. Duane nodded. "We're here to double check, make sure everything is solid. It's my fault for not calling ahead, I'm sure that Dr. Neuland wants an update, but I'll just give him a call later."

I patted Gulliver on the rump, encouraging my hair to swing forward over my face until I got it under control.

"I did hear about the arrest." Ms. Duane said, scratching Gulliver behind the ears. His hind leg started to thump furiously. "I thought that would be the end of it. Except for the trial of course."

"You know lawyers," Harry said. "It's really just a matter of crossing the T's and dotting the I's."

Were we taking dictation now?

"How long have you worked for Dr. Neuland?"

"Almost three years."

"And you were here on Tuesday?"

"Briefly. I had some personal business to take care of that day." She looked periodically towards the back office, keeping an eye out, I imagined for her brute of an employer.

"That's right," Harry said, as if he'd just had a brief lapse in memory. "And Dr. Neuland didn't bother with a temp?"

"No. There was no need. Miss Neuland has been working in the office recently, so she managed everything that day."

"Why is that?"

"I was never informed why."

"Is that what you told the police?"

"Of course that's what I told them. It's the truth." Was it the Absolute Truth?

"You must hear things," Harry said, leaning in, inviting confidence.

Julia Duane glanced around the waiting room before answering. The two patients still waited, respectively absorbed in issues of Time and

Architectural Digest.

"From what I heard," she said, "Dr. Neuland wants his daughter to be more responsible, to start working for the things she wants."

"Such as?" Harry asked.

"Oh, a townhouse she wanted him to buy her. I believe that's what led to her working here. She was supposed to get a job and pay her own mortgage. Of course he was still going to make the down payment." In a moment of perfect accord, Ms. Duane and I exchanged looks. Having your down payment and your job given to you by an overindulgent father wasn't exactly making it on your own.

"So she's still working here?" I asked.

"Sometimes." Must be nice.

"What about patients?" I said.

Ms. Duane gave me a questioning look. "I mean on the day of the murders, what patients were here in the office? I know patient stuff is confidential-"

"Actually we don't see patients in the office on Tuesdays."

"Oh. What do you do?"

"The doctor does rounds for the patients who required a stay in the rehab center after their procedures and catches up in the office. I do paperwork; send flowers, that sort of thing."

"Send flowers?" I said.

Julia looked prim. "The doctor likes to show his patients that he cares."

It was probably easier than actually caring.

"So then," I said, "Dr. Neuland was unaccounted for most of the day?"

"No," Julia said. "Like I said, the doctor was doing rounds and handling some things here in the office. He wasn't alone and the police have accounted for his time. Look, I'm happy to help, but really, I've already answered these questions and I have a lot of work to do."

"No problem. If it's ok, we'll just wait for the doctor and Ms. Neuland to finish and hope for a word with them then." He hit her with the Jedi charm and she smiled back and withdrew behind her partition.

"You know," Julia Duane said poking her head around the computer. "I think maybe Ms. Neuland is allergic. Would it be ok if your dog waited elsewhere? Maybe just outside the door."

How was he supposed to do that? He was a dog, not a kid. I couldn't just set him outside the door and tell him to hang tight.

Before I could marshal my thoughts into something polite enough to say aloud, a delicate series of rat-tat-tats came echoing from the back. It was Reina Neuland tapping down the hall like she belonged in a 20's musical. As the jezebel. She stopped on the other side of the counter and looked us over. She was still L.A. perfect, all ribs and cheekbones. Her boobs were large and perky, and I wanted, so wanted, them to be fake, but they lacked that telltale stillness. She bounced when she walked and they bounced with her. Her almond eyes and pouty lips were topped by a gleaming and expertly cut do, freshly highlighted. Again, I noticed the too perfect nose.

"No. It's not a problem, Julia. It's not like we have any reason to keep things clean in here. This skirt is Marc Jacobs though and I'd hate to get anything on it. Just make sure nothing touches me, if you don't mind. I have a date. Of course I made it before I met you."

She made eyes at Harry. I thought about decking her, but she was definitely the type to press charges for assault. Perhaps I could contrive to wipe drool on her spotless black skirt, and the obnoxious abundance of toned leg sticking out the bottom of it. Gulliver's drool. Not Harry's. If I wanted to be fair, which I didn't really, I'd have to admit he didn't drool. Harry that is. He just looked. Since his brilliant blues were aimed at her face, I tried to go easy on the umbrage. Especially, since we were not a couple and possibly didn't even qualify as friends. I sighed to myself and kept quiet. Not everyone was so well behaved.

"It's you again." She said to me, and she said it in a tone.

I was working up to a dislike bordering on hatred, when she said, "Did I tell you that you have the most gorgeous hair?" I remembered not to judge people based on their looks and man-eating demeanor.

"No."

"Oh." She smiled at me.

Bitch.

"So, I see you're still asking questions. I hope Julia was helpful." Dr. Bobby had joined us, escorting a woman with bright darting eyes and a smooth, immobile face. I was sure the synthetic charm was for the benefit of the botoxed babe.

He was again wearing two pieces of a three-piece suit that had to have been custom tailored to fit that bullish body so well. Unlike Detective Quick, he was not wearing an endearing child-picked tie. This father-daughter duo was big label or bust.

"Not so helpful that she's wasting your money," Harry said stepping forward to introduce himself to Bobby and the woman, who identified herself as Nani Tourney.

Dr. Bobby tried hard to dismiss Mrs. Tourney but she wasn't budging. Julia tried to lure her over to schedule her next appointment, and got a flash from

Nani's gleaming eyes but no success.

"We won't be answering any more of your questions," the doctor told Harry with a look at Julia that made her shrivel. "I realize we tend toward the casual here in the desert, but in the future, don't bring dogs or liars to my office. I don't appreciate the impropriety."

"Get her out of here," Neuland went on, "If I see either of you again, I'll file a restraining order. Ms. Duane, I'll speak to you tomorrow. If in two minutes, they haven't driven out of the parking lot, call the police."

He started to lean in on me until he remembered Gulliver was there. Suddenly, he was a lot more respectful of my personal space. From a safer distance, he looked down at me and said, "You're a little bitch. Now that I don't have a divorce to worry about, feel free to come by the house. You don't have to bother getting dressed up."

"Fuck off," I said, loudly so the whole room could hear it. I liked 9½ Weeks as much as the next girl with daddy issues, but I wasn't screwed up enough for that offer to be attractive.

There was the brief silence that descends when someone violates the rules of society in reasonably polite company. Even Reina had the decency to shroud her bitchiness in subtle one-upmanship, mockery and false compliments.

Harry forestalled Bobby's exit by waving a folder under his nose. It contained some stills we had made from the videos before the printer had conked. Bobby so clearly wasn't expecting what he saw that anyone with an ounce of compassion would have felt bad for him when the blood drained from his face. Not me.

"We should talk privately," Harry said.

Radiating fury, Dr. Bobby escorted Harry into the V.I.P. room pointedly not inviting Gulliver and me. The door slammed sharply behind them. Mrs. Tourney, left out of the action, called out to the two women who'd gone from reading magazines to openly gawping and they all left.

"So," Reina said, "How's the head?" I must have looked startled because she added, "It was in the paper."

"I didn't see it."

"It was only a few lines, way back on page eight."

Bitch.

"Great. Thanks. Since you're a big girl now, do you feel like talking even though your daddy said 'no'?"

"Nope. I'm all set."

We sunk into a hostile silence. It was soon broken by Bobby's voice booming from the V.I.P room. "She was a blackmailing bitch, but I didn't kill her!"

I assumed Harry responded, but I didn't hear it. I looked at Julia whose gaze was desperately fixed to her computer screen. Lack of a better option led me to lock eyes with Reina, who said, "See, that's what kind of person she was. Anyone could have killed her. She must have been sleeping with your stepdad too."

"Jack didn't kill anyone," I snapped, taking a step forward.

"Whatever." She wrinkled her perky little nose. I wanted to rip it off. "That's obviously not what the police think. By the way, I'll be calling that Detective to let him know you're still bothering us."

"If none of you did anything wrong why not just cooperate?"

"We are cooperating. With the authorities. That doesn't include you." Reina looked down her nose at me. "But, at least you're only snooping. The first time I saw you I was afraid you were fucking my father. Or my brother. His last girlfriend was a whore."

"Nice family," I said. "Who was dating the whore? Your father or your brother?"

"I don't remember." She laughed. "But you remind me of her."

Before I could give in to my urge to commit part one of a particularly gory murder-suicide, Harry and Bobby came striding out of the back office. Bobby paused to dismiss Julia, then told Reina he would see her at home before he disappeared out the front door, jacket draped over his arm.

"If you have another minute, I'd love to speak with you privately." Reina had placed a hand on Harry's arm.

"Evin, can you give us a minute?"

Wait. What? I examined his face, looking for the punch line.

"I'll meet you outside," Harry said.

I was too furious to speak. Thirty seconds after we'd been ejected, Julia Duane slunk out the door. Gulliver and I had taken refuge in a bit of shade provided by a cluster of palm trees. Julia took no notice of us. She hightailed it to a little red Prius and fled.

When I looked down, Gulliver was licking ants off the sidewalk. I tugged him away from the busy little hill, apologizing to the fallen.

I sat on a small boulder, imagining Harry and Reina inside, cooing and gazing deeply into each other's eyes.

Ugh. "She's awful," I said to Gulliver. He panted in agreement. "I shouldn't care, I guess." No matter how sexy he is. "Men are bad. Human men I mean," I clarified, mindful of Gulliver's feelings.

"Maybe it's me. I'm just bad with men. It's not Harry's fault he looks like that." I considered. "Well it's partly his fault, I mean, clearly he works out, and that's a fifty dollar haircut. And I don't want him, right? But what if I want him someday, but by then he's been tainted by slutty Barbie?"

Gulliver's tail wagged. I sighed. What did I expect? Harry was a professional, trying to elicit information from the daughter of a probable murderer. Even though she did look like she was selling the girlfriend experience, there was no reason to assume Harry was buying. Not that I could object. Not that I should.

However, my indignation remained strong. I looked at my watch. It had been over three minutes.

"You've been in there for ten minutes," I said to Harry when he came out a moment later.

"Why aren't you in the car?"

"Because I'm here." I could feel my brow crease. I remembered deciding I shouldn't be pissed off. "I wanted to spy on you guys, but no windows."

"How honest. Your mother is rubbing off on you."

Hurtful.

"Didn't you think I'd tell you what happened?"

"I don't know." I looked at him, considering. His face was guileless, his smile open. In the last few days, I'd watched him perpetrate lies varying in degree from omission to blatant, wearing that very same look.

"I don't lie to you. You're not a job. Besides we go way back."

I oozed skepticism as hard as I could. "Not really."

"You kissed me."

"I did not. You tried to kiss me and I let you down as easily as I could."

"Let's see how easily you let me down now."

My half-formed reply was having trouble leaving

my body since I had no breath with which to propel it. Finally I managed, "Don't we have more important things to do? You know, like helping Jack?"

"We do have another stop to make."

We reached the Jeep and Gulliver popped into the back like an old pro.

"What stop? What did you find out? I don't appreciate being excluded."

"Sorry. The whole family seems to hate you, so I thought I'd do better on my own."

"So now you just pander to a family of murderers?"

"I don't think they're all murderers."

"Potential then."

"That includes everyone. Look Evin, like you said, I'm trying to help Jack. Isn't getting information more important than making sure you're included every second?"

"Fine." I didn't even have to think about it for long.

"I didn't find out much from Reina, but Bobby was surprisingly chatty." Yeah, I remembered the yelling.

"So what did he chat about?" I said.

"Mostly stuff we already knew. Candace blackmailed him out of five hundred thousand dollars-"

"That's what he gets."

"Which he says the police never turned up. We didn't find it and we were on the scene before the cops, so if he did pay her then the killer probably took the money."

"If she was killed for the money, why were Hazel and Maggie killed?"

"I didn't say she was killed for the money. It could have happened that way, but she and the others could have been killed over the videos. And we don't know that they were all meant to die. Candace was the first victim. It's possible Maggie and Hazel could have known enough about what happened to her to be a danger."

"And the money was just a lucky break for the killer?" I thought about it. "I still think it was Bobby."

"Based on the facts or on your dislike?"

"The facts make me dislike him," I said.

"You may be right. We're going to go check out Candace's apartment though."

"You know where it is?"

"And I have the key."

"He gave you the key?" Harry nodded. "Why would he do that? He's trying to confuse us."

"That doesn't mean it's going to work."

I wasn't sure we deserved that much credit. "What about Reina?"

"She wants to know what we know. And if we're in on the police investigation."

"I hope you didn't tell her anything."

"Evin. I'm not hypnotized by every perfect pair of boobs that comes along."

I hated him.

"I can still say no to you, can't I?"

Forgiven. I smiled, but I turned my head so he couldn't see it.

"It took you over four minutes to find out she wasn't going to tell you anything?"

"Is that what I said?"

"I think it was implied."

"Only inferred."

"Quit screwing with me and tell me what she said. Unless the two of you were just making plans for next Saturday night." I smiled, to make it clear I was unaffected by any fraternizing with the enemy.

"Not even close. She swears she was with him all

morning, and that he kept his usual lunch reservation."

"Where?"

"She wouldn't say. She did say he expensed it; the receipt went to the cops. A receipt doesn't prove who was there, but we can swing by and see if any of the staff have a clue."

"So to speak. Where was she?"

"She had a lunch date." That rang a bell.

"Right," I said, disgusted. "With Maggie's partner, Eddie."

"How do you know?"

"He was bragging. It seems amazing that all of this went on the day Julia Duane had to take off for personal stuff. Maybe she did it."

"So you're willing to pin this on anybody who isn't Jack?" Harry said.

"Wasn't that always the plan?"

Anne Stinnett

Twenty-three

We pulled into the apartment complex that had been Candace Brown's last home. I removed myself and Gulliver from the Jeep before I noticed my laces flopping around. I bent over to deal with that and when I came back up Harry's eyes were frankly admiring my cleavage.

I flushed happily and said, "Stop staring."

"Don't worry. Until we get Jack out of jail, your virtue is semi-safe."

"My virtue is completely safe, you Neanderthal." I got lost for a second in contemplating caveman behavior. I could do without a club to the head, but a strategically pulled fistful of hair... "Just because I didn't kick your ass for sneak attacking me with a sloppy wet one when we were kids doesn't mean I've spent every minute since dying for a rematch."

He put his lips within breathing distance of my ear and said, "Neither have I. That doesn't mean there won't be one."

In self-defense, I changed the subject. "I hope no one has cleared the apartment out."

"It's in Bobby's name, so they haven't."

"That's nice," I snapped. "No wonder she had to leave."

"That and the blackmail."

I waved that off, "Is he keeping it? Planning to install another woman?"

"I don't know." Harry smiled. "But feel free to post a warning on the door."

The door in question was bright orange, on the second floor, and overlooked a sparkly kidney shaped pool. Deck chairs of iron and green mesh sat in relaxed rows around its perimeter.

The apartment was miserably hot. The oversized windows had intensified the sun's offering from generous to brutal. The place was done in various blues and oranges over laminate wood floors. Impressionist prints, nicely framed, hung on creamy walls. At first glance, there was no personal clutter to catch the eye; a second glance confirmed it.

There were empty hangers in the closet, gaps in the tidy row of shoes, and in the bathroom, no brushes for teeth or hair.

It looked to me like Candace had taken anything she'd considered necessary or valuable. It felt empty even though the furniture was still in place. Despite the upscale quality, it reminded me of the depressing little studio I'd left behind in Minnesota. I didn't think this place had come furnished, but I would have bet Candace had never thought of it as a true home. If she had expected to be the third Mrs. Dr. Neuland, her focus would have been on Bobby's prestige villa.

Gulliver ambled over to press his head against my thigh. He had been panting since we walked in.

"He needs a drink," I said to Harry and headed for the kitchen. On the way we passed the thermostat. I turned the AC on and set it to sixty. Bobby might not even notice a high electricity bill, but I felt a bit of mean satisfaction anyway.

The kitchen looked intact. Service for four was stacked neatly in a cabinet. The bowls were petite and too delicate to trust to Gulliver. I fished a stainless steel mixing bowl from the cupboard below. A folded piece of paper fluttered to the floor in its wake.

"Don't drool on the floor too much," I told Gulliver. The paper was notebook, three holed, college ruled. I unfolded it and called Harry over.

"Look at this."

It was a column of numbers. It started with 500,000 and a list of subtractions and the resulting totals followed. Notations were scribbled next to most of the figures: they included plane fare, house, and car among others. About a third had been earmarked for a CD. The remaining sum was enough to keep Gulliver and me in kibble and veggie burgers for twenty years.

"What a sensible blackmailer," Harry said.

"A lot of good that did her." There was an upside to having no plans. I had no high hopes to be dashed. "It doesn't seem like there's anything else to find."

Harry agreed. "Yeah, it looks like she never planned to come back."

"Why would she? Too risky. Although, if she was hiding out at Jack's to avoid Bobby, why would she let him meet her there? Why not somewhere public?"

"Either he managed to convince her he wasn't a threat, or she was overcome by greed."

I bristled at that. "She was hurt."

"Most people don't go out of their way to ruin lives when they're hurt."

I thought that was giving most people too much credit.

"She got what she deserved then?"

"I'm not saying she deserved it, I'm saying that her actions provoked a reaction. That's all. She blackmailed him and she didn't even do it in good faith. She took his money and still gave all the information he was supposedly buying to his wife."

"Yeah, let's all sympathize with the murderous perpetual cheater."

"What's the problem? When have you ever cared about Candace Brown beyond the inconvenience her death caused you?"

"Me? I'm not worried about me. I'm worried about Jack. And now, you think I'm an asshole because I had a moment of empathy for a woman I found dead?"

"Stop it, Evin."

"Fine." I took Gulliver with me and I stormed out the door, smack into a neighbor.

"Careful sweetheart." He caught me by the arms and steadied me.

"Sorry."

"I'm starting to think that apartment generates crying women."

"I'm not crying, I'm just mad."

He put his hands up in surrender. He was maybe sixty and still handsome, if perhaps stockier than he had been in his youth. He had pulled his hair into a long white ponytail, and he had a beard to match.

"I remember that was Candy's reason for crying too," he said extending a firm hand, "I'm Sam."

"You knew Candace?"

"Of course I knew her, I lived next door."

I wasn't sure where the "of course" came in. I had lived next door to people for years and never known them. Sam was obviously not the curmudgeon I was.

"When did you last see her?"

"Tuesday afternoon." She'd been dead by Tuesday morning. "The Tuesday before she died, it was the seventh." Sam amended, when I expressed puzzlement.

"Was she was upset then?"

"She was heartbroken. Finally broke up with her boyfriend. Said she had to leave. Poor girl had been crying for days. We had coffee together most mornings. She didn't know many people out here."

"Why do you say finally?"

Sam shrugged. "It just didn't seem like he was good for her. Or to her."

"Was he around much?"

"Not at all. I haven't seen him since just after she moved in. Six or seven months ago, I think. They were cute kids, but God knows, and the rest of us too, it takes more than that to make a relationship. She moved out here to be with him," Sam made fatalistic gesture. "I guess it was too big a step so soon, and them so young."

Something was off here. Sam was in the vicinity of senior citizen status, but he wasn't old enough to think of Bobby Neuland as a kid. "Who are you talking about? Bobby Neuland?"

"No. His name wasn't Bobby."

Right. "Robert, I mean. Kind of bulky upper body, you can kind of see he used to be handsome."

Sam laughed. "Sorta like me, then?"

"No." I said, finding a smile for him, "you're still handsome."

He ducked his head and chuckled. "I thank you, sweetheart. I don't like to disappoint a pretty girl like you, but it was definitely a kid she was seeing, at least when she moved in here. Maybe they broke it off and she started seeing your fellow."

I said he most definitely was not my fellow.

"This is your fellow though, isn't he?" Sam said, starting to make friends with Gulliver. "Or is it this one?"

The last had been said in a confidential tone, and I looked to see Harry joining us. I made a face at Sam and shook my head. I did a quick round of introductions and caught Harry up. Harry filled Sam in on what we were doing here.

"So you and Candace were good friends?" Harry and Sam were taking stock of each other in some way. I remained baffled by the meeting rituals of men.

"More like friendly neighbors."

"Do you think the guy she was seeing before Bobby had a motive?" I said.

"Maybe to kill Candace, but not the others," Harry said. "But I think you were right when you said it was unlikely that he would be upset enough to kill her after so long."

"Six months isn't that long," I said. "What if they were in it together and she double crossed him too?"

Sam shook his head at me. "I knew her well enough to know that's not what happened. If Candy made some wrong decisions, it was out of anger and hurt. She was no schemer."

"Do you know where she worked?" I asked Sam. "Maybe someone else remembers the name of the other man."

"She didn't work. She used to dance in a show in Las Vegas before she came out here, but mostly she just waited around for him. He was a partier, worked late nights."

Into my head and straight out of my mouth popped, "Rex?"

"That's it." Sam nodded.

My mouth dropped open and I looked at Harry who had also gone high alert. Gulliver thumped the ground with his tail.

"You're sure?" I managed.

"I'm sure sweetheart. I guess some things happened that Candy didn't tell me about, but when I met her, she was with a young man. I couldn't catch hold of the name earlier, but I remember. It was Rex."

Harry gave me a look and I nodded. Time to go. "It was nice meeting you, Sam. And thanks."

"Bye sweetheart. Take care of this one," he said to Harry.

"I'm not sure she'll let me."

We hauled our butts to the Jeep.

"Rex and Candace?" I said immediately.

"What made you think of Rex?"

"I'm not sure, it just occurred to me. He was so furious when he was talking about her. Way more upset than he should have been about one in a long line of Bobby's women."

"Now we know why."

"Yuck. So what now?"

"It's late, I'm hungry. If you're finished being pissy, I'll make dinner."

"You cook?" It just kept getting worse. "Don't you think we should go talk to Rex again, now that we know about him and Candace?"

"I called his house while you were making your sad attempts to muscle your dog into the car. Trina said he went to work." Harry threw the Rubicon in gear and appealed to me with his eyes. All I could see was blue. "I make the best pasta you'll ever taste."

I expressed disbelief.

"Evin."

"What?"

"Shut up and look pretty."

I knew I shouldn't be pleased, but I was.

***

We whizzed back by the park on the way to Harry's. I'd come through here twice in one day without one glimpse of a pregnant teen or other Palm Springs High defector. Maybe C-school had been relocated. As we sped past, I craned my neck to see the center where my undistinguished high school career had whimpered to an end.

We pulled onto Harry's street two blocks from Mesquite, no more than half a mile from the park where Harry's baseball team practiced in the spring.

"What position?" I said when he informed me.

"Shortstop."

"I played second base. When I was in middle school."

"Before I knew you. You wouldn't have been caught dead participating in wholesome group activities by the time we met."

I laughed. "I wasn't that bad."

"You gave me my first drink, my first cigarette and my first kiss."

"Are you looking for an apology?"

"I hardly ever smoke, and I've never been to Betty Ford."

"Well then, we're good."

"I am."

Twenty-four

My earlier impression had been spot on. Harry's house was a marvel of masculinity. The stereo system was Bose and the television was enormous. The electronics were in serious competition with a huge green sofa for total room domination. By the time I had finished ogling the television, Gulliver was wallowing in the couch.

"Sorry," I said to Harry, trying to push, pull or otherwise shift my hairy beast off his furniture.

"He's fine there, he's not hurting anything."

"He sheds. But it's not his fault," I added when Gulliver looked at me woefully.

"Leave the poor dog alone."

"Whatever you want."

"Sounds good. Wine?"

"No." I shouldn't drink around Harry.

"You sure?"

"I'm good." In his house.

"Ok." He poured himself a glass.

"Well, maybe." Probably mere yards from his bedroom.

"Red?"

"No, nevermind." From his bed. Dammit, I had needs.

"Evin?"

"Ok, just one." To take the edge off.

I looked at Gulliver who was looking back at me. I thought about a book I had read on the psychic abilities of pets. I hoped it was all lies.

"Here," Harry said, handing me a glass of red. I accepted and took a slug. Classy. I rolled my eyes.

"Problem?" Harry said.

"Nothing to do with you."

"You were rolling your eyes at yourself?"

"I was having a mental debate and it wasn't going well."

"What were you debating?"

"Nothing."

"How do you debate nothing with yourself?"

I took a shallow breath. Somehow, Harry had ended up in my personal space. Oh. Yeah. That had happened when he'd handed me the wine.

I took another sip, so I'd have something to blame if I gave in to my base instincts instead of virtuously resisting like a good girl should. Though the truth was, it never had time to hit my system.

"Sorry about the cigarette," I said.

"And the drink?"

"That too. I shouldn't have been contributing. To your delinquency."

He took the glass out of my hand. My eyes followed it to the end table where he placed it and they followed his hand back. It didn't land on me.

"You don't have to worry about my delinquency anymore."

"I'm not worried, I just mentioned it."

"Why not mention everything?"

"What everything?" We were so close I was almost whispering. My voice felt husky. Stomach, fluttery.

Palms damp.

"There was the first smoke, the first drink and the first kiss."

"Yours." I was throbbing. My Private Arts panties would betray me if I were in an accident right now. Best just to stay here.

"True. And I never forgot it."

"Never?"

He moved his hand around to the small of my back and slowly, too slowly, pulled my body against his. I sighed.

"No." He bent his head and I tilted mine up to meet him; it was too late for coy. Our first kiss had been an exploration, stolen from one uppity kid by another. It had been warm, friendly, curious.

The kiss in the jeep had been notice: *I'm coming for you.*

There was nothing exploratory or playful now. The first touch of his lips to mine drove reason screaming away; with it went every trace of softness. My fists were clenched in his shirt, trying to force him closer though we were pressed so tightly together he had nowhere to go but inside. Clothes. Bad. I snaked my arms around his neck trying to pull him down. His hands moved down from my waist, lifted me easily up and against him. Now he was pressed right there and I wanted to divest us of every garment, but I couldn't do it without dislodging myself. I may have whimpered.

"Bedroom."

"Yeah."

I unbuttoned my sweater on the way in, let it drop to the ground. Harry was carrying me, our lips and tongues still exploring, contesting, mating.

He kicked the bedroom door shut behind us.

I don't know what the bed looked like, didn't care.

It was soft beneath me and I sank in just the right amount when Harry added his weight to mine.

I pulled his shirt up and had to stop kissing him when it went over his head. I ran my hands over his chest, down his stomach. It was warm, hard. I fumbled for the buttons on his jeans, but he moved back, peeling my own denim down my legs and tossing it away.

"Those are nice," He said, looking at the hand-painted design on my panties. "Nice material. Soft."

I gasped.

"Wait!" I said, when he stopped.

"Wait?"

"Keep going."

"You sure?"

"Could you shut up and take off your pants?"

He did. He took my remaining bits of attire while he was at it, slowly, with frequent stops along the way. I clutched his hair, trembled, exploded inside.

He mumbled something into my thigh. It sounded like a compliment.

I watched him move over me and said, "Ditto."

We were perfectly aligned, our mouths came together again and everything else followed.

I was still panting, from exertion now. We were sheened in sweat. Harry was blowing gently on my stomach, cooling down my skin, heating me up again elsewhere. There was a low keening moan coming from the other side of the door.

"When did that start?" Harry asked.

"I didn't notice, but maybe I should go out there."

"He'll be ok. He can snack on the couch."

"He's lonely. I should check on him."

"Poor guy." His hands were moving again, bringing my topography to blistering attention. That was before he went back to work with his mouth.

Ok, but after this for sure.

***

The pasta, when we got to it, was delicious. Not as delicious as what had gone before, but mushroom ravioli, no matter how beautifully prepared, can never compete with multiple orgasms.

We made it up to Gulliver with an array of tidbits while we polished off the wine Harry had opened earlier. Harry was critiquing my interviewing skills, a sure sign that I'd put on too many clothes before we'd come out of the bedroom.

"So now you're going to tell me I'm not charming?" I said.

"You have other fine attributes." He started listing them. I flushed and swatted him. "You have to remember you have no authority."

"You were singing a different tune an hour ago."

"I'll do whatever you want when you're naked." He threw on a thoughtful look. "Maybe Bobby Neuland would too."

"Shut up."

"If you wanted, I could take one for the team as far as Reina's concerned."

"Let's consider that a last resort. At least for now." I added, because he was far too pleased with my original answer. "What's our first resort?"

"We keep working." His hands were doing something that couldn't be classified as work.

"Doing what exactly?" I said. "What about Jack? Maybe we should visit him. Maybe he has something to contribute."

"Besides this mess?"

I leaned my head against his chest. "Yeah. You probably want to wrap this up and get back to your real life, right?"

"This is my real life. Beisdes, my backstroke still needs help."

"So you're in it for the free golf lessons?"

He ran his hand up my thigh and said something. I missed it. Probably nothing important. I reveled briefly in the hedonistic then gathered myself and shoved him away.

"What? Gulliver isn't watching."

I laughed. "It's not that. I just want this to be over. Poor Jack."

"Shouldn't your mother have called with an update?"

"Shit. I left my phone in my purse."

Sure enough. Seven missed calls, all from Leonie. I had one new message. I touched in my code and played it on speaker.

"Evin, I have had enough." Leonie's recorded scold filled the kitchen. "If I had had any idea your stepfather would get into this much trouble on his own, I would have chosen a method of punishment that would have allowed me to keep an eye on him. He is making friends in there, Evin. It's unacceptable. That stupid man wants to start a golf program for inmates. I don't know what I did to deserve a husband who thinks it's wise to pass out clubs to murderers. I will be at home. Expecting an update from you. And I will not be berated for the number of times I called; I left a message."

I deleted it.

"Evin?"

"What?"

"You look glazed."

"I was thinking about the phone. Candace's. If we knew the number maybe we could figure out her pass code and listen to the messages."

"Getting the number isn't a problem."

Gulliver and I trailed Harry into the office. Harry used his P.I. ways and produced the number. We took turns guessing codes. Mine were random, Harry's contributions were based on variations of significant numbers in Candace's life, such as birthday, social, alphanumeric combos. Both methods failed. I was kicking the leg of Harry's desk so my frustration wouldn't come out as a scream. We hadn't guessed the voicemail code, hadn't identified the killer, and couldn't exonerate Jack. All we had done was stumble upon body after body.

"Why do you think the bodies were just left around?" I said. "If I went on a killing spree, I'd have the decency to dispose of the bodies properly."

"They did try, don't you think? Hazel was hidden under the pool cover. If the killer knew the situation with Jack's condo, they would have thought Candace wouldn't be discovered for much longer. Lots of the places in the Mystic are seasonal."

"It is the season."

"Yeah, but if you hadn't come to town, it's possible neither body would have been found yet."

"Thanks."

"Yeah, that was me blaming you."

"I know."

"If I hurt your feelings," Harry said, moseying into my personal space, "I'll make it up to you."

I decided my feelings were very, very hurt.

***

I woke up as usual, with a heavy head resting on my stomach. Also as usual, it was Gulliver's head.

"Where's Harry?" I said to Gulliver after I'd muddled around the bed enough to be sure he wasn't there.

My purse was on the floor, I fumbled my phone out, pressed a button and found out I had missed three more calls.

Two were from Zuzu, one from Leonie. I called Zuzu back.

"Evin! Where are you?"

"I'm at home. It's one-thirty in the morning. What's up?"

"What's up is you're a liar. I just drove by Leonie's and your crappy car was there in the driveway and all the lights were on, so I stopped in, but guess what?"

"Uh... I didn't come to the door because I was asleep? You know, societal mores dictate that you shouldn't pop up on someone's doorstep at one in the morning."

"Screw the mores. You're always up late."

"Not always. I was asleep until five minutes ago."

"Oh my God. You're at Harry's. I knew it was going to happen."

"Zuzu, shut up. You're not still there are you?"

"I left before I called you, but it was Leonie who said that you'd be with Harry. So you can go ahead and admit it now."

"Only if we don't have to talk about it."

"No deal. How was it? Does he look as good without clothes?"

"Better. We did dirty things and fell asleep. At least I did." My hair was a mess of tangles. I tried to finger comb it into some kind of order. The dirty things had not been kind to the 'do.

"What's that supposed to mean?"

"What? Oh." I gave up on the hair and chewed a nail. "I'm not sure where he is. Maybe the kitchen. Guys like food after right?"

"You woke up in his bed, but he's not there?"

"Well, Gulliver is here."

"That was creepy, Ev. I hope you know they're not interchangeable."

"Ok, bye."

"No, wait. I'm sorry. Go see if he's there."

"I'm naked."

"So? Go look anyway. Put something on if you want."

"Shit. Hang on." I couldn't find a light or my clothes, so I crept out of the bedroom, phone to my ear, my free hand covering not nearly enough of my nudity.

"Well?"

"Hang on, I'm looking." Besides the stint in the office earlier, my exploration so far had been limited to the living room, kitchen and master suite. There was a second bedroom sparsely furnished with a foldout couch, and an unvarnished dresser with a small flat screen on top. The windows were untreated so I backed out quickly, not wanting to expose my naked silhouette to any nocturnal neighbors.

The hall bathroom was empty, as was Harry's office; empty of Harry at least, still crammed to the rafters with everything else. The computers, file cabinets and bookshelves were, presumably, stuffed with information on who was doing what to whom in the desert.

"He's not here," I whispered, feeling like an intruder. A naked intruder. "Hang on." I wrapped myself in a throw from the couch and stuck my head out the front door. "His jeep is gone."

"Shouldn't you have been the one to slink out and disappear into the night in shame after *he* fell asleep?"

My sentiments exactly. I had played hard to get with the guy who peed in the shower; although not hard enough. Even Cory, whom I'd expected to be with for the rest of my life, (or at least a year or two) had a long, proper wait for the goodies. Although I had given it up to Jason the would-be porn star; that obviously didn't count. Full disclosure had certainly not been made, rendering the sex null and void. Now I was a cow who had not only given away the milk, but baked cookies to go with it.

"Thanks Zuzu."

"Sorry. Maybe there was an emergency."

"Yeah."

"Ev, stop panicking. Harry has a mad crush on you, and he's a nice guy with a rocking body."

"I'm not supposed to be dating."

"Technically, you're not."

"What are you trying to accomplish with this conversation?"

"Nothing. Just stop thinking that Harry is like every other mistake you ever made. If you don't trust your judgment trust mine."

"Maybe." Gulliver came tottering out of the bedroom, stretching and yawning massively. He shook his head, and drool flecked my bare legs.

"Call him," Zuzu said.

"No." I scratched Gulliver's head; he groaned and thumped his leg on the floor.

"Ok, I'm done with this. What's going on with Jack and the growing body count?"

"The count remains three. Jack is still in jail in Banning. Leonie's been visiting him. Did she tell you?"

"Yeah. Just go from there." I sat on the couch and

tucked the throw around me. Gulliver hopped up too and rested his head on my curled up legs.

"I was sure it was Bobby Neuland." I told her about our visit to the office. "But now I don't know."

"Could you knock off the dramatic pauses?" Zuzu said. "Why don't you know?"

"We found out that Rex and Candace used to be a couple. She came out here to be with him. We knew he hated her, and now we know why. But... I don't know, it was six months ago."

"Candace was with Rex and she left him for his father?" Zuzu said. "That's gross."

I agreed.

"So you're wondering if Bobby killed Candace and Hazel over money, or if Rex killed Candace because of the jilted lover thing?

"Right," I said.

"Either way, I don't see why Maggie was killed."

"Maggie helped Candace hide out. Hazel stayed at Maggie's when she left Bobby. She knew enough to make her a risk. I think that's why she was so desperate to find the letters and stuff. She wanted to protect herself."

"That strategy had no flaws," Zuzu said.

True.

"So what were the Neuland alibis?"

"According to Reina and his receptionist," I said, "Bobby was at work, then at his regular lunch spot, although no one would share where that is. I have no idea about Rex."

"So maybe the daughter's lying. She's spoiled right? He does everything for her. Maybe she's trying to protect him, whether or not he did it."

"Spoiled or not, I don't think she'd put herself at risk for anyone else. Rex wouldn't talk to us, but I don't know if that's because he's hiding something or because he doesn't know anything. His roommate was helpful, kind of. Maybe we should go see her again and hope she's all stoned and chatty like last time."

I heard the rumble of an engine outside and the jaunty slam of a car door. Gulliver picked his head up and started to bark, deep, throaty and loud as hell. I dropped the phone in my futile efforts to shush him. Giving it up, I jumped up from the couch, and found myself bare to the world again because half the blanket I'd been wearing was pinned under Gulliver. I fished the phone from between the sofa cushions and told Zuzu, "He's back. I have to go."

I heard her say, "Wait-" as I hung up and scrambled back to the bedroom in bare-assed glory. I flung myself into Harry's big bed and arranged my hair in a becoming spill across the pillow. The pretty picture was complete, but I was breathing like an out of shape marathon runner. I struggled to calm my respiration.

I waited. Gulliver had stopped barking, and now I couldn't hear anything at all.

I snuck a look at the time on my phone. It read 1:58. I shoved it back under my pillow. It was incongruent with my portrait of a sound sleeper.

I waited some more. My breath had calmed, the time was 2:07. I was tense with anticipation. I could feel a headache easing through my shoulders and neck, inching up the back of my skull. Enough.

I got out of bed and fumbled around in the dark for something to make me decent. When the lights came on, I was caught, crouched on the floor, digging under the bed in search of my panties. I straightened immediately, hoping Harry, standing in the doorway, hadn't noticed the roll across my middle that had been created by my awkward posture. In the wrong light, it could have been taken for fat.

Ok, in light.

"Hey," I said, as casually as I could. Being the only one in a room sans clothes makes casual a stretch. Even Gulliver, who was faithlessly fawning around Harry, had a collar on.

"Did you get up to watch some Sportscenter or something?" I said.

"I would never leave you naked in my bed to go watch TV."

That's what you say now.

"Do you want me to pretend I don't know you were just out in the living room?"

I shrugged. His eyes fastened on my breasts, which had bounced obligingly. I crossed my arms and glared at him, which didn't have the withering effect I'd hoped for. I thought it was time for a little cover so I plucked the corner of the sheet, pulling enough from the bed to conceal everything important.

"Shy?"

"Nope."

He had the nerve to smile as though he hadn't just snuck out and left me vulnerable and alone in a strange house. "You look a little uncomfortable."

"I have this weird dislike of being the only one in the room who's naked."

Harry laughed. "I know the feeling."

"Yeah, I'm sure you do."

"It gets better."

"When?"

As it turned out, then.

Anne Stinnett

Twenty-five

"I'm still pissed," I said after a brief, but not too brief, interval. Harry's hand was lazing around my back; I was sprawled face down, my voice muffled by the pillow.

"I can't wait to see what I get when you're happy with me."

"Never happen. Where were you?" I was too relaxed to be really pissy, but I was doing my best.

"I have good news."

"Perfect. Save it for after you answer my question."

"I found a gun."

"That's not where you were."

"I was in Bobby Neuland's office."

"You broke into his office without me?"

"We can't all end up in jail," Harry said. "Besides, I didn't break in. I had a key."

I raised my head to inspect him. Everything looked good.

"How did you get a key? Doesn't he have an alarm?"

"The key I stole this afternoon; the alarm I tripped."

"Stealthy."

"I meant to."

"No you didn't." I let my head plop down. "Ok, why?"

"So the cops would come, basically."

"Basically?"

"A security patrol showed up and they called the police. Someone in all that mess noticed the gun case in an open drawer."

I scrambled up from my prone position and said, "The gun that almost shot me? And Maggie was killed with? You found it? How did you know it was there?"

"I didn't. I was looking for anything helpful."

That was helpful.

"Did you trip the alarm before or after you found the gun?"

"Before."

He'd been right not to take me. But that was no reason to let him off the hook.

"Sounds iffy."

"If it hadn't worked, we could have gone with an anonymous phone call."

"If it hadn't worked you could have signed up for Jack's inmate golf program."

"You worry too much."

"You worry me. What if you'd broken in and there hadn't been a gun?"

"There might have been something else." He hauled me on top of him and kissed me. It was on the chaste side, as naked kisses go. "Haven't you heard of the power of positive thinking?"

"Ick. If you're going to talk like that, get away from me." I shoved him gently. Warmth radiated from his skin.

"Shouldn't you be slightly less uptight by now?"

"Yeah." I smiled and tapped his chest. "Unless

someone is overestimating himself."

"Should I try harder?"

"Right now? No! I'm tired. You're killing me."

"Thanks."

"Seriously. How did you know?"

"Told you. Didn't know. Had to check." He was kissing my neck and I was on the verge of a second wind.

"How sure are you, that it was our gun?"

"It was the right caliber. I didn't touch it, but I think it's the one."

"So Jack should be released?"

"I hope so. Then we can celebrate."

"You, me and Jack?"

"He can celebrate with Leonie. I want to celebrate with you." I could tell he was ready to start the party now.

"What did I say about you killing me?"

"That you liked it?"

"I don't remember that part."

"Are you sure?" He held me tighter. I struggled. He had his way. We both did.

***

"Harry. Harry, wake up." I nudged his shoulder with my knee. Gulliver helped by dragging his tongue across Harry's ear.

"Harry!"

He muttered something that sounded like, "I'm coming." Then, "Who licked my ear?"

"I have to go to the police station. Are you coming?"

"What's the problem?" He sat up and shoved his hair off his forehead.

"Quick just called and said he needed to see me. I told him I could be there in an hour."

"Ok."

"And also," I said, nearly bursting with self-importance, "I accessed the messages on Candace's phone."

"You mean her voicemail."

"Yes, I mean her voicemail." Always with the details.

"You figured out the code?" Harry was all sleepy and sexy with his bare chest and bare... I prodded myself mentally. I'd thought he was more of a morning person, but we had been up late.

"More like found it. You know the apology letter Candace wrote?"

"What about it?"

"The date wasn't right."

"It was dated February eleventh."

"It wasn't a date," I said.

"Who says smart isn't sexy?" Harry said, making a lazy grab for me.

"Stop it. Sam said she left on the Tuesday before she was killed, and Candace wrote in her letter that she was leaving her apartment that morning. I was just sitting in your office, the calendar was right in front of me and I noticed that the day she left her apartment to go to Jack's was the seventh. Well, Sam actually said that, but I didn't realize the significance at the time. The point is, the letter was dated the eleventh. I couldn't see why she would post date the letter, plus there was no break between the month and day. So I tried it as the voicemail code, and voila."

"Where's my phone?" I stood by and watched Harry dial Candace's number and key in the pass code. The messages were primarily from Bobby espousing his ardor. Candace was the one he loved, the one for whom he would leave his wife, the one who touched his soul. The messages also contained some graphic filth, both reminiscent and anticipated.

"I can't believe none of these women killed him," Harry said. I motioned for him to shut up and keep listening. The seventh message was the zinger.

I had been catching a word here and there, as Harry listened, but the next one I knew by heart.

Candace had sounded giddy with excitement when she contacted Hazel for the last time. I watched as the message played for Harry. "Bobby just left. I have the money and he didn't give me any trouble. I gave him the letters and the card. He'll be so pissed when he finds out you have copies. I wish I could see his face." Candace swore and said, "Hang on." There was a brief pause and then she said, "He just drove back up. I bet the asshole wants a receipt. I'll leave a message if anything else comes up." At this point, the doorbell chimed. "If not, good luck."

There were no more messages.

"What do you think?" I said.

"I don't know. I can't see why he would leave and go back."

"Buyer's remorse? Maybe once he saw the blackmail evidence it didn't seem worth it."

"He must have checked it out before he left. And if he never intended to pay her off, why bring the money?"

"Maybe he had to show it to her to get in," I said.

"It's his leaving that I'm having trouble with," Harry was dragging his gorgeous self out of bed. It distracted me.

"Evin, are you listening?"

"Uh-huh."

"When are you supposed to be at the station?"

"Soon."

While Harry showered, I dialed De la Cruz. He answered on the first ring. Not out of eagerness, it turned out.

"What now?"

"Hey, it's Evin Hart."

"I know. What I don't know is why you think we need to talk every day."

"Don't be like that. Have we done anything to screw you over?"

"Not yet."

"Haven't you heard of the power of positive thinking?" I said shamelessly, since Harry couldn't hear me.

"You're one of those?"

"No, I swear, I'm not. Everything sucks."

He laughed, barely. "Ok, that got you two minutes."

"You rock. Here's what I'm wondering."

***

I was in the interview room again. If I had to come back one more time, I was going to bring a framed picture of Gulliver with me, to make things homey. The dog himself was outside with Harry.

I had filled De la Cruz in on the significance of the non-date on the letter we had handed over the day before. In return, he allowed me to finesse the information that Bobby Neuland was finally being questioned regarding the shooting of Maggie, and that a warrant had been issued to search his home.

I asked what that meant for any wrongfully incarcerated stepfathers lying around, and that's when the conversation ended on a rather sharp note.

"So Ms. Hart, are you well?" Quick's eyes were gleaming and so were his teeth.

"I'm ok." I was jumpy. The air in the interview room was crackling with tension. I felt like something important was happening, but I had no idea what.

"You look on edge."

"I'm not sure why I'm here."

"No? Where were you last night?"

"At a friend's place." My face was going hot.

"The entire night?"

"Yeah. The entire night."

"And your friend stayed with you?"

"Yes."

"I'll need the name and address of your friend."

I gave Harry's name, squirming slightly. I didn't actually know the address. Not at all mortifying. I caught myself fidgeting with the frayed hole in my jeans and forced my fingers still.

"You'll be interested to know, I'm sure, that the gun that was used to kill Margaret Connor was found."

I took a deep breath. "Did it come with whoever shot her?"

"We're looking into it."

"Ok. I don't really know what that means. Where was the gun? Who had it?"

Quick regarded me without wavering. "It seems strange, that the person in question wouldn't have disposed of a murder weapon. Or, would have used a gun registered in their name."

"Who?" I said again.

"Oh, of course, no reason you would know," he said, still regarding me with his daunting eyes. "Dr. Neuland is the owner of the gun, and it was discovered by officers responding to a break in at his office last night. It was a fortuitous break-in. For us, that is, not for Dr. Neuland. I find his lack of savvy perplexing."

"He's crazy. He killed three women and almost killed me. But you have Jack in jail. Maybe crazy is going around."

"Mr. Dekker clearly was not the perpetrator of the attack on you and Ms. Connor. However, other than the loose connection between the murdered women, there is no evidence that the shooter in your case is the same person who committed the earlier murders."

"Bobby Neuland knows all the women who have been killed. And he knows me."

"He knows you because you went to his house, lied about who you were and questioned him. You have tracked down every member of his family. Has it occurred to you that he felt harassed, that perhaps you were the intended victim and Maggie Connor was an unintentional one? It could be that you and she were stalking Dr. Neuland together. Maybe he felt your attentions were a danger and he had to take the safety of his family into his own hands."

"Is that what he said?" I went on, trying to reduce the tremor in my voice as I spoke, "That's ridiculous. He would never be afraid of me, even if he had reason to be. Which he didn't."

"You weren't trying to gather proof that he committed murder?"

"I wouldn't put it like that."

"Feel free to use your own words."

"Look, I have the advantage of knowing Jack would never hurt anybody. That's why I knew you had it wrong when you arrested him. I just want Jack to be out of jail. I talked to a couple people. I can talk to people."

"Not if you are interfering with, or obstructing, a

police investigation. Not if you withhold evidence."

"I never-"

"I'm talking about the letter, the phone and the memory chip you turned in to Officer De la Cruz after keeping them in your possession for over twenty-four hours."

"I was in the hospital. I had a concussion. I couldn't get in touch with you, so I contacted another officer I was familiar with as soon as I realized what had happened."

"I got no message that you were trying to reach me."

"Well. That's strange." We looked at each other for awhile.

"I can't say how much the department appreciates your conscientious behavior." He leaned forward; I struggled to stay put. "But if you ever find yourself in a similar situation, which we all pray you won't, do everyone a favor and call us instead of removing evidence from a crime scene. In fact, call us if you even suspect there is something to find. You haven't done any good by proceeding on your own."

I sat there with my hot welling eyes and churning stomach and refused to allow myself the luxury of fidgeting. Of crying. Or throwing up. Harry had left me out of the break in because we couldn't all go to jail. We wouldn't all go to jail, it was just going to be me. I wouldn't even have Jack for company. He would be in the men's facility, golfing with inmates, and I would be elsewhere with a bunch of large, angry, depilatorily deprived women. I would never see Gulliver again.

All I could do was nod.

There was a tap at the door, and Quick excused himself. When he came back, he scrutinized me for a long few moments. He never seemed to tire of making me uncomfortable.

"Good. Then you can go."

I goggled at him for a second then I scooped up my purse and got out of there. I didn't run, but my walk was brisk.

Harry and Gulliver were right where I had left them in a shady spot across from the station. I hopped into the passenger seat, urging Gulliver into the back. He went willingly, but about-faced to stick his big head between the seats and slurp my face.

"That's what happened to my ear this morning," Harry accused me. "Although I'm happy that wasn't you waking me up. A little too sloppy."

"Your ear is fine. You're fine. I'm the one who was almost hauled off in shackles for interference and obstruction. Oh, and withholding evidence."

"Want me to kiss it and make it better?"

"No. Get away." I punctuated that with a delicate shove. "I'm inconsolable."

"I guess you really did major in theatre."

"How is that helpful?"

"Fine. So it's Rex and Trina's for now then?"

"I don't know."

"What's the problem?"

"They've got to let Jack go now, maybe we should wait and see what happens." I hated what I was saying, but I continued to say it. "I don't want to go to jail. You should see my hair without a good conditioner."

"Ok." He put the jeep in gear and off we rolled.

"Ok, what?"

"Ok, I'll drop you off."

"You're going out there by yourself? No. You can't go by yourself."

"Someone has to. Look, sorry. I know being

questioned by the cops can be unnerving. You're not used to all this. I'll be fine."

"Forget it. I'll go." I hadn't meant to scream. I took a breath, but didn't use it to apologize. If I ended up going to jail, I was going to kill someone. Screw Harry and his selflessness and his impossible standards. He probably didn't even need conditioner.

"You don't have to."

"You don't have to either. Maybe I'll just go by myself. Like you said, we can't all go to jail."

Harry suggested I quit using my words, until I was more myself. I informed him that I was myself and if he didn't like it he could go to hell. He critiqued the lack of originality in my insults, and the conversation rolled merrily downhill from there.

In the end we both went, Gulliver in tow, stony silence filling the jeep.

The day was warm and bright, the mountains were topped with snow, in short, beauty abounded wherever the eye should rest. I wanted grey skies and hail to match my inner landscape.

The desert did not oblige.

Anne Stinnett

Twenty-six

As we pulled up to Rex's house I saw two people in the driveway approaching a flashy SUV. They were Rex and Verona Neuland. By the time Harry came to a halt half blocking the driveway, Verona was ensconced in the passenger seat. Rex saw us coming and stood beside the car, looking like he'd been waiting all day for a fight.

"Hey," I said.

"What?" Harry did not sound friendly.

"What if he rams the jeep? Gulliver's here."

"He won't."

I took a glance out of the corner of my eye and saw a clenched jaw. The sexy scruff it was sporting was wasted on me. Mostly. Before I could say anything else, Harry was out of the car. I got out too, placing myself between the big BMW and the Rubicon.

"I guess it's your dad who's going to jail," I said, not to cause trouble, which I did, but because Rex seemed the most deserving target on whom to unleash the pent up fear and fury that were boiling away inside me.

"You need to shut her up," Rex said to Harry, "Because I have no problem doing it myself."

Harry was between me and Rex. Annoyed as he

was with me, I trusted he wouldn't step aside and let Rex beat me to death. I felt free to taunt further.

"Violence against women must run in the family. Did you kill your girlfriend?"

Rex went white.

"Don't call her that," he said. "She was a mistake. She was a gold-digging whore."

"That's redundant," I said.

Verona was out of the car now, on Rex's side, both figuratively and literally. She held his arm and spoke to him urgently. The polite, motherly gist was that he should shut up.

"I don't appreciate you coming here to provoke my son," she said.

"We didn't," Harry said. "We came to find out if you knew about the blackmail."

We got a long unified look from the duo. Finally, Verona asked, "What blackmail?"

"Candace was blackmailing Bobby."

"You mean he paid her money? For what?"

Harry explained about the extortion. Rex was looking at the ground now, and I was starting to feel bad for him. Maybe he and I should take a trip to the Spa and play some cards. Unlucky in love.

Verona informed us that they had nothing more to say, which wasn't entirely true. I didn't take any of it personally, no one can help their ancestry and it's not like she called me fat. Finally, they loaded themselves into the car again and maneuvered around Harry's car and down the street.

As we stepped up to the house I could see that this time the front door was wide open with only a screen, fronted with a simple wrought iron design, keeping out the world. It looked good but was doing nothing to contain the cloud of smoke, which oozed pungently through to assault our nostrils.

I waved it away from Gulliver's face. The last thing I needed was for him to get a contact high and pass out. I was in no mood to lug a hundred and a half pounds of stoned dog. I breathed deeply; I needed it.

Trina pushed open the door in all her pierced glory. Her eye makeup had been liberally applied, although it looked like last night's leftovers. She had a fresh tattoo smeared with Vaseline or something like it, on the inside of her forearm. She was wearing ripped jeans, nearly identical to my own and a wife-beater with no bra. I had a hard time keeping my eyes off the dark nipples trying to poke their way out of their cotton prison. It's not like I was some doe-eyed innocent; I'd frolicked naked with Harry, that jerk, for hours the night before without so much as being taken to dinner first. Still, I couldn't see myself answering the door to virtual strangers, in a see through shirt, with my high beams on.

"Hey," she said to Harry, "I know you right?"

"We're old friends," he said, and gave her his hand. Instead of shaking it, she used it to pull him inside after her. Gulliver and I followed in their wake, through the house and out the back to the patio table where we had spent our previous time with Trina.

Memories. My face felt sour, so I tried to straighten it out. No reason for Harry to know I gave a shit about him staring at Trina's slutty little chest. Observation soon trumped assumption; he was apparently oblivious to the rampant ta-tas. It was almost enough to make me want to make up.

"So what's going on?" Trina asked, packing a bowl. "You just missed Rex again. And his mom." She pulled a little face.

"They looked like they were in a hurry," Harry

said.

"Holy shit, man. Verona came down this morning like before the sun even came up, you know? Like it was urgent." She stopped to fire up and draw urgently on the colorful glass.

I took the opportunity to say as nicely as I was able, "Rex tells you a lot, doesn't he?"

"Some he told me and some I overheard when I was kinda zonked on the futon in my room." Of course, she sleeps on a futon, I thought before remembering I didn't even have a real bed of my own.

Trina shrugged. "I think Verona thought I was sleeping or whatever, you know?"

Harry and I nodded in unison. Gulliver yawned. Trina took another hit and coughed enormously, not bothering to cover her mouth. I cringed and tried to look casual while leaning as far back as I could. A burst of laughter escaped Harry and when I met his eyes, I couldn't help but smile.

"Can I use your bathroom?" I asked Trina.

"Go for it." She waved an arm adorned with various cause bracelets, displaying a veritable rainbow. "Down the hall, first door on the left."

I handed Gulliver's leash to Harry, slid the screen door and shut it again behind me. The house was dim and cool.

The carpet was beige and plush, boring color but good quality. It seemed to be the only thing in the house that wasn't original. I walked softly across the living room, Trina's voice rasping through the screen door after me.

"So it turns out, he like totally did it. Dr. Neuland, you know?" I turned my attention to the mantel over the fireplace.

"Really?" It was Harry acting surprised at Trina's

little bombshell. There was no way I should date a guy who's that comfortable with deception. In the spring of seventh grade, Paul Leeds was my boyfriend for almost two weeks. In spite of the rumors, and in spite of the fact that he turned bright red every time he told a whopper, I allowed myself to be convinced that he wasn't holding hands with Susie Kanter every day on the bus ride home.

The fireplace was pristine. Everything was pristine. No pictures on the mantle. There was a little arrangement of tie dyed candles that I would have bet my dog Trina had contributed to the décor. I did the old white glove test with my bare finger and brushed up against something that wasn't dust. It was a card. I pulled it down hoping for something amusing, but no. Just an outpouring of sentimental greeting card garbage outside and in. Opposite the factory sentiments was a cute little note to Trina.

It was signed, "Love, Mom." I hadn't seen "Love, Mom," on a card since I was five, when Leonie had decided motherhood did not define her as a person and suggested I start calling her by name.

I left the card and headed down the hall. I saw the bathroom; went on by. The next door was also ajar. There was no futon in sight, so I dipped in, guessing it was Rex's. I listened. The voices on the patio were faint but flowing. I flew through the dresser drawers, reaching into corners, feeling underneath. I checked both nightstands and looked under the bed. A quick rummage of Rex's bathroom yielded more nothing. I was looking around for another possibility when I heard the screen on the patio door screech open.

I took the five steps from the bedroom to the hall john in just under three seconds. I shut the door silently, flushed the toilet and turned on the tap.

There were no hand towels, only a wrinkled bath sheet slung over the top of the shower stall. I turned off the water, happy I hadn't actually needed the facilities. The last thing I wanted was to dry my hands on the same towel Trina used to slough the water off her overly decorated anatomy.

I pulled the door open and shrieked when I found Trina on the other side.

Fuck. Who does that?

"Dude," she said. "You've been gone for awhile. Are you having, you know, like a problem? There's some Pepto in the medicine cabinet, you know, if your stomach is kicking your ass or whatever."

"I'm fine, thanks," I said, trying to edge around her. "How sweet of you to ask." And *so* appropriate.

She was walking backwards down the hall in front of me saying, "I just came in to grab a beer and you were still in there, you know, so I thought maybe you had some bad Mexican or something."

I looked past her to the patio hoping she would shut the hell up. If I had to confess to snooping in order to deflect accusations of catastrophic gastronomical dysfunction in front of Harry, I would.

"At least there was a bathroom close by, you know? One time-"

"Trina, I'm fine."

"But dude, you were in there so long-"

I racked my brain for something to squelch the conversation. "I had to throw up."

"Oh," she said nodding. "Trying to lose weight, right?"

I said nothing, just squeezed myself and my apparently fat ass past Skeletor's bride and out the patio door. Rude I know.

Although, not as rude as a left hook to the jaw.

I flung myself down across from Harry, fuming. Trina rambled out after me offering a stick of gum and a wink. The most thoughtful girl I had ever wanted to strangle.

I took the gum to prevent further discussion of the state of my insides. As an extra precaution, I asked Trina what they had been talking about.

"You won't believe it," she said, popping a stick in her own mouth and proceeding to smack away at it. "Dr. Neuland is like totally nailed. They found that powder on his clothes from when he shot some other woman, and now I guess the lawyer is there. Dr. Neuland isn't talking."

That was to be expected. A doctor should know enough to invoke his right to counsel. My brain got around to the phrase, "powder on his clothes...," and I looked a question at Harry who nodded and said, "Gunshot residue."

"Yeah," Trina chimed in, "he managed to scrub it off his hands, but he didn't get it off his suit. And there was the whole car thing. Crazy, you know?"

I knew.

Trina gave a little jump and pulled a phone out of her pocket. "Oh hey, it's Rex, I'll tell him you're here." She flipped the phone open and said, "Hey man, what's good? No shit?" She cut her eyes to Harry then me. "Yeah, yeah dude. Sounds like way too much. We'll bounce. Later."

"Hang on," I said, trying to reign her in. "What did you say about a car?"

She put the phone away and stood up, "Dude, I'll totally tell you later, but Mary Jane and I gotta jet you know?" Moving faster than I'd ever seen her, she disappeared into the house. I looked at Harry and said, "What the hell?"

He shrugged and followed her. Gulliver and I followed suit. We found Trina stuffing her mightily resisting cat into a carrier. She seemed nonplussed at our reappearance.

"I almost forgot you were here," she said, hand to chest. "But look, I gotta go. I know you wanted to see Rex, but I wouldn't be here when they get back if I were you. Mary Jane and I are gonna chill elsewhere, you know, 'til things are mellow again." I assumed Mary Jane was the indignant feline in the crate. "We do not want to be here for a Neuland family reunion."

"Rex and Verona are coming back?" I said. Harry and I preceded her out the door, Harry carrying the crate and its yowling occupant. "Why does that mean you have to leave?" I was holding Gulliver back from inspecting the crate too closely. Mary Jane had worked a paw out and was taking swipes at anyone in reach.

"It's not so much that I have to, but avoiding unpleasantness is my main thing you know?"

I thought a well-packed bowl was her main thing.

"Anyway, they found out they can't bail Dr. Neuland out yet, so everyone is pretty pissed. Rex is awesome, well you know that, but family stress is a bitch." She shrugged.

"Anyway, we're outtie, dudes." She gestured at Harry who was still holding the carrier and its yowling occupant. "If you'd be so awesome."

He hefted the cage onto the worn backseat. Trina planted a kiss on Harry's cheek leaving behind a smear of recently freshened black lipstick. He tried to avoid it, but he could have tried harder. He hadn't thrown one punch.

Trina climbed behind the wheel, gave a cheery wave and screeched out of the driveway, leaving behind a substantial puddle of the Saab's vital fluids.

Then she was gone, driving down the street straight as an arrow. Of course she was only going about ten miles an hour.

"Do you think she should be driving?"

"Technically no, but she seems to be doing all right. I'm sure she gets plenty of practice."

That was certainly true. We loaded into the jeep, and Harry related the beans Trina had spilled while I had been officially powdering my nose.

"So Bobby's in jail," I said.

"He is."

"I'm calling Leonie," I said, and did.

She answered on the first ring. "Darling, I can't talk now, Jack is being released."

"Jack's getting released," I told Harry. "So are you going to pick him up? Hello? Mother! Leonie!" I screeched into the phone. I threw my head back against the headrest. I told myself that I loved my mother, she nurtured me, gave me life, all that jazz. I'm sure she had a perfectly good reason for hanging up on me. No, I wasn't buying it. I mean really, what a bi-.

I stifled the thought and huffily redialed. "Don't you dare hang up," I snapped when she answered.

"Of course not darling," she said gently, as though she were speaking to a mental patient.

"You just did."

"Yes darling, but now I won't."

I was tempted to delve into her reasoning, but I pulled my shit together and headed for the pertinent. "When?"

"Now darling, I'm on my way to pick him up. Don't you listen? If that's all-"

"It's not. Why and when did they decide to release him? They arrested Bobby Neuland for shooting

Maggie, but what about the others?"

"Darling, the car. Pay attention."

"To what? You didn't say anything about a car." I wanted to scream. Oh. "Did Trina say something about a car?" I asked Harry.

"Who's Trina?" Leonie said in my ear. "Nevermind. I don't care. Your stepfather needs to be retrieved and possibly deloused."

"In the movies they delouse them when they get there. What about the car?"

"The car that was at your stepfather's condominium. When that horrid woman was killed. One of the neighbors came forward and identified it as Dr. Neuland's. They charged him with that murder as well. Then of course they had to release your stepfather."

"What did the neighbor see exactly?"

"I have no idea, darling. I'll have Jack give you a ring back when I collect him. Will that do?"

It would have to.

"We need to know which of his neighbors would be likely to be hanging around being generally nosy."

"If you mean his neighbors at the condominium, I have no idea. I told you, I will have him call you back. I think we should all meet for a celebration. Now things will be normal and we can forget about these atrocious women."

"Mother."

"What darling? They're nothing to me, why should I pretend they are? I plan to put all of this behind me."

"I want to put it behind me too," I said giving Harry a look of exasperation. "But I'm curious. Why didn't this neighbor pop up before? And what did they see exactly? I just want to make sure nothing is going to bite us on the ass later."

"I have no idea what that has to do with us, darling, but if it makes you happy, go have fun interrogating people. I thought all this stalking of strangers was to benefit Jack, but I understand that pure altruism is scarce in this world. By the way, are you sleeping with Harry? Because if all this is so you can spend more time with him-"

"It's not. Bye."

"Jack's out," Harry said.

"Jack's out," I agreed. "Well, almost out. They've connected Bobby to the shooting and to Candace's murder, which will also connect him to Hazel's death. Also, my cracked skull. He probably won't get much extra time for that."

"Because of a car?"

I laughed. I knew I was still mad in theory, but I couldn't remember exactly why and I wasn't feeling it. "Don't you even pretend not to listen in on other people's conversations?" I said.

"Occupational hazard."

I filled in the blanks. "So, I'm a little curious about this neighbor who saw the car, and why they're just popping up now. Leonie wants us to meet them after she picks Jack up, but how do you feel about taking a ride in the meantime?"

"Who's the neighbor?"

"I don't know.

"Sounds like a waste of time," he said. But he said it with a smile.

Anne Stinnett

Twenty-seven

We were at Mystic Springs twenty minutes later. Harry was cruising at a moderate twenty-five mph, which wasn't sedate enough to prevent his getting the finger from an irate golfer, who almost sideswiped us in his little Cadillac cart. Harry was too polite, so I took it upon myself to reciprocate. We made it through the maze of courses, pools, and senior athletes physically unscathed. Emotionally, I was a bit damaged after exchanging the finger with someone's granddad.

Jack's street had a deserted vibe. We parked outside his garage and extracted ourselves from the jeep. No sooner had Harry beeped the lock, than a voice from above said, "You can't park there. I don't know what's wrong with people that they think they can just park wherever they please, without any regard for others."

Harry looked annoyed, but not quite willing to shout the woman down. I too, opened my mouth but nothing came out. The voice had come screeching out of an indigenous desert species: the sun-dried human.

"What's that poor Mr. Dekker supposed to do if he wants to come home and use his garage, but he can't because you've got that big red monster parked in front of it? We don't need any more trouble around here. I don't know you and I don't know what you're up to, but there was a murder here last week. Here! Right in Mystic Springs. Do you know how much our association fees are?"

I did know, because Jack groused every time they were due, but the question seemed rhetorical.

"And they went and let a murder happen like we're living on the North End or something. I'm not afraid to tell you, I wrote a strongly worded letter. Well?"

Part of me wanted to flee the scolding, but the rest was mesmerized by the spectacle she presented. She had to have spent every day of the last fifty years slow roasting in the sun. Brown as can be, she was a mass of leathery wrinkles except for where her larger-than-life boobs protruded from her liver spotted chest. The woman I estimated to be mostly in her sixties, the twin peaks were probably just about old enough to sell Girl Scout cookies.

"Hellooo? I asked you a question?"

"So you're friends with Jack?" Harry to the rescue.

"I wouldn't go that far," she said. "He's not so bad mind you, and the man is a looker, but that wife of his thinks she can say whatever she wants and we should be grateful to hear it."

I didn't think now was the time to admit my relation.

"We're here on behalf of Mr. Dekker. This is Evin, his stepdaughter."

Thanks Harry.

"That woman is your mother?" She worked it out instantly; all that and brains too. "Do you believe she had the nerve to comment on my breasts?"

I believed.

"Let me tell you," she said. "It's nobody's business if I want to look good for Lester here."

Lester? I peered up and around, straining my neck and finally managing to catch a glimpse of what had to be Lester. I accidently caught his eye; he leaned forward and grunted.

"Would it be ok if we came in for just a minute?" Harry asked. "You are the ones who saw the Mercedes outside Jack's place on Tuesday, right?"

"I'm the one. I already talked to the police about that though."

"I completely understand, but-"

"We're busy, can't you see? We garden." There was a riot of potted greenery crammed onto the balcony. If Lester didn't get up from time to time, he would be engulfed within the month.

I could see that he had dozed off. Or something. Rough morning, I guess. Harry agreed that he could indeed see how busy they were, and promised to take mere moments of their time.

He got a huff and a reluctant invitation to come in for a moment, but only a moment mind you, because there was so much that needed doing, and nobody else was going to bother with it all.

We waited at the door for so long that I thought she'd decided against talking to us, but finally she appeared, flinging the door open and treating us to a martyred smile. At close range, her artificial endowments seemed even larger. Her mouth was freshly lipsticked.

"What kind of dog is that?"

"He's a Leonberger," I said. "His name is Gulliver."

"Humph. Beautiful animal. Well, come in, come in, already," she said, waving us inside. "Wipe your feet, why don't you? You're tracking who knows what all over my clean floor. Have a seat on the sofa there. Don't sit in the recliner whatever you do, Lester will have a fit. I suppose I should offer you some coffee or iced tea."

We eased ourselves onto the creaky wicker loveseat and assured her we were fine.

"Lester! Get in here. There's company. Some of Jack Dekker's people."

We all waited expectantly and after a painful interval, our reward waddled into the room. He looked like an elderly gnome, bowlegged and squat. His hair could have been any color once upon a time, but it was all gone now. A spray of liver spots, blending together like mutant freckles, adorned his cranium. He wore a crew neck sweater, shorts and slippers.

"I'm Wanda Glatz and this is Lester."

I found my voice and introduced Harry, Gulliver and myself. Lester let out another grunt. I chose to interpret it as a cheerful hello.

I struggled through the telling of the bodies, Jack's arrest, the shootings, Bobby Neuland's arrest and Jack's eventual release. I fumbled for a tactful way to ask why they had waited so long to provide the police with the information about Bobby Neuland's presence at Jack's on the day of the murder, but came up blank.

"Obviously, you came forward as soon as you were able," Harry said, in a freaky display of mind reading, "We were just wondering-"

"Ha. Why we didn't speak up sooner? Well, damned if we knew what was going on. If we had, we certainly would have come forward. What happened was, we were out of town for a bit. Drove all the way up north to see our daughter and grandkids, almost eight hours each way. We don't fly anymore, Lester and me. I won't let some pervert guard pat me down or scan me with those machines. And then they touch your under-things." Wanda paused; I nodded. I didn't like my under-things touched by strangers either.

"So that's what happened," she went on. "Spoiled, those kids, but cute as anything." She nodded decisively. "The boy just turned sixteen and got a spanking new car. An Audi. I ask you. But it's not our business, she says."

"Who says?" Lester had stirred himself to take part in the conversation.

"Your daughter, that's who says." Wanda patted her hair with a bejeweled hand.

"What does she say?"

"Nevermind that Lester. We were talking about the police." She dismissed him and continued. "They were here early this morning knocking on all the doors. This area is empty now except for us. Jack was staying occasionally, well, I don't have to tell you that, but not lately, even before they hauled him off."

Since Jack hadn't exactly been hauled off, this made me wary of Wanda's observational acumen.

"So, when they made it to your door you told them about the car."

"And the man. Some guy in a fancy suit. He looked like someone had gone and dressed up a gorilla. I don't mean that he was unattractive, mind you. More that he reminded me of one of those mafia dons in the movies. The police kept asking if I was sure about the day, like I couldn't remember the date of our trip."

"It was the day before we left to go see Janet," Lester said, jumping into the game.

"That's exactly right Lester," she praised. I wondered if she'd toss him a treat.

"He got here sometime after noon, that's when we do our gardening, right after we watch Rachael Ray."

Lester looked apathetic, I couldn't tell if he was down about the gardening or Rachel.

"How long was the car there?" I asked.

"We don't know to the minute, but we go inside and have our lunch, usually around twelve-thirty, and it was still right there afterwards."

"Was that the last time you saw the car? Or the man?"

"I didn't see him leave, if that's what you mean, but the last time I saw the car was, oh, probably about a quarter after one, when I left to go to the market. It was gone by the time I got home again. That's usually around two or so."

"So neither of you noticed exactly when he left?"

"Like I said, I didn't, and I don't believe Lester saw him leave either, did you?"

Lester shook his head dutifully. I wasn't entirely sure he was following the conversation.

"Did you see anyone else?" I said. "Like a younger version of Dr. Neuland. Early twenties?"

"Doesn't sound familiar."

"It might not have been the same day."

"Like I said."

I felt my phone vibrate in my back pocket. I pulled it out and tried to ignore the call but was outwitted by the damn touch screen.

I resigned myself and said, "Hello?"

"Evin," Leonie's voice sounded in my ear like a clarion. "I asked Jack who would have been likely to be lurking around spying on people coming and going and he said the most likely possibility is the dreadful couple across the way, although I wouldn't expect much help from them. I question the woman's intelligence, and the husband actually grunts. You wouldn't believe it."

I believed. Half of the dreadful couple was giving me the evil eye like I'd never seen, and the other was resting quietly, chin on chest.

"Ok, thanks, I need to go."

"What darling? I'm in the car, I can hardly hear you. Can you hear me?"

"Yes! We can all hear you." Harry was glaring right along with Wanda, but I could tell he was fighting laughter. My yell roused Lester who fished some pistachios out of his shorts pocket and began to placidly open and eat them. He either concurred with Leonie's assessment of his wife or hadn't heard it. I shouted into the phone, "Harry's with me, we're talking to the nice couple who live across from Jack."

"Hello? Darling, if you can hear me, avoid the woman who lives across from Jack. She's a harpy. She has absolutely no appreciation for people who try to give her desperately needed advice. A woman that age with implants the size of footballs-"

"Ok. Bye," I yelled and hung up.

"I think your phone was on speaker," Harry said.

Our welcome, so hard-won, had vanished.

Out we went onto the doorstep. Harry, undeterred even now said, "Just so you know, I think you look great." Sincerity shone from him like a beacon. If I could learn to do that...

"Humph. Well, I like a man who appreciates a woman with a figure," she said, "these girls today are all skin and bones. I like to say, real women have real figures."

Yeah, and big fake boobs. Hypocrite.

"Anywhoo," Wanda patted Harry's arm, "I'll tell you this because Jack Dekker has always been a fine neighbor and the Good Book says you can't hold the mistakes people make in their personal lives against them."

That was a bible I could get on board with.

"Well, let me tell you, Lester and I know what we saw, but that detective gentleman, was taking notes the whole time, and I saw in his little book that this Dr. Neuland said he was somewhere entirely different."

"And you know where?" Harry said.

She nodded and patted her hair. "He told the police he was having lunch at Oliver's. I was a secretary for forty years, I can read anybody's bad handwriting."

She gave Gulliver a pat on the head, Harry a lingering handshake, and me a curled lip and a curt nod.

The sins of the mother.

***

The three of us trundled out to the Rubicon, pausing for Gulliver to hydrate a young palm tree.

I looked at Jack's door. I'd always loved the condo, I wanted to live somewhere just like it when I grew up, but my last visit had taken the bloom off the rose.

"Maybe we should check on the place," Harry said. "Jack needs to get a biohazard cleaner to come out. Johnny's No More Smears is the best with blood."

"How do you know that? No. Nevermind. Please, nevermind." I took a breath. I didn't want to go inside. I didn't want to look like a baby either. Crap. "I think Gulliver might need to walk some more, to, umm... So if you want to just run in for a minute that's ok."

"Won't be long."

I handed over the key and Harry disappeared inside. Gulliver and I ambled down the street. It turned out he did have to, umm... I riffled through my pockets in search of a bag. Zilch. I cast my eyes around ever so casually to assess my options.

Wanda was leaning over the balcony, boobs resting on the rail, arms folded across them, looking at me expectantly. I held up a hand intending to wave, but Wanda's medusean gaze petrified the gesture. My hand just hovered at the end of my wrist until I pulled it down again.

I pointed at the gently steaming pile and raised my finger to indicate I would be right back. Gulliver and I tramped toward Jack's in search of a bag. I felt eyes between my shoulder blades like the bead of a sniper.

"Harry," I called as we stepped inside the door. I felt stifled, unable to utter any sort of lusty, attention grabbing hail.

No matter. Harry came clambering down the stairs shortly, phone to ear saying, "Great, I owe you one." He saw me and grinned. "Oh that's right. We'll call it even then. I'll leave a key outside for you. The doormat is as good as anything. It won't be for long anyway. Thanks, man."

To me he said, "I thought you were having none of this place?"

"Gulliver had to..."

"I thought that was an excuse to avoid the leftover carnage."

"Yeah, well, it was. I need to find a bag or something, I'm getting judgmental looks from Wanda. I can't take it."

Gulliver wiggled and thumped his tail against my leg. I told him not to worry. I had it all under control.

The kitchen gave up a host of old grocery bags. I stuffed a couple in my pocket for later, and took one to deal with the mess, scooping it up and depositing it in the bin by the garage. Wanda nodded sharply then retreated inside.

"We ready?" Harry asked when I strolled back into Jack's.

"Yeah, I guess. Let me wash my hands."

"How does it look up there?" I called from the sink in the kitchen. I made a face. Shouldn't have asked. I didn't really want to know.

"Not as bad as when you last saw it. Just needs some cleaning. A few things need a little throwing away, but overall it's salvageable."

"I don't think Jack's going to be here much anymore anyway. Maybe he'll sell it."

"Maybe." He looked at me, cool blue eyes in a warm, concerned face.

"I always loved this place. Too bad it's ruined." I looked around and sighed. I could have lived here, if not for the human goop upstairs. There was no question I had to get out of Leonie's now that she was back in residence. We got along much better from a distance.

We left Jack's. Harry locked the door behind us and concealed the key under the mat.

"That's the best you can come up with?"

"Shut up," Harry said and threw his arm over my shoulder.

"So off to Leonie's?" I said when we had settled in the jeep.

"Almost. Just one more stop."

Twenty-eight

The stop was at Oliver's, Bobby Neuland's lunch restaurant of choice. I perused the menu behind glass out front; I hate to be lowbrow, but I thought seventeen fifty for a salad was a little much. Plus the menu boasted veal. Ugh. Bobby probably had it every day.

I was waiting for Harry. After two drive-bys had failed to yield a parking space, he had stopped, briefly holding up traffic, for me to jump out while he went in search of the "parking in the rear," promised by a discreet brass plate.

From where I was standing, I could glimpse the dim interior. Not dim in a grungy, bring your own silverware kind of way, dim in a softly lit, exclusive, can't get in without knowing the secret handshake kind of way. The walls were lined with old literature that wasn't for sale, and local art that was.

Harry and Gulliver came striding around the corner, both adorable, in entirely different ways. Harry was casual in jeans and a rugby jersey, but still, I found myself standing straighter, shoulders back, boobs out, hips forward.

"Let's skip it and go back to my place," he said, after looking me over.

"We couldn't anyway," I said. "We'd still have to go to Leonie's."

"They'll have a better time without us."

"Eew. You ruined it." I wrinkled my nose and shoved him away, feeling his warmth through the jersey. When things went south, I would miss that chest.

"I'll run in," he said. "See if anyone knows Bobby for a start. We'll see if there's anywhere to go from there."

"Ok."

He hauled open the door and ventured inside. I could see it was mostly empty, the lunch rush over. A couple of men in power suits were propped against the bar, gin or vodka tonics sweating gently in front of them. Then the door shut behind Harry, and Gulliver and I were standing on the sidewalk looking at each other.

"It's almost over," I told him. "Soon we'll move out of your grandmother's house and find a place of our own. Maybe we'll even go somewhere else."

He responded by sprawling on the sidewalk, legs apart, head between them. Eyes shut.

"I know you like it here. I do too, sometimes. You haven't seen it in the summer though, it's brutal. You would probably need to be shaved, and I'm not sure how good that would look. It's been great having Zuzu around though. I don't know, we'll see-"

"When you're done scaring the tourists meet me in back."

I snapped to attention and saw that indeed, I was collecting wary looks from passers-by. Hypocrites. Who didn't talk to their dog occasionally? In public? On the street? Oh well.

I nudged Gulliver and around the back we went, to

find Harry and a pudgy waiter type having a smoke a few yards away from the kitchen door.

"I thought you didn't smoke?"

"I said hardly ever." Harry inhaled and let out a series of perfect rings.

I rolled my eyes. I had quit six years ago and I hated casual smokers. I was so jealous of casual smokers.

"This is Cecil." I greeted Cecil and he offered me a cigarette. I sighed, and declined.

Cecil was staring at my eyes; I lifted an eyebrow at him and stared right back.

"I didn't mean to stare," he said, and smiled at me. "Your eyes are beautiful."

I smiled back.

"I work the lunch shift. Harry here says you guys have some questions about Dr. Neuland?"

"Yeah, just wrapping a few things up." I looked at Harry, who nodded at me. I guess that was my go-ahead.

"So, you work the lunch shift, every day?"

"Yeah. Well, every weekday."

"And Bobby Neuland has lunch here every day?"

"Monday through Friday, for years."

That was a lot of overpriced salads.

"He usually has the veal," Cecil added. I knew it.

"We're really just interested in the last couple of weeks, I think."

"Well, I've been here and so has he," Cecil said. "Around twelve-thirty, every day."

"Sorry, what do you mean by around, exactly?"

"I mean he shows up every day between twelve-thirty and twelve-forty-five. I think his office is somewhere around here."

I agreed that it was.

"Every day though? Doesn't he ever have patient emergencies?"

Cecil shrugged, put out one cigarette and lit another before responding, "I have no idea. It's not like I'm friends with the guy."

I was starting to flounder. I looked at Harry.

"Does he ever meet anyone here?"

"Different girlfriends over the years. There was a hot blond, that he saw pretty consistently for like six months but she hasn't been in for weeks. His daughter has been in with him a couple times lately."

"Reina?" I asked, and made a face. Of course Reina, what other daughter was there?

"I didn't get her name," Cecil was saying, eyeing my facial contortions impassively. An experienced waiter could ignore a variety of questionable behaviors. "She's hot though right? Long hair, short skirts, high heels?"

I confirmed that and added "nose job," to the list.

"She was here Thursday. Dr. Neuland was already here and she joined him. Seemed happy about something."

"Herself?" I suggested. Cecil laughed.

"I don't know. She's usually pretty reserved, kind of above it all, but Thursday she was excited, happy. Kept hugging Dr. Neuland and straightening his tie, things like that. I thought maybe he got good news and she was congratulating him."

"You didn't hear what they were talking about?"

"Sorry, not really."

"But maybe a little," I said, all charm.

"It sounded like they were making up or something. I'm not sure, I have other tables, I can't just sit there and eavesdrop."

"If they were making up, what was the fight

about?"

"I have no idea." Cecil laughed and checked his Movado. I guess fifteen to twenty percent of lunch receipts at Oliver's wasn't too shabby. "Sorry. And also, I've got to go."

"Wait, you said a couple of times, have you seen her since then?"

He considered and said, "No. That was the last time. Before that was a couple of weeks ago."

"You sure she wasn't here Tuesday?"

"I'm sure. Tuesdays we have shrimp bisque."

"And?"

"That's the only soup Dr. Neuland eats here. Otherwise he has a salad, bleu cheese."

"And Reina hasn't been in on a soup day?"

"Nope."

We thanked him for his time and he disappeared into the kitchen.

"He was helpful," I said to Harry.

"We tip well."

Bribery. I liked it. I looked at Gulliver and he thumped his tail on the asphalt. He liked it too.

"You park back here?"

"Yeah," Harry said, pointing me in the right direction.

He opened the door and I hopped in after Gulliver. Harry leaned in and kissed me on the neck. I shivered. I turned my head and brushed his lips with mine. Addictive.

My stomach churned. When Harry and I were over, I'd have another ex in the same small town. I wriggled out of his arms, away from his lips, too nervous to enjoy the moment.

"You smell like smoke," I said.

"Sorry." He took his place in the driver's seat and

off we went, headed for Leonie's.

"What do you think?"

"About?"

"Everything. Well, about the discrepancies. Between what Cecil says and what Wanda and Lester say."

"It could be any number of things," Harry said.

"Someone lying? Cecil sees Bobby every day. Maybe Bobby bribed him to support his alibi."

"It could be some mistake about the time. Neuland could have been at Jack's earlier than Wanda thought."

I agreed. "It does feel iffy for everything to be timed on when Wanda and Lester eat lunch."

"It doesn't matter. Jack is off the hook. That's what we wanted right? Life goes on. We have a celebration to get to."

"Do you think Bobby will go to jail?"

"You mean be convicted?" I nodded. "I don't know. It seems like a slam dunk, but then so did O.J."

I snorted. Bobby probably still had the money Candace had tried to extort. A ready-made defense fund with more where that came from. I hoped Bobby-call-me-Robert's trial had a better result than O.J.'s had.

"Want to grab dinner later?"

"Yeah. I don't know. Maybe." I felt my insides squelching. I glanced at Harry, made accidental eye contact and whipped my face around towards the window.

"Don't let me feed you against your will."

"I'm not good at this."

"You're not doing great right now." Harry's voice was tight.

"I know. I don't want another ex right now. It's a

small town and I might be here for awhile."

"We're on the verge of breaking up, then? How does that work? I just got a firm 'maybe' for your attendance of our first date." When I glanced sideways, from the corner of my eye I saw white knuckles on the wheel. Harry's voice was tight. "What makes you think I'd want a second?"

"That wouldn't be much fun either. I'm sorry," I said again. "You've been amazing. You're a great friend to Jack. To all of us."

"I'm not sure I'm your friend," Harry said. He looked like he might have more to say, but he didn't say it because we had arrived at Leonie's. Gulliver, unaffected by the tension, shook himself vigorously and stretched.

Jack and my mother were oblivious to anyone's angst. The party atmosphere prevailed, alcohol flowed, and veggie burgers sizzled on the grill.

"Darling, and Harry darling. What took you so long?"

"We just got back," Jack clapped Harry on the back and passed him a beer.

"It's been twenty minutes," Leonie said. "If I wasn't so thrilled I would be furious at your lack of priorities."

Lucky me.

I found myself engulfed in Jack's arms, breathing in the familiar scent of Cool Water while Leonie beamed.

"Didn't I tell you Harry would be helpful?" Jack said when we broke apart.

"Yeah, you did. And he was." I smiled all around, blinking away the blur.

"Drinks darling?"

"One for now."

"Where's Zuzu? You should invite her."

I should. I made the call. Left a message. There.

"So he's fine?" I said to my mother. "Not traumatized or anything?

Leonie let out a sparkly laugh. "Not that he mentioned. What worries me is that he made friends in there, and I feel uncomfortable thinking of them showing up for a visit."

I couldn't deny it was a possibility. Our best hope was that Jack's prison buddies were fraudulent bankers and shoplifters rather than murderers.

We went outside to join the menfolk.

Afternoon turned to evening and so on. Zuzu called at some point to say she couldn't make it, but she'd love to congratulate Jack, which she did when I passed him the phone.

I could feel Harry's gaze from time to time, it felt like he was expecting something. I wasn't sure what it was; if it was even anything I had to give.

Finally, the party wound down. All I wanted was to crawl into bed and sleep, sleep, sleep. Gulliver was lounging next to the couch with a fat belly from all the treats he'd wolfed down.

Leonie was kissing Harry goodbye. I waited my turn, thinking I might walk him out, but as usual, no one followed the script in my mind.

"Ok, darling," Leonie said to me, "I've booked you a room at the Riviera and Gulliver is welcome there."

"What?" I said.

"Harry darling, I made the reservation for two adults, in case. Of course, it's up to Evin. Don't worry if she's troublesome at first. She has terrible taste in men. Traditionally. I'm sure she'll come around soon."

I was speechless. It was one thing to be Absolutely Truthful about your own life, but she needed to leave me out of it.

"Why am I going to a hotel?" I asked, because I was ignoring the issue of Harry along with my attendant mortification.

"Well darling, I know you hate it when I'm explicit, but the truth is we don't want anyone else here tonight. I find it rather selfish that you didn't volunteer to go. Besides, children don't like to be around when their parents are having sex. It will just upset you. Not that we have anything to hide. If you'd like I'll tell you all about it tomorrow."

"No. Thanks though."

"Think of it as the adult version of movie money."

"What am I supposed to do about therapy money?"

"I don't care, darling. I paid for your therapy when you were twelve." When I was twelve, Leonie had been a nudist for three months, two weeks and six days. Jack and I had refused to participate. "This round is on you."

I gathered my dog and twenty-four hours worth of belongings and loaded my little car.

When I turned back to the house, I found that the door had been firmly closed against us. Talk about unseemly haste.

"That was ridiculous," I said to Harry.

"Leonie knows what she wants."

"Hey," I said.

"It wasn't a shot."

"It sounded like one." Felt like one.

"You're imagining things."

"Are we really not friends?" It seemed harsh after everything.

"Are you really turning down dinner?" I'm sure that had never happened to him before.

"You know my family," I said. "I would still have to

see you when things…"

"What do you think I'm going to do to you?"

It was what he wouldn't do. Continue to put up with my moods. Find jealously charming. Love the neuroses.

"Nothing."

"Whatever you want, Evin."

"I want you to stop being mad."

"I'm not mad." He shrugged. "I'm not impressed with your reasons."

"My reasons are fine."

"There's only one. And it's not a good one."

I ignored that.

"Why can't we be friends?" I said. Maybe Harry could get fat and give up on hygiene to make things easier.

"Friend friends, or friendly friends?" He looked me up and down as though he'd never seen me naked, but had a yen.

"Friend friends," I said, and then, "for now," slipped out after.

"Ok. If you want to be friends, we're friends. I'll see you." He walked away. I heard his footsteps heading down the driveway, but I didn't turn my head. I listened to a door slam, the motor catch, and finally to the Rubicon roar away taking Harry with it.

"Bye," I said to the taillights.

Twenty-nine

Check-in was a nightmare. While Leonie had called ahead to make a reservation and find out if the hotel accepted dogs, the fact that the dogs were expected to weigh in somewhere under thirty pounds had escaped her. Once I had hauled the bags, Gulliver and myself inside, I had to spend half an hour explaining my tale of woe to everyone from the girl at the front desk to the general manager. In return for their generous accommodation, I was charged a onetime fee of two hundred dollars, twice the usual rate for a pet. I would have been slightly better off if they had charged me by the pound. I also had to sign a two page contract outlining what was, and what was not, acceptable behavior for dogs and their guardians at the Riveria.

Throughout the ordeal, the front desk girl was sweet as could be, which was more than I could say for myself.

An adolescent bellboy led us to our third floor room. I'd considered upgrading to a suite, to punish Leonie for my exile, as well as all the confusion, but had managed to pull some maturity out of my ass at the last minute.

The room we were assigned topped two hundred,

before the pet charge. A suite would have been close to twice that. It was jazzy and plush though, worth every penny, especially since they weren't my pennies.

I dredged some cash out of the depths of my purse for the kid who'd hauled my bags and handed it over. He stammered something without meeting my eyes and backed nervously out the door. Maybe Gulliver concerned him.

We were hungry. At least I was, and Gulliver can always eat. In short order we were strolling leash and hand down to Palm Canyon to see what we could find to sustain ourselves.

We settled on Hamburger Mary's. It's pricey, but they have a decent veggie burger, and those of the canine persuasion are welcome in the patio area.

I was sipping my coke and perusing the menu; Gulliver had already been served. He was having a bone and a bowl of water.

"Does your husband let you go out of the house dressed like that? Or your boyfriend?"

I turned to find myself being examined by a string-bean sexagenarian. Most of his hair was AWOL and what was left made a frizzy circlet around the back of his head. He was clad in a Hawaiian shirt that was unbuttoned a pair too far, revealing bushy white chest hair. The growth on his chest matched what was sprouting from his ears. His pinky was adorned with a large gold ring, which was bad, but nothing compared to the scaly feet encased in Tevas.

Physical revulsion aside, I lacked the patience to suffer the sad mating dance of some guy whose approach to romance was to imply that I was a subservient slut.

My dream lover was leering down my tank top, begging for some elder abuse. If I had been a man, I could have kicked his wrinkly ass, but since I am slight and untrained in physical combat, the odds of me delivering a successful beating to anyone were discouraging.

I was also hampered by the inconvenient notion that beating children and seniors is plain wrong.

No matter how much they deserve it.

"Both. I have both," I said. "They don't let me do anything though, so I snuck out. I'm actually supposed to be barefoot in the kitchen right now. And pregnant. But ever since I started wearing these pants..."

He chortled. Spittle flew. I cringed.

"You're an uppity little thing. But that's a fine rack you have there, so maybe we can work it out. That your dog?" He peered down to assess Gulliver, then took a step back.

"Yes."

"He bite?"

"Yes."

"You know, that's my Caddy over there." He nodded toward a powder blue monstrosity in a curbside handicapped space.

The best thing I could say about it was that it looked expensive. It did nothing to elevate my suitor from unsavory to alluring. That vehicle didn't exist.

He leaned toward me as far as his decrepit body would allow and said, "What's wrong with your eyes? You lose a contact lens or something?"

"Nothing's wrong with them." I was pulling out a five to cover the coke, in preparation for a speedy getaway.

"Well sweetheart, I don't want to alarm you," he said, using his age thick nails to scratch parts best left unscratched in public, "but one of them is blue and the other one's brown."

The only thing alarming about this encounter was the thought of the chest hairs he was loosing upon the world with his energetic scratching.

"You're right. I'd better take a look. Excuse us," I said, edging past.

"You're missing out."

"On what? Spoon feeding you fiber sprinkled with little blue pills?"

My aged Lothario leaned down and said, "You're a vain little bitch, you know that?"

My love life never works out.

Now that he was closer, I could see he had white goo in the corners of his mouth. I wondered if it was residue from his denture cream or something organic. Either way, it deserved a shudder. I took my dog and fled.

Back in the room we watched TV. I looked for a movie, but there was nothing good that I hadn't already seen, and nothing that I'd seen was good enough to watch again.

I went with reruns. And commercials. I almost ordered a new mop, but I had nothing to mop. I considered the Perfect Puppy Harness, but when I brought it up to Gulliver, he wasn't impressed. The Mercedes commercial was kind of a downer; SL class nicely equipped from the low 100,000's. The things I wanted, I couldn't afford and the things I could afford no one wanted.

The room phone rang. It was Zuzu.

"Hey Ev," she said before I could speak.

"Hey. How'd you know we were here?"

"Jack told me before. We is...?"

"Gulliver and I. He told you before what?" I was on the verge of pissed.

"Before, when I talked to him on the phone. You

were there."

"He told you before I knew?"

"I don't know when you knew Evin. No Harry?"

"No. I'm stuck with no one to talk to."

"So talk is what you're missing?"

"Yeah. Talk." Maybe Jack would buy me a Benz to make it up to me. I asked Zuzu what she thought the chances were.

"Of Jack buying you a car?"

"Leonie could chip in too. This was her idea."

"You need a night in a nice hotel made up to you?"

"Kind of. And don't put it like that." I fiddled with the phone cord, wrapping the coil round and round my pinky.

"Why?"

"Because it makes me sound…"

"Spoiled?" Zuzu offered.

"Shut up."

"Ungrateful?"

"I'm hanging up."

"Obnoxious? Ok, sorry, I'm done. Why isn't Harry there?"

"Because. I don't know. I don't know what's wrong with him."

"With *him*?"

"There's always something. Or it really is me, in which case I'm doomed."

"Doomed?" Zuzu said.

I sighed and flopped back on the bed. Gulliver licked my face. "I don't want to talk about it."

"Then don't." Instead, she proceeded to talk about it. "Harry is a doll. I know you don't trust your judgment, but there's nothing wrong with mine."

"You went out with a toe-sucker."

"Irrelevant. Harry's perfect."

"I'm not, though."

"So? It will all even out."

"I wish it worked like that." I said, and made excuses to get off the phone.

"It doesn't work like that, right?" I asked Gulliver. He had nothing to say.

Harry seemed good. Really good. Harry wouldn't cheat. Probably. He would never kill me over money. Definitely not. He didn't seem like a crier. I felt sure he relieved himself only in appropriate places, though I found it disheartening that this was now something I had to consider. He seemed happy with his job, so probably he didn't have a secret yen to do porn. But, there was always something.

With my record, I'd probably end up with a Dr. Bobby of my own. Bobby Neuland showed no signs of loving anyone, certainly not the women he slept with. And still Verona had come like a shot when he'd been questioned. Of course that was probably more for the twins' sake. Children tie you together forever. That reminded me to take my birth control pill.

Because eventually, children will turn on you, although admittedly sometimes they had good reason. Take Rex. But was Rex so hostile he'd kill the woman his father had stolen from him? No. It was pointless from that angle. Bobby wasn't heartbroken. Grossly inconvenienced sure, but in spite of the slow-growing pile of evidence, I thought Bobby had a decent chance of getting off. If Rex had killed Candace, it was because he still hated her.

And unless they'd had proof that Rex killed Candace, there'd been no reason for him to kill Maggie or his stepmother. There had been reason for Bobby. They had conspired to blackmail him.

I didn't care. Jack was on the loose and I could go

back to fixing my own life. Tomorrow. I finally found a decent movie to watch and settled back. At some point, my appetite returned. Room service snappily agreed to bring sustenance and I ordered extra for Gulliver.

Shortly, yet another cute young thing arrived with a laden tray and arranged it appealingly on the table. He wasn't afraid of Gulliver so I upped his tip.

"I appreciate it, Ma'am," he said.

I raised an eyebrow at the *Ma'am*, and he caught my meaning.

"They make us say, 'Sir' or 'Ma'am'," he said. "It's not like you look like one. You're like twenty-four right?"

"Twenty-five," I said easily. Thus vanity does make liars of us all.

"I was close."

I smiled and said, "The fries are amazing." I hadn't had the decency to wait until he had gone before indulging myself.

"I have them almost every shift," he said. "Have a good night."

"Hang on," I said. His tie was askew. I reached out to fix it and found out it was a clip on. I tucked it back in and ran it through my fingers to straighten it.

"Crap. I'm sorry." My fingers had left behind smudges of grease and salt.

"Don't sweat it. I'm almost off anyway."

He gave Gulliver a pat and me a jaunty wave and was gone.

As we ate I smiled to myself. Cute waiters thought I was twenty-four. I considered one a solid representative sample. Maybe I was vain. Just a little. Certainly not as vain as some people. Like Eddie Daigle.

Like Eddie Daigle. My thoughts were whirling

around, fitting together, and then not, like a puzzle in a cyclone. I pulled up Google on my phone, and started searching. Either the information wasn't on the web, or I wasn't stringing words properly. After ten minutes of fruitless skimming, I screamed and hurled my phone across the room.

I was sure it was possible. I hoped it was possible. I chewed on my lip for a minute and realized I could just call Harry, he would know. As would Detective Quick. De la Cruz. Of course better to ask someone who wasn't currently pissed at me. A stranger on the street would suffice. I'd just go with Harry. He couldn't arrest me for interfering with an investigation. I steadfastly ignored my other motivations.

My phone, when I retrieved it, was dead. I mentally condemned the brand. If technology can't take an occasional impact with a hotel wall, it's not for me.

That meant Harry was out, as were Quick and De la Cruz. I had none of their numbers committed to memory.

I dialed Leonie on the hotel phone and listened while the call went to voicemail. I left a message saying I needed Harry's number.

I upended my purse on the bed and found a business card. I used the hotel phone one more time. Eddie picked up right away and I asked my question.

I pictured the shamed expression he would be wearing on the other end of the line. I was right about the vanity. Liars of us all. Or, at least, a key some of us. Male pride would be the undoing of our semi-civilized world.

"And that's what you told the police?" I wanted to be sure.

I listened to the panicky affirmative, said, "Idiot,"

to both of us, and hung up.

I stewed and paced around the room. I decided I would just go over to Harry's. Not that I'm a fan of women insisting men do all the dirty work. However, when it came to me not being murdered, I was ready to embrace my inner hypocrite.

"I'll be back," I told Gulliver, but he stood up and whined softly through his nose.

Damn.

"Gulliver. Can you hold it?" In his doggy way, he told me that he could not. "Ok, ok. But please pee fast."

I hustled Gulliver into the elevator and out through the lobby. The door was opened for us by the same frosty haired little hard body who had been working when we arrived.

"Still working?" I said. It was inane, obviously he was. Nothing made me feel more like an asshole than trying to make polite conversation with a stranger.

"Yes, Ma'am."

Gulliver pulled me away from the door. We headed down Indian toward Ramon. We were barely out of sight of the hotel's front entrance when my beloved dog produced one of the biggest piles of poop I had ever seen. I fished a bag out of my pocket. It had a hole. I tried to focus on the fact that I'd noticed in time to avoid getting shit all over my bare hand. I dug deep in my pocket for another bag, which was intact and sufficed.

We about-faced. Gulliver had one more trick up his... anyway. I was out of bags, so I scooped up the new mess as well as I could, using the torn bag to transfer the latest heap into the intact one.

I tied it all up gingerly, managing to keep the biohazard on the inside. Gulliver sniffed the bag and wagged his tail. Whether he was relieved or proud, I had no idea.

"Good job. Now let's go," I told him. "I'm going to drop you off in the room, because, well it will probably be fine, but I want you to be safe just in case, ok? And look for a trash can, would you?"

The first one I spotted was outside the hotel door. It was the stone kind with an ashtray on top. I took it as a sign that the doorman had abandoned his post, and I tossed the odorous bag right in as we sailed by. Tacky as hell, but these were closely akin to desperate times. The elevator was waiting on the other side of the lobby to whisk us up to the room.

I washed my hands, situated Gulliver, and put the room service leftovers in the hallway on my way out.

When I got down to the lobby, the doorman was back at his post. He watched me approach, intently. Either he was suddenly into me or I was busted.

I was busted.

"That's not mine," I said as I approached. He held the familiar bag between two fingers and away from his body. His expression didn't change.

"I love dogs myself," he said, "and it's wonderful that so many places are able to accommodate them. It's a shame when people take advantage, don't you think?"

I glanced around to see if anyone was witnessing my dressing down. The lobby was scantly populated and the few people who were within sight weren't focused on me.

"Look sweetie, I don't mean to put you on the spot, but the smell was wafting in and we can't have that. Ok?"

I thought he was supposed to call me "Ma'am."

"Sorry," I said. "But I'm really in a hurry, so do you think maybe-"

"Did you read the contract you signed pertaining to the care and supervision required for pets on our premises?"

"Fine," I said, and took the bag.

"There's a dumpster around back. At the west edge of the parking lot. You self-parked I believe?"

"Yeah, thanks." It seemed I was expected to feel bad about that too. The thing is, the Thunderbird is delicate. I'm the only one who understands how it should be driven. I wanted to tell him that at least I wouldn't steal the towels.

Anne Stinnett

Thirty

I took my bag of poop and my humiliation and followed the drive around to the parking lot behind the hotel. When I spotted the dumpster I hesitated, it was across the lot from my car. I debated whether walking all the way across the lot was worse than driving a massively stinky bag of excrement to the bin.

I sighed and trudged away from my car; it had enough problems without adding a revolting smell.

It was nearly pitch here, away from the lights of the street. The moon glowed faintly from behind a bank of clouds; shedding minimal light. I heard an engine rev somewhere behind me and was relieved not to be alone. When I heard the tires squeal, I glanced back and quit being relieved. The car was speeding towards me, bright lights on and blinding. I had time, barely, to throw myself behind a lonely little Accord. My surprise when the Honda was rammed was nothing to the shock I felt when I hit the ground fifteen feet away. The second-hand impact forcibly expelled every whisper of breath from my body. There were lights flashing now and something was blaring. I hoped for the police, for Quick with his condescending looks and suspicion, for De la Cruz and his perpetual annoyance with me.

It wasn't the cops. It was just the alarm blaring from the little Accord, doing its damndest to attract some sort of attention. I wished it luck.

I couldn't breathe, but I rolled, aiming my battered self for the line of cars behind the crippled Honda.

I didn't make it. I heard footsteps coming fast behind me and I tensed for a bullet, still trying to get air. Trying to get away. When the bullet didn't come, I remembered that the gun was safely in police custody.

Instead, something dug brutally into my back. Not a knife. I would know if there was a knife in my back. Belatedly, I realized that it was a knee. It wasn't helping my wind any.

"I'm going to kill you, bitch." *I* was a bitch?

Before I could squeak a reply, I lost what little breath I had gathered to a jab from the knee that was pinning me down.

I struggled to leverage myself slightly off the ground. I was getting shallow breaths now. Not enough. I got my hands under me and heaved, twisting my torso as it left the ground. I was on my knees now. Better. Still not great. I reached out, groping for a weapon of some sort, but I was having trouble because she'd captured a fistful of hair and was wrenching my head back.

I gasped for air. My neck felt like it was tearing.

My fingers were still seeking something with which I could hit, stab or shoot. I strained in another direction and made contact. It wasn't a traditional weapon, but I grasped it with the tips of my fingers. I wiggled it closer; finally got a grip on it. All my might went into the upswing. My arm flew over my head, my hand holding tight to my makeshift bludgeon. A sock full of quarters would have done more damage. Sometimes, you have to make do.

I made contact. With a "POW" and a "SPLAT" that would have earned me an honorary cape from Adam West, I hit Reina Neuland smack in the face with the massive bag of shit. It couldn't have done much damage. The whole thing was smooshy as hell. Damage or no, she shrieked and jumped off me like I had just spontaneously combusted.

I got a foot under me, then another, and staggered around until I was leaning against the battered Honda Accord. It was blue. I gave it a pat for being there for me.

A stream of invective was flowing from Reina's mouth and a quantity of excrement was dribbling down her person. So much for L.A. perfect.

"You ruined everything, you fucking bitch! I'm going to kill you and your stupid boyfriend and I'm going to kill your disgusting dog."

Too far. "At least I won't die smelling like shit." Although really, that was less than comforting. Definitely better to smell like shit and live. What I needed to do was run. I didn't feel up to it.

"You got my dad arrested."

"You planted a murder weapon in his office," I said. "You rubbed gunpowder residue on his suit."

"That was just in case." She sprang. I evaded as well as I could.

"Just in case what?" I said. Reina was between me and my car, between me and the hotel entrance.

"In case they let your stupid stepfather go." She scrambled over the hood of the car and threw a kick at me. I ducked it and tried to get the car between us again. Before I had completed a stride, I felt an impact and my head rocked on my already tender neck.

Reina Neuland, daddy's girl extraordinaire, had punched me. My head ached out of proportion to the blow. Whether by chance or choice her fist had landed on my stitches.

Without thinking, I hauled off and gave her my best shot. Thanks to my half-assed attendance of a college self-defense course, my best shot was a kick to the crotch. I missed. My foot glanced off a toned thigh and I lost my balance.

I managed to stagger right back up.

By then she was on me, screaming, throwing girlie blows. They still hurt. My back was against the Honda. I managed to get a leg up and used my knee to push her away. She staggered back and I wasted no time scrambling around the car.

She lunged. I sidestepped. My only goal was to keep something between us.

I patted my ass, looking for my phone and remembered I had sent it sailing across the hotel room. It might be time to think about cutting down on the tantrums. Reina's certainly wasn't attractive. Of course, some of her lost appeal was due to the shiny new fecal coating.

The Honda still stood bravely between Reina and I. I kept trying to get to the other side so I could break away and run for the hotel, but Reina was anticipating that obvious move. We were still feinting back and forth, trading curses, when the buff little doorman made an excellently timed arrival, with a uniformed security guard in tow.

The guard was female and unarmed. She was tall though, and muscular. Her hair was bound in a jaunty ponytail that was at odds with her serious face. She came equipped with handcuffs and with the help of the doorman, Reina was soon gingerly but adequately, restrained.

"I called the police," he said, "Are you ok?"

"Mostly." There was some blood on the outside that should have been in, but I seemed essentially intact.

"You look a little... Your face needs attention, I believe."

I felt like my entire body needed attention.

"I came out immediately when I heard the crash, but I thought I needed help, so I ran back to get Michelle."

"Do you have a phone?" I said, then sat down on a parking stop. He produced a cell and handed it to me. I nodded my thanks and dialed Zuzu.

When she heard what had happened, she said I was to come over immediately and stay with her. I couldn't leave yet, and asked if she would let Leonie or Jack know what happened. Of course, she offered to come, but I told her everything would be drawn out and boring and there was no reason for her to sit through it. We hung up after I promised to call back shortly.

"Maybe we could wait inside for the police," I said, because I was getting cold.

"We're not taking her inside," my little doorman said.

Right. Reina was quite unpleasant, a genuine olfactory assault. I probably wasn't much better.

"Anyway, I think I hear them coming."

I listened and when Reina stopped ranting to breathe, I heard them too.

"What's your name anyway?" I said.

"Charlie."

"Thanks, Charlie."

The first thing I said to Quick was, "If you want me to go to that damn station again, you're going to have to arrest me." I'd meant to sound brave and humorous; if I succeeded, the effect was completely ruined when I burst into tears.

"I don't think that will be necessary tonight." Quick produced a crisp tissue from an inner pocket and handed it over.

The paramedics arrived and someone ushered me over to sit in the ambulance. I could see De la Cruz was on scene. I could hear him arguing with another officer. It seemed no one wanted Reina in their squad car.

"You got here fast," I said to Quick. "Usually I have to wait for you."

"If it's inconvenient, feel free to stop participating in my murder investigations. I got here fast because I was having dinner down the street."

"That's lucky, I guess." I saw an officer, who I thought was Hoffman, putting Reina in the back of a car.

"This is not great for us. The department or me personally." He was rattling something around in his pockets.

"You mean all the false arrests."

"Previous arrests."

"Well, it looks like this one's the charm," I said.

"On the bright side, we haven't released any information about Dr. Neuland to the press so we saved some embarrassment there. However, it would have been better if you had come to us instead of acting on your own."

"I would have come to you if I'd actually known anything. I just watching TV and there was this commercial and I wanted a new car, but I can't afford one really, and then I ordered room service, and the fries were greasy, so-"

Quick held up a hand. I stopped.

"I'll be back," he said. "I'd rather get the entire story in one sitting. If you would prefer to wait inside, once they're finished with you here, I'll be along shortly."

I preferred.

The paramedic fussing with my face told me it wasn't so bad. The stitches had somehow come through intact. He cleaned and sterilized the areas that needed it and I was good to go. In theory.

What I really wanted was a hot shower followed by a hot bath. If I hurried, I might have time to grab one of those.

I made my way inside. Charlie wasn't at the door. I went through the lobby, up in the elevator, and on to my room, where I headed straight for the bathroom. With the shower turned to boiling, I gingerly scrubbed everything I could reach without cringing and hoped the flow of water would take care of the rest.

When I was done, I donned a plush hotel robe and flopped down on the bed next to Gulliver with my head pillowed on his side.

Twenty minutes later there was a knock on the door.

"When I said you could come inside, I meant to the lobby," Quick said.

"It's good to be specific."

Quick pulled a chair out from the table and settled himself in it. One of the posse of two he'd brought with him stood inside the door, the other stayed in the hallway. Neither was familiar.

"Reina Neuland says you've been stalking her and her entire family. She says you set up first her father, and then her."

"I say she murdered three women for money."

"The money that Candace Brown extorted from

Dr. Neuland?"

"Yeah." I was too tired for this. I was sick of the whole mess, sick of people all around me, sick and unbelievably tired of hurting. I just wanted to be alone. Maybe forever.

When Harry arrived, I was still sick of everything, but I thought maybe, I didn't want to be completely alone. Not always.

"I got three separate calls saying you were in dire need," he said from the doorway.

"I think I might be. He can come in," I said to the cop at the door, but it wasn't until Quick gave a nod that Harry was allowed by.

I reached out a hand to him before I really thought about it, he quirked an eyebrow that I knew was meant to let me know he hadn't forgotten about earlier. He took my hand though, and sat next to me, which was enough for now. I started talking.

Thirty-one

Twenty minutes later, I was still at it. To be precise, at it again. Quick had asked me to run through what I knew in chronological order. The first telling had been rather disjointed. As was I.

"Six or eight months ago," I said, "Rex Neuland was a typical rich kid. He worked, but he was living in a house his dad had put the down payment on. He went to Vegas whenever he had the time and cash which was often. Then he met Candace Brown who was a showgirl in Vegas."

"Who wanted to get out of that lifestyle," Harry said.

"He must have loved her," I said. "To still be so angry."

"Then she left him for a bigger meal ticket." Quick, once again, was making good use of his notebook.

"And the meal ticket happened to be his father. That's why Rex stopped speaking to Bobby, and started working all the time to pay him back. He wanted Bobby out of his life."

"Simple," Quick said.

"We thought it could be Rex," Harry said, "When we found out about his history with Candace." That history, I had eventually realized, had been why

Verona had reacted so strongly to the news of Candace's death. Verona had feared her son would be implicated in the demise of his ex.

"But he had no motive for killing Hazel or Maggie." Quick's pen was still scratching away, as Harry talked. "Unless, they had stumbled on proof he had killed Candace. And with Hazel and Candace being stabbed within hours of each other, it seemed far-fetched."

"Did it?" Quick's voice was dry.

"Yeah. Ok, next twin," I said. "When Reina came back from college, Bobby bought her a graduation present, a new Benz. Then she wanted him to buy her a townhouse, up on the hill, in Rancho Mirage. I mean, why not? It would seem like a reasonable request, I suppose, if you and your dad are driving around in matching hundred thousand dollar cars."

During our first go-round, Quick had admitted that the matching cars had never come up. Wanda Glatz had supplied a license plate number that matched Bobby's and there had been no reason to suspect a ringer.

"But he didn't give in on the townhouse."

"I think he would have, but by then Hazel had started to have suspicions that Bobby was cheating on her. They had a pre-nup, which was nullified by cheating."

I paused, and Quick nodded. "So that's when he dumped Candace. He was hoping to mollify Hazel, and avoid the divorce so he didn't lose half of everything to the community property laws."

"And Mrs. Neuland was willing to forget."

"Until Candace contacted Hazel and told her Bobby had been promising to leave her so he could marry Candace. Or at least, live in sin with her in

Hazel's house. And Candace had proof."

"So the blackmail scheme was born." It wasn't quite a question, but I nodded anyway.

"Hazel left Bobby and stayed at Maggie's. They'd been friends forever. Candace needed to take off too, but she didn't have anywhere to go. Bobby leased her apartment and had a key, so you can see why she didn't want to stay there once she started blackmailing him. She was conspiring with Hazel, but Hazel didn't want her around. Since Hazel was staying with Maggie, Maggie put Candace up for a few days at Jack's place, because she knew Jack was staying at my mother's. Maggie was the go-between for Candace and Hazel."

"When we found out about the blackmail, we thought it was Bobby," I said. "But, I wondered, why both of them? I mean, if his motive was solely financial, killing one or the other would have done the trick. He could have killed Candace to keep her from feeding Hazel fun facts about the affair, or he could have cut out the middleman and just killed Hazel."

"And where did you come in?" Quick said to Harry.

"Friend of the family," Harry said a bit too pointedly. "I've known Jack since I was a kid. I wanted to help clear him, but other than that I'm not overly concerned with what the Neulands were doing or who they were doing it to." He looked at me and added, "Until now."

"The blackmail was intended to hurt Bobby, and give Hazel and Candace what they felt they were owed. One of the side effects was that, for the first time, Reina didn't get what she wanted. According to Trina, Rex's roommate, there was quite a ruckus." I looked at Harry for confirmation. He nodded.

"So you have Reina Neuland finding out her condo

money has gone to pay blackmail to her father's mistress."

"That's what I think, yes. I don't know exactly how she found out. It could have been any number of ways. She was living with him, and she was working at his office, so she could easily have intercepted a phone call, or come across an email or note. It could also have been that she was snooping. From what everyone says, he had never denied her anything. I'm sure she wanted to know why it was happening now."

"You could have asked her." Harry treated me to his infectious grin. "How she found out about the blackmail. What were you doing all that time in the parking lot?"

"It didn't come up," I said, and hid my smile.

"So you figured it was Reina because…?"

"I never really thought of Reina," I said. "I mean not past the fact that she's a bitch. I thought from the beginning that she had an alibi."

"When I talked to Eddie, that day at the salon, he told me he had lunch plans with Reina on the day Candace and Hazel were killed. But when I thought back, his phrasing struck me. He only mentioned plans, not the actual lunch. So I called him." Thinking about the vain little lie I had told the waiter about my age had led me to wonder if Eddie was so vain that he would mislead everyone about his date with Reina, rather than admit she'd stood him up.

He was.

I watched Quick jot a note about Eddie and went on.

"We were stuck until the gun was found in Bobby's office." I squeezed Harry's hand. I had majorly glossed over anything having to do with De la Cruz. "We did go out to talk to Rex again anyway, when we found out about him and Candace."

I was tired of talking. Harry took over when I nudged him.

"While we were there, we talked to Trina again. She told us about the powder residue that you found on Bobby's clothes."

"And then when you released Jack," I said, "we found out about Bobby's car being at the condo the day Candace was killed. So we figured we were done."

"You never should have started." Quick said.

I shrugged that off.

"I did wonder if Bobby could have been telling the truth about being at the restaurant," I said. "I remembered that Wanda and Lester had gone inside for lunch. After that, I wondered if someone could have been there after Bobby. But I didn't put it together with Reina having an identical car until later."

The last voicemail Candace had left had said, "He just drove back up." But it had been Reina, who must have waited around the corner for Bobby to leave.

"So it was room service that led to your revelation?" Quick wasn't exactly ridiculing me, but he wasn't about to give me a pat on the head either.

"I got grease on my fingers, and salt." I sighed, so Quick wou ld know I was ready to wrap this up. "I straightened the waiter's tie, and I got it all over him, which made me think about the residue, and Cecil the other waiter, telling us that when Reina came in Thursday she was hugging Bobby and fussing with his clothes, straightening his tie."

"Transference is a problem," Quick said. "The courts haven't considered residue conclusive for quite some time."

Well, good for the courts. But I had thought of it all on my own.

"Reina and Bobby had been fighting about the townhouse," I went on. "Both Trina and Julia mentioned it. But the day Maggie was shot, she showed up at Bobby's usual lunch spot. According to the waiter, she was very affectionate. Gave him a hug, straightened his tie. So I thought, if she had just shot Maggie and she went straight to the restaurant, she could have transferred some of the powder residue to him."

I felt pleased. I waited graciously for my credit.

Quick waited for me to go on. I gave in.

"However she found out about Candace, Reina showed up at Jack's place shortly after Bobby left, killed Candace and took the blackmail money. You never found it, did you? The money?"

Quick regarded me briefly before shaking his head.

"We will," he said.

"From the letters, we know that Candace kept copies of everything. But the copies-" I stopped because Harry was crushing my fingers. Quick was looking sterner than usual. I tried to figure out what I'd said wrong. Finally, my fried brain put it together. I shouldn't admit we had searched Jack's condo or Candace's things.

"But the copies," I said again, "I never heard anything about the copies. Were those found?"

Quick let me know he knew I was full of shit, in his official, mannered way. Then he admitted that Candace's copies of the letters had not been found.

"So Reina found Candace's copies, took the money and headed off to Maggie's house because she knew Hazel was there from the letters." I let out a breath. I needed a drink.

"Unbelievable."

I felt like I was included in that condemnation, so I took exception. Gulliver woke up and took exception too. Harry helped me calm him down, before the nervous looking cop on the door got trigger happy. It was lucky we weren't dealing with the LAPD.

"What I don't know," I said, "is why Reina cared about getting Hazel's copies of the evidence when she had Candace's."

"All she took was the phone."

That was true. We had thought it had been lack of time, but Candace's throwaway phone had yielded only one number. If Reina had seen or heard Candace talking on the phone as she approached, she might have been worried. She would have wanted to know to whom Candace had been talking. I shared these thoughts and we kicked them around for a minute before I went back to the setup of Bobby.

"At first, I thought she was trying to get back anything that might point to her father, but she'd so clearly done things that would implicate him, like putting the gun in his office, that it was impossible she was trying to help him. Outside, she was screaming at me about how everything was my fault, that Bobby would never have wanted her to go to jail. She said it was just in case. It was like she thought he would want to take the fall for her. I bet now he won't give a damn what happens to her."

"Maybe she was going to blackmail him too," Harry said. "Something along the lines of, buy me the townhouse or I'm turning evidence of your motive for committing these murders over to the cops."

Cynical. But knowing the players, not incomprehensible.

"She could have just bought the damn place with the money she took from Candace."

"Not right away," Harry said. "She would have needed to sit on the money. Or launder it, and I doubt she'd really know how."

"She worked out how to kill a bunch of people without too much trouble."

"I think you gave her plenty," Harry said.

Quick wasn't interested in praising me or in Reina's future plans. "The District Attorney will push for no bail," he said. "I think the judge will go along with him."

"She has a rich father." Even as I said it, I hoped her rich father would leave her to rot.

"He might not be so willing to help her now," Quick said.

"Well, that was just in case," Harry said. I rolled my eyes. Ouch.

"Do you think," I said to Quick, "you could leave now? Please."

"We'll need you to come in tomorrow for a formal statement. I hope by then you'll have changed your mind about making us arrest you."

I assured him I would be there and he left, taking his minions with him.

Harry was heading for the door as well.

I pushed myself off the bed. "You're going?" I said, like an idiot, because obviously he was. I guess "don't go," is what I meant to say, but it didn't come out.

Harry stopped, but didn't speak.

"I just wanted to make sure..." I stopped talking because nothing was going to come out of my mouth that made sense. I tried starting over.

"So we're friends then? That's what we decided, right?" That still wasn't it. He liked me didn't he? There was the sex. Except he was a guy, so that didn't necessarily mean anything. There was the dinner invitation. I had turned it down. It was probably too late. He had come tonight. That could be a good sign. My brain was getting nervous and it was having a bad effect on the rest of me. My stomach was fluttering, and I felt like I needed to wipe my palms.

"That's what you decided. Friend friends, nothing more."

I never made good decisions. Didn't he know me at all?

"For now. I definitely said, 'for now'."

"It isn't now anymore?"

"I don't know. What if now was just then? Maybe I think I was too hasty." I looked down at my bare feet and spoke intently to them. I needed a pedicure. I was never going to seduce him with such unkempt toes.

"Maybe, you think?"

"I mean, yeah, I was too hasty with the sex, which is why I said we should be just friends and not friendly ones. Friendly friends. Then I made it worse by being too quick to stop. With the sex. Because that was..." When I finally pried my eyes up Harry was smiling.

"Nevermind," I snapped.

"So you regret your haste?"

"No. Not regret." I would regret this conversation when it caused my head to explode. "I'm just saying it's possible that friendly friends got taken off the table too soon. Maybe."

"What should we do about that?" Harry fixed his eyes on me and I was having trouble breathing again, but for an entirely different reason.

"I like dinner. And I feel friendly."

"Me too." Harry pulled me against him. My body reacted favorably from head to toe, but mostly somewhere in the middle. I could tell he felt the same.

"What happened?" he said. "You seemed sure

earlier."

"I thought I was." I stretched with my whole body to bring my lips within reach of his. "But that was hours ago."

...Three Dead Blondes

Anne Stinnett

About the Author

Anne Stinnett was born in Los Angeles where she spent her first decade reading books and playing in traffic. Due to the professional obligations of her own personal Leonie, Anne found herself, at the tender age of ten, sweltering in Palm Springs, CA. Learning to deal (cards not drugs) led her to Albuquerque where she graduated with a degree in English from the University of New Mexico. Thanks to her finely honed and practical ability to discuss fiction, Anne found herself so overwhelmed with offers of employment that she was forced to retreat to Palm Springs where she now lives with a pack of rowdy dogs who are occasionally kind enough to let her get some writing done. She is currently at work on Evin's next adventure. *I went to Palm Springs and all I got was Three Dead Blondes* is her first novel.

Anne Stinnett

For updates on Evin's soon to come antics, as well as a glimpse of the beauty and variety of Palm Springs, visit www.iwenttopalmsprings.com.

Anne Stinnett

www.ingramcontent.com/pod-product-compliance
Lightning Source LLC
Chambersburg PA
CBHW030405180626
46812CB00005B/1933